"Okay, who is he?" Morgan demanded.

"First, I want you to know that I have absolutely no obligation to tell you anything at all about this pregnancy. According to my attorney—"

"Screw your attorney. I want a name."

"I can't give you a name, Morgan," she said quietly, in spite of the flurry of nerves in the pit of her stomach.

"If I have to, I'll get it myself, but I'd rather you tell me."

"Why?"

"Why the hell do you think? You're mine, Raine. You've always been mine."

Dear Reader,

With the coming of fall, the days—and nights—are getting cooler, but you can heat them up again with this month's selections from Silhouette Intimate Moments. Award winner Justine Davis is back with the latest installment in her popular TRINITY STREET WEST miniseries, *A Man To Trust*. Hero Cruz Gregerson proves himself to be just that—though it takes heroine Kelsey Hall a little time to see it. Add a pregnant runaway, a mighty cute kid and an opportunely appearing snake (yes, I said "snake"!), and you have a book to cherish forever.

With *Baby by Design*, award-winning Paula Detmer Riggs concludes her MATERNITY ROW trilogy. Pregnant-with-twins Raine Paxton certainly isn't expecting a visit from her ex-husband, Morgan—and neither one of them is expecting the sensuous fireworks that come next! Miniseries madness continues with *Roarke's Wife*, the latest in Beverly Barton's THE PROTECTORS, and Maggie Shayne's *Badlands Bad Boy*, the newest in THE TEXAS BRAND. Both of these miniseries will be going on for a while—and if you haven't discovered them already, you'll certainly want to come along for the ride. Then turn to Marie Ferrarella's *Serena McKee's Back in Town* for a reunion romance with heart-stopping impact. Finally there's Cheryl St.John's second book for the line, *The Truth About Toby*, a moving story about how dreams can literally come true.

Here at Intimate Moments, we pride ourselves on bringing you books that represent the best in romance fiction, so I hope you'll enjoy every one of this month's selections, then join us again next month, when the excitement—and the passion—continue.

Yours,

Leslie J. Wainger
Senior Editor and Editorial Coordinator

Please address questions and book requests to:
Silhouette Reader Service
U.S.: 3010 Walden Ave., P.O. Box 1325, Buffalo, NY 14269
Canadian: P.O. Box 609, Fort Erie, Ont. L2A 5X3

Paula Detmer Riggs

Baby By Design

Published by Silhouette Books

America's Publisher of Contemporary Romance

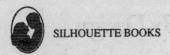

SILHOUETTE BOOKS

ISBN 0-373-07806-4

BABY BY DESIGN

Printed in U.S.A.

PAULA DETMER RIGGS

discovers material for her writing in her varied life experiences. During her first five years of marriage to a naval officer, she lived in nineteen different locations on the West Coast, gaining familiarity with places as diverse as San Diego and Seattle. While working at a historical site in San Diego, she wrote, directed and narrated fashion shows and became fascinated with the early history of California.

She writes romances because "I think we all need an escape from the high-tech pressures that face us every day, and I believe in happy endings. Isn't that why we keep trying, in spite of all the roadblocks and disappointments along the way?"

Prologue

A paper end to a paper marriage.

It seemed fitting, Morgan Paxton decided as he tossed the letter from his wife Raine's attorney to the floor of the tent. All very neat and tidy, just the way he liked his life. No more ties. No more responsibilities.

No more Raine.

Closing his eyes, Morgan focused on the night in an attempt to assuage the sudden pain that lanced through him. Beyond the canvas walls of the tent, the booted feet of faceless men pummeled packed clay as the communal meal was prepared. The scent of spices that would be considered exotic back home in the States filled the air, mingling pungently with the acrid heaviness of campfire smoke and the occasional whiffs of camel dung.

Ah...the joys of being on assignment. Visiting foreign shores. Sleeping on a cot. Shaving without water. What more could a man want? Excitement, challenge, living on the edge. Morgan Paxton, journalist extraordinaire. He had the world by the tail.

A bitter smile twisted Morgan's mouth. Knowing he shouldn't, he slipped his hand under the pillow on the bunk where he was sitting to touch the dog-eared leather folder that had been his constant companion for almost eleven years—since Raine had sent it to him a few weeks after their wedding. Inside, in one of the compartments was their wedding picture. He drew it carefully from its niche, the pad of his thumb caressing one corner where eleven years of handling had worn away the edges of the photo. Not that he adored the woman, or anything. Hell, no. According to Raine, he was too consumed with passion for his work to care deeply about anything or anyone else.

The backs of Morgan's eyes burned as he studied the wedding picture. In direct contrast to her name, Raine was all sunshine and sweet warm silk. As Morgan gazed down at her precious visage, the photo lost definition and his memories of her took over.

In his mind's eye, he saw her almost as clearly as if she were in the tent with him, her sable dark hair glowing with golden highlights, shimmering around her small face whenever she moved. A lovely fire burned in her big brown eyes, drawing him closer with its promise of warmth. Warmth he'd craved since the age of seven when his gentle, careworn mother had walked out of their roughly constructed cabin into the wild, briar-covered Kentucky hills and disappeared.

Raine. She had been the ultimate prize. A gentle spirit to soften the hard corners of his personality. A caring nature that forgave his faults and flaws, many though they were.

What had he given her in return? A child she'd adored, but who had worn her out with his hyperactive ways and inexplicable tantrums. A home and enough money to allow her to give Mike the kind of constant attention he had required. A husband fighting his way to the top, who was gone more than he was with her and their son.

At the time he'd told himself he was doing the right thing. The decent thing. Zebulon Paxton had grudgingly given his only child, Morgan, a shack with a leaking roof and a dirt floor. In direct contrast, Morgan had provided increasingly lavish houses for his own family, houses that Raine transformed into lovely havens.

Now, when it was too late, Morgan realized his mistakes. Okay, so he'd made sure Mike had a fat college fund—his son was to have had the first-class education Morgan had secretly coveted—but did money make up for his not being there while the boy had cut his first tooth or taken his first step?

Hell, no, it didn't. Nor had any of his other offerings. Cards and phone calls instead of his presence. Visits at Christmas that were over almost before they'd started. Awkward conversations with a child who had changed from visit to visit.

Reluctantly, dreading the hard punch of guilt he knew to expect, he shifted his gaze to the other picture in the folder, the last photo of Mike ever taken. His son at eight, only a few weeks before his death, smiling up at him, his blond hair mussed as always, his brown eyes alight with mischief.

A miniature Morgan, everyone said. The image of his daddy, with Morgan's wanderlust and rebellious bent.

Mike would have been ten in a few weeks. Poised on the edge of manhood. Probably would have been as tall as his mom by now. Close, anyway. Filling the house with his clutter and noise and energy. A house that had to seem terribly empty now.

Not that he would know.

It had been eighteen months since he'd been home. Eighteen months of trying to smother his grief, of driving himself so fiercely, he was teetering on the edge of massive burnout. A year and a half since Raine had asked him to leave and not come back. Having him there, seeing Mike in his every expression was only exacerbating her grief.

Besides, without Mike, she had no claim on him. No right to demand anything from him but her freedom. As an observer of life's twists of fate and odd symmetry, he had to appreciate the irony. After all, wasn't that the one thing he prized above all—his freedom.

"Yo, Pax, you awake?"

Lanky and leathery and pushing fifty, Dave Stebbins was reputed to have ice water for blood and a computer for a brain. As a producer he had no equal, as he never failed to remind the suits at the network come contract time. He was also the closest thing Morgan had to a friend in the dog-eat-dog world of network journalism.

"Yeah, I'm awake. What do you want?"

"Your presence, O Mighty Media Star. In thirty minutes."

Morgan muttered an obscenity that had Stebbins grinning. "A thousand bucks says you don't have the guts to repeat that on the air."

"Don't tempt me," Morgan muttered as the tent flap dropped, blocking Stebbins from sight. The man's footsteps receded, then blended with the muffled cacophony of camp activity.

Though it was several hours before dawn, the desert air was already heating. The crew would be sweating as they prepared to establish the satellite uplink for his live report on the nightly news. Though blessedly brief, the skirmish in the desert he'd been covering had been as violent as he'd ever seen, with one sect battling another over possession of a strip of hot, arid sand no larger than Rhode Island.

God, but he hated war. The noise and smells and the waste. The pain. Pain he'd experienced up close and personal in Southeast Asia. He'd fought that war rather than observe it. His own physical wounds had healed, leaving

him with a few scars here and there and a constant dull
ache in his shoulder, the one ripped apart by a Vietcong
bullet a lifetime ago.

Lord, but he had been young and innocent in those days.
An idealist willing to die for the "greater good." Just like
those poor kids who'd bled out their short lives into the
sand only a few hours ago. According to their religion, they
were now in heaven, revered as martyrs.

Once the uplink with the communications satellite was
completed and the camera readied, he would go before the
world to reveal yet another exclusive snippet of information
previously unknown about one of the terrorist leaders trying
to provoke another unholy war. It would be an additional
coup for a man whose place in the history of broadcast
journalism was already secured.

Oh yeah, Morgan Paxton was one great journalist all
right. Just his face on the screen guaranteed the network a
good four or five more rating points for the nightly news.
He had the contract to prove it, signed almost three years
ago with fanfare and celebration, guaranteeing him an obscene amount of money.

At the time he'd signed it, he'd thought it was the pin-
nacle of a long uphill climb, a real coup for a moonshiner's
kid from Hound Dog Hollow. Every poor boy's dream of
success. A quintessential power trip.

Raine used to call him her proud lion. Undaunted. Un-
defeated. Her protector. Another sharp, agonizing pain ran
through him at the thought. Instead of protecting her as he'd
promised, he'd left her alone and vulnerable while he went
off to prowl the world, looking for bigger and better stories
to lay at the altar of his much-coveted success.

But hadn't that been what had drawn her to him in the
first place? His fierce ambition? His drive to make his mark
on an increasingly complex world? To reveal the insanities
of war and oppression for what they were so the powers-

that-be would be forced to make changes? In short, he had been a card-carrying idealist. A crusader for truth, justice and the American way.

Why else would a gently reared, brilliantly accomplished professor's daughter have been interested in a guy who'd quit school at fifteen in order to help his daddy turn out the best sour mash in Hanks County, Kentucky? Who'd lied about his age and joined the army at sixteen in order to evade the net of federal agents who'd hauled Zebulon Paxton off to jail for bootlegging? Hell, at first, even his fellow soldiers thought he was little better than a hill rat, a hick who'd never owned more than one toothbrush in his life and thought that bathing regularly was for sissies.

By the time he'd met Raine Connelly, however, he'd been thirteen years older, a lot more cynical and a great deal more polished. The ignorant country boy had still been there, all right, buried under the changes he'd forced on himself. Persistence, practice and steely determination had changed the all-but-illiterate mountain twang into a lazy drawl. Constant reading and study had taken the hard edges off an education that was at best third rate. And a heretofore undiscovered acting talent had helped him fit into any crowd when the notion struck him.

Because they'd met on a college campus, where she was a student and he was delivering an address to an honors journalism class, and because she was an American lit major, he made it a point to talk about books. Mark Twain was his favorite author, he'd told her, and *Huckleberry Finn* his favorite book. Because Huck reminded him of himself, he'd admitted with one of those engaging grins that proclaimed to the world it no longer stung him to talk freely about his lowly beginnings.

Something in those soft brown eyes of hers had told him she'd seen through the sophistication and bravado to the ill-clothed, ill-fed, neglected boy he'd been. That realization had both touched and scared him. He'd told himself to make tracks fast. Instead, he'd asked her to dinner. And that night he'd taken her into his arms and kissed her.

Though he'd bedded his fair share of willing women by the age of thirty-five, he'd felt like a virgin that night. Trembling inside that he would make a mistake and drive her out of his life forever. Instead of catching the plane to Tahiti where he'd planned to spend his much-needed vacation, he'd stayed in the little Oregon town of Bradenton Falls where Raine had been attending college.

Every night for three weeks he'd told himself he was "leaving first thing tomorrow." And every morning he'd found another reason to stay one more day. No matter what words he'd used, however, the reason was Raine. Her smile. Her twinkling eyes. Her bright wit and clever mind. And most of all, her total acceptance of the man beneath the image. More than anything he wanted to please his gentle princess who thought he was special.

But now...

Maybe he should just let her go, he thought, staring down at the laughing face of his bride. Free her to find her happiness with another man. A man who wasn't wandering the globe more than he was home. A man content to live a quiet, ordinary life. A man who could give her the security and serenity she now claimed to need.

In short, someone not obsessed with himself and his precious career.

A better man than Morgan Paxton.

Oh yeah, a better man would do the right thing, all right. Give her up for her own good. Let her get on with her life in any way she chose.

On the other hand, a selfish bastard like Morgan Paxton would fight to keep her. Fight like the very devil, no-holds-barred, because to lose her would be like ripping a part of himself away. The best part.

A cynical jerk like Morgan Paxton would use any weapon, devise any strategy to make her love him again.

Because he needed her. Because without her he was only half a man. Because he was too much of a coward to even contemplate living the rest of his life knowing he'd held sunshine and joy in his hands and, like the ignorant country boy he really was under all the polish, he'd been too stupid and too clumsy to keep his lady safe and happy.

No wonder she'd asked him to leave.

Night after night as he'd lain alone in a strange bed in some distant part of the world, he had comforted himself with plans for the new start they would make. This time he would take special pains to cosset and cherish her.

He'd been so sure she'd just needed time alone to heal.

Give me a chance, Raine, he pleaded silently. I swear I'll make it up to you.

Please.

His only answer was silence—and the hard, steady agony of guilt.

Chapter 1

Three months later

Morgan was going home. And he was scared.

His stomach was giving him fits, and his mouth was cotton dry. He knew his hands would be ice-cold to the touch, even when the rest of his body was drenched with sweat. It was the same feeling he had whenever he went into combat, the same feeling he'd had when he'd gone on the air for the first time. And when he'd asked Raine to marry him. When he was younger, he'd spent some time trying to overcome it. Now he simply accepted it for what it was—a deeply ingrained fear of failure.

Fear, hell, he thought as he stared through the tiny window of the 757 at the cloud bank below. It was a full-blown terror.

He'd tried to drown the sucker in Scotch, only to add a pickled brain to the mix.

Exercise sometimes helped, but it was damned inconvenient to go for a run at thirty thousand feet.

So he pulled inside himself and brooded behind a polite mask.

About the mistakes he made and flaws in his character he hadn't bothered to correct. About grief so deep, he'd wanted to die, and the numbness he'd embraced to escape the pain and the guilt.

But mostly he thought about the woman he was traveling halfway around the world to see.

He'd thought about asking her to meet him at the airport the way she'd always done in the past. He considered it during the noisy, butt-jarring helicopter trip out of the desert, the endless transatlantic flight, the layover at Kennedy with the predictable delays.

When he should have been grabbing some much-needed sleep in the VIP lounge, he'd found himself staring at the gleaming pay phone, trying to talk himself out of placing the call to her new number, the one he'd had to move heaven and earth to wangle out of her father, who lived in Salem, Oregon.

Hell of a note, he thought. Not only was he being divorced, but his wife hadn't bothered to send him a change-of-address card when she'd left the East Coast.

Probably her father's idea. The overprotective bastard.

He scowled as he reflected on his relationship with his father-in-law. Arthur Connelly was overeducated, even tempered and fussy about details—the exact opposite of Zebulon Paxton. He was also devoted to his only child. Though Arthur never said it aloud, Morgan had sensed the older man's dismay at his daughter's choice of husband.

Arthur had still been half-asleep when he'd picked up the phone, his cultured professor's voice reflecting equal parts fear and annoyance at the middle-of-the-night intrusion. At the sound of his son-in-law's voice, Arthur's tone had turned icy.

Though it hurt, Morgan couldn't very well hold that against the man. If he ever got lucky enough to have a daughter of his own, he sure as hell wouldn't want her tied up with a self-involved, ambitious, success-driven jerk.

No, Arthur was right to be wary.

It would take more than a multimillion-dollar contract and a high Q rating to turn Morgan Paxton into a valuable human being. No doubt Raine's father had strongly supported her decision to file for divorce.

More times than Morgan cared to count during the last leg of his flight to Portland, he'd pulled the leather folder from his pocket and opened it to stare down at her face. Each time, he'd studied every precious line of her features until his tired eyes had lost focus and his mind had begun to substitute an image of her waiting impatiently for him by the door to the Jetway.

She'd always been easy to spot. A slender pixie not quite five feet three inches tall, radiating energy, dressed in one of those bright, gauzy dresses she loved. Small on top, generously curved below the waist, she fitted his image of the perfect woman to a T. Soft and yielding where a man needed softness, her skin like silk beneath his skimming fingertips, her dark shining hair smelling like spring.

But it was the welcoming excitement in her eyes he craved. The eagerness in her smile. He was never really home until he touched her. Until he felt her sigh into his mouth as he kissed her.

Looking forward to taking her into his arms and swinging her around had become a ritual, one of the many that had gotten him through some pretty tough times.

Rituals had been important to him for a long time. He'd discovered their power during the miserable months he'd spent in Letterman Army Hospital, playing one-handed poker with the other hollow-eyed vets while he'd endured an endless series of operations to reconstruct his destroyed shoulder. Boredom. Pain. Physical therapy. He'd suffered through it all because he'd had no choice.

It was then that he'd discovered a hard truth. When a man didn't have nice warm memories to sustain and anchor him, he clung to his silly little self-imposed practices when times got rough. Small things, like eating the same breakfast every day whenever possible, and putting on his clothes in exactly the same order. Reserving the same window seat in first-class when he flew. Never throwing anything away if he could help it.

A deliberate, conscious arrangement of his world.

A sense of control when everything else had gone to hell in a handbasket.

Ritual.

Like stopping on the way home from the airport to have a hot fudge sundae, he reflected as he studied the ice cubes in his glass of club soda.

What he'd come to think of as Mike's special time had started when their son had been four and acutely unhappy at having to go meet the father he scarcely knew at the airport. His hyperactive son had pitched one of his ear-shattering tantrums right there in the midst of the disembarking passengers, embarrassing Raine and amusing Morgan.

Raine had tried diplomacy. Morgan had bypassed that and gone straight to bribery tactics. He'd placated his conscience by telling himself how infrequently he managed to spend time with the boy. Which is exactly what he'd told Raine when she'd accused him of spoiling him.

What should he have done? Step off the plane and immediately assume the role of stern disciplinarian? No way.

Because the visits with Mike had been so precious, Morgan had been a firm believer in quality time, which he hadn't wanted to taint with unpleasantness. Hoping his son might have inherited his own sweet tooth, Morgan had suggested stopping for ice cream. It had worked like the proverbial charm. Slick as sweat.

Just like that, another ritual had been born. First a kiss and an exuberant hug for Raine, then ice cream for the kid. Somehow it had been easier to slip himself into the fabric of their lives over gooey hot fudge.

Between bites, Raine had caught him up on domestic trivia. The status of the current house she was renovating— her job, she'd always called it. From the distance of an observer, Morgan thought that it was more like a crusade. Her way of contributing. Find a ramshackle derelict with promise, cut away the dross to reveal the gold, then make it shine—that was her strategy and her passion.

Once she'd described the precise status of each room, she'd invariably moved on to Mike's most recent humorous antic, always perceived by his doting parents to be an indication of the boy's brilliance.

Yes, he was a handful, but he was also a lovable kid, full of fire and curiosity and generous with hugs and kisses. All boy, with a white-blond cowlick that refused to be tamed, a spray of freckles on his blunt little nose and a knack for collecting scrapes and bruises, he'd been blessed with a grin that softened even the hardest heart. Naturally, he was destined for great things—once he settled down. Great things like his dad, Raine would always add with an impish grin that invariably made Morgan want to strut.

That settled to her satisfaction, she'd invariably moved on to the state of her father's always shifting state of well-being. All the while Raine talked, Mike would watch his father with big golden brown eyes lined with thick dark lashes tipped with gold on the ends just like his mom's. And then, slowly, Mike would begin to add his comments, until finally, by the time he was scraping the bottom of his dish for the last taste of fudge, the boy had been jabbering away a mile a minute.

Then, and only then, had Morgan really felt welcome.

Accepted.

Wanted.

Since Mike's death, Morgan hadn't been able to stand the taste of ice cream.

"Mr. Paxton? Sorry to disturb you, sir, but the captain has turned on the Fasten Seat Belts sign."

Lost in thought, it took Morgan a moment to focus on the sleek blonde leaning over his seat. The head flight attendant, his mind registered. The senior attendant always worked first-class. One of the perks of the job, he'd been told once. No dealing with crying babies or nervous first-time flyers.

Morgan couldn't begin to list the number of flights he'd taken, beginning with that first cold, endless, gut-twisting trip to Nam on a military transport.

"Where are we?" he asked as he released the reclining mechanism on his mauve-colored seat and clicked the belt into place. After shoving up his tray and stowing the leather case with Raine's picture in it, he flicked his gaze to the small silver nameplate pinned over the attendant's right breast.

Cheyenne. He figured it wasn't the same name that appeared on her birth certificate. He'd run across too many wannabe actresses with similar names.

She leaned past him to glance out the window, offering him a closer look at her chest. A frequent opportunity to score was one of the perks of *his* job. One he didn't particularly want or need.

"Looks like we're just going over the Rockies," she said, turning to look him in the eyes. "We're about an hour from Portland."

He acknowledged that with a smile.

"Are you familiar with the city?" she asked, straightening with the lazy grace of a cat stretching in the sun.

"Never been there," he admitted.

Raine had moved there from Connecticut after they'd separated. She'd grown up sixty miles south in Salem. And like a little homing pigeon, she'd returned to the nest. Or close enough. Her father was only an hour away by car—and no doubt a steady, reliable presence in her life.

The thought had his mood darkening even more. Family was important to Raine. It was just a concept to him. A vague ideal. Personally, he had no desire to return to Kentucky. Ever. Since he and Raine had separated, he'd listed the network's New York City address as his official residence.

"If you're free, I know a great place for dinner," the attendant murmured, her voice pitched low and her blue eyes dark with sexual promise. "Marvelous seafood and a great wine list."

"Thanks, but I'm not free."

He held up his left hand in a gesture that had become automatic over the years. Her face didn't change. Obviously she'd already noted the wide gold wedding band. He'd never removed it since Raine had slipped it on his finger.

"If you change your mind in the next hour, the offer's open," she said before disappearing into the forward galley.

Unlike a significant number of his colleagues, both male and female, he'd never particularly relished this aspect of his success. Not even when he'd been single.

One-night stands had always seemed too much like the mindless rutting of animals he'd seen everyday growing up in the hills, the same kind of rutting his father had forced on his mother.

Morgan had grown up listening to his daddy's piglike

grunts coming through the thin walls of the shack, agonizing over the small gasps of pain that were all his mama allowed herself during the ordeal.

May Paxton might have been small, sickly and helpless, but she'd also been proud. Not even Zebulon Morgan's crude cruelties had reduced her to begging.

Morgan drew a long breath and forced his mind away from the black memories. He had his daddy's big hands and powerful build, but not his temper or his cruelty. He was his own man, older now than his father had been when he'd died in prison.

Realizing he was scowling, Morgan forced his facial muscles to relax. Deliberately he let his eyelids drift closed, forcing his attention on the white light he envisioned flooding into him.

Light to counteract the dark and murky pull of the past.

Sunshine.

Raine.

His mouth quirked as he remembered telling her that her name was all wrong. There was nothing gloomy about her. Nothing to dampen a man's spirit. Just the opposite. Which was why he'd immediately started to think of her as his Sunshine Girl.

Sunshine Woman, you chauvinist, she'd corrected with an imperious grin. *A liberated, independent, enlightened woman.*

His fierce little fighter.

His wife.

Now he was on his way home to her. Hopefully to restake his claim. It had taken patience, a lot of slick maneuvering and a generous portion of bluff on his side, but in the end he'd managed to persuade the suits at the network to let him take his considerable sick leave and vacation time in one four-month block.

The divorce papers were in the bottom of his duffel,

unsigned. He knew Raine could process them without his signature, but he was counting on her sense of fair play to give him a chance to plead his case before cutting him off at the knees.

His conscience stung a little whenever he thought of the pressure he intended to apply. First he intended to plead burnout and play on her sympathy to let him hang around her place for a while. Just until he got back on track.

Hell, truth to tell, he was pretty much teetering on a knife edge, had been for months now. The headaches he'd suffered for nearly a year after his mother's disappearance had returned after Mike's funeral. Sharp talons tearing into his brain, blotting out sight and reason for hours on end. A pain so vicious, he was utterly helpless until the agony finally eased off. Most of the time they came in batches, sometimes daily. And then they'd disappear for months on end. Fortunately, he hadn't had one since he'd decided to fight for her.

The pain he felt now was more primitive. The sooner he made love to her the better.

His fierce hunger for her had started gnawing at him the moment he'd boarded the Concorde at Heathrow. If he hadn't been dragged down by the nearly twenty-four hours he'd gone without sleep, he might have spent the entire flight with his coat draped over his lap to hide the physical evidence of his arousal.

By the time he'd switched planes at Kennedy, he'd psyched himself into a more patient frame of mind. This time Raine deserved a proper courtship, with flowers and moonlight strolls and all the trappings that he'd been too besotted to bother with the first time around.

He'd already resolved to pay whatever price she exacted from him to get her back. Anything—including begging for her forgiveness, if that's what it took.

His mouth twisted in a grim, self-deprecating smile.

Morgan Paxton, on his knees. Never in his life had he grov-
eled, not for anyone. He had a little too much of his mother's stubborn pride braided into his backbone to bend, he
guessed. But for Raine, he would gladly beg and consider
it fitting punishment—his penance, so to speak.

Wasn't that what those crotchety old guys in the Bible
had had in mind when they talked about cleansing one's
soul? Confess your transgressions, resolve not to sin again.
Stand up and take your punishment like a man, no matter
how much it hurt.

Okay, if that's what it took. No matter what Raine flung
at him, Morgan figured he had it coming. The only penalty
he wouldn't accept was losing her.

According to the talkative cabbie who'd recognized Morgan on sight and thus considered him a celebrity rather than
just another airport fare, 372 Mill Works Ridge was in one
of Portland's oldest and most historic sections.

Built on a bluff high over the Columbia River, six Vic-
torian-style bungalows were all that remained of a once-
huge complex that had comprised a log yard, lumber mill
and railroad spur. Originally owned by the Waverly family,
the bungalows had once housed the mill's managers and
executives. As Portland had grown and prospered, the mill
had, as well, but gradually the value of the land had out-
weighed the profit from the mill and the property had been
subdivided.

A sprawling, upscale mall now occupied the spot where
the mill had stood and a freeway traced the route of the
old railroad line. Running east and west, Raine's street was
only two blocks long and dead-ended into a barrier of
gracefully arching river birches at the western end. As far
as Morgan could see, there were three houses to a block,
all made of wood and painted white, lined up like sparkling

gingerbread cottages plopped down in the midst of a crinkle of lush green velvet.

It was a scene right out of a book on charming Americana. Slice-of-life stuff, the Norman Rockwell kind he'd done early in his career. Feel-good segments, soft news. Nothing remotely like the gritty, hard-edged pieces he did now.

Nostalgia rolled over him. Though he'd never lived this kind of halcyon life, never wanted to, he sometimes wished that he had the patience and staying power such a life required.

Watching a robin diligently pecking at something buried in the well-tended grass, he thought about the months he'd spent looking at sand and more sand. Suddenly he had a strong urge to slip out of his boots and run barefoot through the neatly cropped thatch that seemed to beckon like a cool drink in the dog days of August.

It struck him as damned pathetic that a kid who'd grown up wishing for a pair of shoes that fit had become a man who waxed sentimental over running barefoot through a strip of lawn not much wider than the average news studio.

"Like I said, this is a real nice neighborhood, even being so close to the mall and all," the cabbie declared as he opened the trunk of the taxi.

"Bet you can smell the river when the wind's right," Morgan agreed, flexing his stiff shoulders. Dead fish, diesel fumes and all.

One of two houses in the entire neighborhood with a second story, Raine's home stood like a graceful sentinel at the corner of the first block, the gingerbread shutters at the window and the front door painted an aggressive slate blue. Pretty lace curtains that made him think of hot steamy nights draped the first-floor windows. An elaborate wreath of dried flowers tied with a jaunty pink bow hung on the door, a pale reflection of the vivid blossoms tumbling from the beds artfully interspersed amid wildly blooming bushes.

A damned rainbow come to life.

Ruefully he glanced down at the cellophane-wrapped bouquet of yellow roses in his hand. Coals to Newcastle. Hell, he should have remembered how much Raine liked to putter in her garden, like a fussy little mama coddling her babies.

A born mother, that was Raine. A natural nurturer. All living things thrived under her care. Certainly he'd felt stronger after spending time with her.

"Good place for kids," the cabbie added. "Not much traffic."

"Wouldn't take much for a kid to tumble down that bank," Morgan pointed out as he shifted the roses to his left hand and reached into the trunk with his right to retrieve his garment bag and laptop computer.

"Yeah, guess you're right. Not having kids, I never thought of that kind of accident." The cabbie glanced toward the river. "Guess you never know."

"No, you never know."

A shaft of pain shot through Morgan, and he drew a hard breath. Though Raine had never come right out and blamed him for Mike's death, he knew he would never feel free of guilt, no matter how long he lived.

"Just leave the rest of that junk by the curb," he told the cabbie who shook his head as he hefted the last suitcase from the trunk.

"No problem carrying 'em to the door. In fact, I consider it a privilege. Like I said, I'm a journalism major myself. Only got two semesters to go before I graduate. I'm hoping to be a foreign correspondent like you, you know. We've got a lot in common."

"So you said."

The trip from the airport had taken forty-seven minutes.

The kid had used damn near every one of them to give Morgan his entire life story, complete with a rundown of all the menial jobs he'd taken to keep himself in school. Not that Morgan minded. There was something likable about the kid. Probably the Huck Finn freckles and wild carroty mop of hair poking out from under a sweat-stained Blazers cap.

Morgan had always been a sucker for a hard-luck story, possibly because he had one of his own to tell. Unlike this kid, though, he seldom spoke about it, and he tried never to look back. Unless, of course, his celebrity status and the widely publicized chronology of his humble beginnings forced him to do so. Like now.

"Way I figure it, I'll probably have to start at some local station like you did." The cabbie grinned up at him as they climbed the two steps from the sidewalk to the brick walk. "In Montana, wasn't it?"

"Idaho."

Morgan frowned at the memory of that brutal winter he'd spent in Coeur d'Alene. He hated snow, always had. He could never seem to get warm enough. Too many reminders of the miserable years he'd spent huddled in a cold, wet shack, trying not to shiver, lest his old man think he was complaining.

"I've already made a demo tape."

"Good idea."

Morgan stifled a sigh. In a year or two the kid's natural optimism would already be hardening into a jaded cynicism. No one stayed innocent for long in the news business.

"I put a little bit of everything on it. Weather and sports and straight news reporting. Show my versatility, you know?"

"Couldn't hurt."

The cabbie had to skip a step to keep up with Morgan's long strides. "You started out doing weather, right?"

"Right."

And had had a devil of a time keeping the blasted, poly-syllabic meteorological terms straight. Even with the read-ing he crammed into every spare minute, his hit-and-miss education had been a definite handicap.

"And then you went to outside reporting?"

"Yeah."

Mostly county fairs and horse auctions. Anything that had to do with dust and manure ended up on his schedule. KSPD News Director T. Graham Piggot hadn't been his biggest fan.

Hey, that kind of gig goes with that redneck accent of yours, pal. Besides, you got a real feel for cow dung.

Last he heard, Gray Piggot was still holding down the same messy desk, a major power in a very minor market, which just happened to be an affiliate of the same network that now paid Morgan Paxton the big bucks. No doubt good ol' Gray darn near bit through the stem of his ubiquitous pipe every time his former grunt reporter's face hit the screen. It wasn't much in the way of revenge for the thir-teen months of hell he'd put in at KSPD, he thought as he climbed onto the porch, but it would do until something better came along.

"It's been great talking to you, Mr. Paxton," the kid said with a grin as he carefully lined up Morgan's scuffed leather bags along the porch railing.

"You, too, son."

Morgan had to set down his computer in order to snag his wallet from his pocket. A scowl crossed his face as he tucked the roses under his arm to free both hands.

The cabbie shook his head. "You already tipped me, remember? Helping with the bags is part of the service."

"Got something else to give you," he said as he plucked a business card from an inner pocket and gave it to the kid who accepted it with an embarrassing reverence.

"What's your name, son?"

"Paul John Frazier."

Morgan filed that away. An all but infallible memory had been one of the few innate skills he'd brought to his job. That and a face that tended to look a whole lot better on camera than it did in his mirror.

"When you're ready to send out that tape, give me a call and I'll give you some names."

Paul John turned bright pink from the point of his cleft chin to the lobes of his ears. "I'll do that, Mr. Paxton. And thanks."

Morgan gave him a hard look. If the boy thought he'd just lucked into a free kick up the ladder, he was dead wrong.

"I'm just planning to give you names, kid. If you get your start, you'll get it on your own merit."

"Yeah, sure. I understand. And I won't let you down, I promise."

Morgan stifled a sigh. "Just worry about yourself, okay?"

"Okay." Paul John grinned, shifted his feet and nodded. "Well, uh, enjoy your vacation."

"Thanks. I intend to give it my best shot."

The cabbie backed down the steps to the walk, Morgan's card still clutched in his hand. Lord, had he ever been that green? He didn't need to search for the answer. He'd been worse. Much worse. He'd gone into broadcasting with only his raw craving to succeed and an ignorant confidence in his own ability to bluff backing him up.

"If you need a ride to the airport, just ask for me when you call in," the kid said earnestly.

"I'll keep that in mind."

The sound of the young man's footsteps receded behind Morgan as he shoved his wallet into his back pocket and retrieved the flowers from under his arm. The half-open buds were already drooping. Dumb idea, buying them at a kiosk at the airport, he thought as he heaved a sigh of disgust. What did an airport florist care about attracting repeat business anyway?

He heard the cab's engine start and glanced back to return the cabbie's farewell wave. Eyes squinting against the sun, he watched the yellow sedan roll to a stop at the corner, then turn right and disappear behind the solid white barrier of the first house in the row.

Squaring his shoulders, he turned to face the blue door again. As he did, he felt his heart pounding and his palms growing icy. Scowling, he jabbed a long finger at the bell and kept it there. He heard a muted chiming through the door, repeated over and over.

"Hell," he muttered, dropping his hand. Now what?

Sit on the doorstep like a damned orphan, waiting for Raine to invite him in from the cold?

The image was far too apt to be anything but distinctly annoying. Not bloody likely, he told himself as he descended the steps and headed for the back of the house. Over the years he'd learned a thing or two about getting into places where he wasn't particularly welcome, but he preferred to do his breaking and entering in as much privacy as possible.

As he neared the rear of the house, he heard the sound of high-pitched giggling, followed by a childish squeal. Somebody's kids were playing nearby, he thought as he approached the gate built into a privet hedge that bordered the back part of the lawn.

The closer he got to the backyard, the louder the squeals seemed. He wasn't much of a kid person. Never had been, except with Mike. And even then he'd been mostly thumbs with the boy until Mike had started walking. From there his son had gone straight to running.

Energetic, the pediatrician had said initially.

The hyperactive bit came later. After Raine had all but worn herself out trying to keep the boy safe. Along with Morgan's fair coloring and gold-brown eyes, Mike had inherited his father's restless spirit. Tell the boy "no" and Mike considered it a challenge. Tell him "yes" and he considered it permission to push for more.

The gate was closed, latched on the inside. Before flipping it open, he stopped and surveyed the scene in front of him with hungry eyes. From what he could see he'd dropped smack-dab in the middle of a typical pool party—except the pool was only six feet wide and a foot deep, with cartoon characters stenciled onto the bright blue interior. It had been placed in the dense, cool shade of a huge sugar maple, and presently contained three little girls, all chattering and giggling at once.

Seated around the pool in mismatched sun loungers were three females in various forms of beach attire. His gaze skimmed the group until he found Raine.

Gloriously tanned, as though just back from a lazy vacation in the South Pacific, she wore a baggy shirt the color of lime sherbet with a scoop neck that had slipped over one shoulder, revealing the thin strap of a yellow bathing suit. Her tanned legs were bare and sleek and shiny with a coat of suntan oil, and her toes had been painted a bright green to match the shirt.

Her head was slightly turned to the left as she listened to the woman next to her, her rich dark hair pulled back into a thick, curly ponytail that gleamed like softest silk in the sunshine. Wisps of the same soft curls framed a face that was perfection itself. Or close enough to make little difference to a man who'd lived on memories and one lone photograph for eighteen long months.

Standing unnoticed, he watched her speaking in animated tones to one of her friends, a petite woman with a riot of coppery curls piled atop her head and a bubbling laugh.

One of the little girls in the pool was obviously hers, with the same fiery hair. A soon-to-be older sister since the lady with the bright hair was obviously quite pregnant. The other woman in the cozy little group had hair nearly as dark and glossy as Raine's and a serene expression that reminded Morgan of a fifteenth-century Madonna painting he'd seen on one of his R and R trips to Rome.

Three pretty ladies in a row, he thought with wry amusement. His chest swelled with pride to realize that his lady was definitely the prettiest—and the sexiest. She was also more voluptuous than he remembered. Sweetly rounded in all the right places. A lush treasure for a man who considered himself anything but deserving.

"Tory, what's that in your sister's mouth?"

The oldest girl, a little creature with dark hair and eyes, glanced over at the Madonna and shrugged.

"I think it's a rock."

Even from a distance, Morgan could see the woman's exasperation. "Shelby, spit that out right this instant."

"Sit still, I'll get it," Raine insisted as the harried mother started to rise.

Morgan felt his breath catch as Raine slipped her bare legs to the side of the chair and stood up. He started to smile, then froze. He felt staggered, his breath knocked from his body as though his muscle and sinew struggled to absorb a vicious blow.

Stunned, he watched her hurry toward the pool. The sun turned her hair into a shimmering brown halo and gilded her delicate features. She was laughing, her arms already reaching for the little tiny mermaid with pudgy cheeks.

The green shirt clung softly to her body, the hem hitting her at midthigh. But it was the ripe, round belly the bright material outlined that riveted his gaze. The truth burned in his gut, nearly doubling him over. No doubt about it. His wife was very, very pregnant.

Chapter 2

"Come on, punkin, give Auntie Raine that yucky old stone."

Like a plump little bird in a wet nest, two-year-old Shelby MacAuley obediently opened her small pink mouth to allow Raine to remove the round white stone tucked in one chubby cheek.

"Thank you very much, Miss Shelby. I will treasure this always."

Shelby giggled, then patted Raine's tummy. "Baby," she said in a firm little voice.

Raine smiled as she felt a familiar thrill run through her. After nearly two years of alternating between deepest despair and searing anger, she was suddenly alive again, waking up each morning eager to see what surprises the new day would bring. In two and a half months she would be a mother again. Whole, instead of empty. Needed.

Nothing would ever bring Michael back, but life did go on, and she'd finally come to terms with her grief. Now she was ready to rejoin the living. That felt good, so incredibly good.

Only one dark cloud marred her sunny skies.

Morgan had yet to return the divorce papers she'd had sent to him over three months ago. According to her attorney, it was vitally important that the divorce be finalized before she gave birth. Otherwise, Morgan would have a legal claim to custody of any or all children born during the marriage.

A wave of sadness ran through her, as familiar to her now as the sound of her own breathing in the dark. She hated the very idea of divorce, and yet she had no choice. Still, it hurt.

Her father claimed she was too stubborn to admit she'd made a mistake falling for a man who worshiped danger the way others worshiped a more traditional deity.

The fact that she'd fallen in love with the man on sight didn't mean diddly to someone as well versed in diverse cultures as Arthur Connelly. Love was simply a form of self-hypnosis. A way for civilized human beings to rationalize a primitive urge to mate. Although in Morgan's case, Arthur considered the veneer of that civilization to be whisper thin.

The man his colleagues called Pax had been a part of her life, a major chunk of her identity for over a decade, and yet in all that time, she and Morgan had actually lived together for a little less than a year. Three hundred and forty seven days, in fact. She'd counted them once in a moment of dark despair. A week or two here, a month there. Never long enough to be totally easy with one another.

Bottom line, she and Morgan were scarcely more than strangers who'd had a passionate affair, resulting in the creation of a wonderful little boy. Once Mike was gone, they'd had little in common to hold them together. No, truth to tell, they weren't dissolving a marriage so much as a partnership. And a rational, emotionally tough woman did not get all teary-eyed over the end of a business association.

"Uh, Raine, I think you have company," her quixotic redheaded friend and neighbor Prudy Randolph said quietly from her spot nearest the hedge.

Raine glanced behind her to see her friend gazing toward the side gate. As she followed Prudy's line of sight, she expected to see a stranger standing there, someone looking for directions, perhaps, or an electric company employee searching for a meter to read.

It took her an eternity to realize the man staring at her from the other side of her hedge wasn't another figment of her overactive imagination, but instead, solid flesh and bone.

He looked worn-out, drained of that marvelous animal vitality that lit up the television screen, his angular face pale beneath the layered bronze of his skin. Only the golden eyes between thick blond lashes were alive, raking her with a simmering anger that was in vivid contrast to the deeply etched lines of weariness.

Raine uttered her husband's name in a breathless tone that seemed to echo like a shout in the sudden stillness that surrounded her. Sights and sounds faded. Her mouth went dry and her heart thundered.

"Why's that big man staring at you like that, Auntie Raine?" Tory MacAuley asked with a child's utter lack of subtlety.

"He's...surprised that I'm pregnant," she answered with a truth that sounded simple—and was anything but.

"Why? Because you're not married."

But I am, she started to say, then realized that what little was left of her marriage existed only on paper. And that, too, was about to end.

"Tory, give Auntie Raine a chance to catch her breath," Stacy MacAuley murmured to her daughter.

"But Mom—"

"Help me gather up the toys," Stacy ordered gently as she rose to her feet. "It's time for Shelby's nap."

"Same goes for Chloe," Prudy Randolph said, smiling at the pint-size replica of herself happily slapping the water with fat little hands. "Case promised to take us out to Tony's for an early dinner."

Raine turned to glare at them. "Some support system you two are, bailing out on a friend in her moment of need," she muttered in a low tone.

"I thought you said he would be happy to have his freedom," Stacy murmured as she lifted a protesting Shelby from the pool.

"So?"

"So he doesn't look happy." Stacy wrapped her daughter in a towel before dropping a kiss onto her damp curls.

"Trust me, it's only jet lag. Morgan's very susceptible."

"Uh-huh."

"That has got to be one of the most interesting men I've ever seen," Prudy murmured, her voice tinged with purely female awe as she struggled to extricate herself from the sagging webbing of the lounge chair.

"Not to mention extremely intimidating, masculinity-wise," Stacy chimed in as she rubbed Shelby dry.

"Awesome," Prudy contributed. "I love my husband dearly, but I suddenly have this wild urge to preen."

"Behave yourself, Prudence," Stacy muttered, grinning as she adjusted the strap of her bikini top. "The man's a big-time TV star and you're a lowly nurse."

"*Charge nurse* to you, Mrs. Dr. MacAuley. Presently on maternity leave, thank goodness."

"Hush, both of you," Raine ordered in a low voice, suddenly terribly aware of her bare legs and tumbled hair.

In every one of her imagined scenarios of this reunion, she'd been impeccably dressed in a power suit in a subdued color, complemented by Italian pumps and pearls. Instead of sodden kids and panting females surrounding her and Morgan, she'd pictured the dingy walls of a dreary domestic courtroom and a judge in a black robe, perched high above them like a disapproving crow.

Morgan at least was dressed in his usual attire for traveling, or so she assumed from the wide expanse of khaki shirt visible over the arching top of the cedar gate. Whenever she pictured Morgan, she almost always saw him in that same shirt with the sleeves rolled tight against his biceps, comfortably worn jeans and boots scarred by dirt and wear.

As he reached over to open the gate, longing swept through her, an irrational kind of wishing that their marriage had been real. But it hadn't been—and that, as the man said, was that.

"Hello, Morgan," she said as he came toward her, his long-legged stride just shy of a predator's swagger. A lion on the prowl, eyes gleaming and dangerous. He'd looked very much the same striding across campus on the morning they'd met. Late for a talk he'd been scheduled to give to a group of would-be investigative journalists, he'd stopped to ask her the way to the lecture hall. She remembered how her stomach had taken a fast roller-coaster ride.

It was the same now, only worse.

She hated the way her blood seemed to sing through her veins and her senses sharpened. Just being in Morgan's presence unnerved her.

It wasn't just a matter of his size. At six-two he wasn't the tallest man she'd known, nor the brawniest, though she had no doubt he could hold his own against bigger men in a brawl. More steely than pumped, his muscles were the product of good genes and hard work with a generous measure of brutally tough army conditioning thrown in.

The most private of men when he wasn't on the air, she'd never known him to raise his voice or deliberately court attention. He didn't have to. Morgan Paxton could command the attention of an entire room of powerful people by simply showing up.

"This is a surprise," she said when he stopped a few feet from her, his booted feet braced wide. One side of his mouth quirked as he deliberately lowered his burning gaze to her protruding stomach.

"You might say that, yeah." The soft drawl that had become as familiar to the world as the unruly mane of sun-streaked hair was suddenly edged with a harder twang, one of the few remnants of the impoverished childhood Morgan never discussed.

She took a hold of her wildly careening emotions and forced a cool smile. "When did you get in?"

"From the looks of…things, not soon enough."

Raine felt heat scorch her cheeks. But before she could reply, Morgan had shifted his attention to the two women hovering behind her.

"Hi, I'm Pax, Raine's husband."

"Ex-husband." she corrected.

Morgan glanced at Raine over the top of Prudy's coppery curls. "Not yet, honey," he drawled, his gaze flickering to her briefly before he extended his hand to Stacy first, and then Prudy who had finally managed to extricate her very pregnant body from the low chair.

Raine realized that both women had introduced themselves and their kids and were now chatting with Morgan like old friends.

"Was Desert Storm really as slick as it seemed on TV?" she heard Stacy ask in an uncharacteristically rushed voice.

Raine nearly groaned. Her next-door neighbor could handle a classroom of wild kindergartners with unruffled serenity. She ran her household the same way, managing to juggle the demands of her husband Boyd's long hours as a trauma surgeon and the needs of their two energetic daughters with aplomb. Raine knew for a fact that Stacy was wildly in love with Boyd, and yet, it had only taken Morgan a scant two sentences to have her giggling like a schoolgirl.

"No war is slick, Stacy," he said with a quiet conviction that spoke far more eloquently than the simple words. "Or as sanitary as it appeared on film."

"Did you really capture a bunch of Iraqi soldiers single-handedly?" Raine heard the awe in Prudy's voice and wanted to throttle her usually levelheaded friend.

"Naw, the poor sods were looking for someone to put them out of their misery. Darn near begged me and my cameraman to take their weapons off their hands."

Prudy laughed. "I have to admit I was glued to my TV set the whole time."

"Me, too," Stacy admitted as she slanted Raine a worried look. *Should we leave?* her dark eyes telegraphed.

Raine allowed herself a tiny nod, which Stacy returned. "Speaking of war, I'd best put this wet little soldier down for her nap before she starts hollering bloody murder."

Stacy shifted her towel-swaddled daughter to the other hip, eliciting a faint protest from the sleepy-eyed little girl.

"Oh, Mommy, girls can't be soldiers," Tory piped up, her gaze darting between her mother's face and Morgan's.

"Says who?" Stacy demanded, arching her eyebrows.

"Lance says." Tory craned her neck to give Morgan a sober look. Her wet ponytail bobbed wildly, and she threatened to overbalance backward. "Lance is a dork."

Morgan's mouth slanted. "Lance is also wrong, sweetheart," he said, crouching down to the four-year-old's level. "I've met quite a few terrific lady soldiers."

Tory watched Morgan with big, curious eyes. Raine's

heart turned over. Mike used to look at his father like that when he was Tory's age. He thought his dad walked on water. Little did anyone know just how disastrous hero worship could be.

"Really and truly?" Tory demanded.

"Really and truly." Morgan reached out to smooth a lock of wet curly hair behind Tory's ear. He had the hands of a peasant, and yet his touch was as deft and gentle as a surgeon's.

"Did they have guns and stuff, like on TV?"

"Sure did. And some of the women I met were pilots, too. Had their own helicopters. Cobras."

Tory frowned. "Cobras are snakes."

Morgan's lopsided and just-a-little-stiff-at-the-corners smile put stars in the little girl's eyes. "That's true, but some Cobras are helicopters. Big black ones."

"With lady pilots," Tory declared with an emphatic nod of her dark head.

"Terrific lady pilots," Morgan emphasized as he rose.

"Well, well, an enlightened man. I'm impressed," Prudy said with a dimpled grin.

Don't be, Raine wanted to shout, but she contented herself with a warning frown. Morgan caught the change in expression and slanted her a thoughtful look.

Patience, she told herself as she bent to hand Prudy a towel.

"Chloe's definitely outgrowing the baby pool," she said as Prudy snuggled her daughter into the soft terry cloth. "A natural water sprite."

"It's Case's fault," Prudy said with a sigh before adding for Morgan's benefit, "Case is my husband. He spoils our daughter shamelessly, of course, which is bad enough. Much to my dismay, he also taught her how to turn on the hose when she was barely old enough to crawl. She loves water, especially with a generous measure of mud thrown in."

Morgan grinned. "Sounds very relaxing."

"Oh it is—for Chloe. Not for her long-suffering mom."

"Can I help you with that?" Morgan asked as Prudy reached for her tote bag.

Prudy looked bedazzled. "Just put it over my shoulder, thanks."

Raine drew a breath as Morgan did as Prudy asked, then reached out to run a finger over Chloe's soft cheek.

"Is it true what they say about redheads and temper?" he asked.

"Damn straight it's true," a male voice answered before Prudy could open her mouth.

Case Randolph came striding over the grass from the direction of the rear carports, his charcoal suit jacket slung over one broad shoulder and hooked on one finger, his tie askew beneath the open collar of his pale blue dress shirt. Smiling a greeting, Raine decided he looked hot and harried and more than a little dangerous, with his black hair flopping over his furrowed brow and his hard chin shadowed by a day's worth of stubble.

"Now, Case, you know that's not completely true," Prudy protested, her face aglow at the sight of her husband. "Chloe and I only lose our tempers around you."

Case slung an arm around his wife and kissed her soundly before planting a smacking kiss on his giggling daughter's cheek.

"Hiya, tootles. How's my girl?"

"Wet," Prudy muttered before glancing at Morgan. "In case you haven't already figured it out, this guy belongs to me. Meet my husband, the homicide cop."

"I figured you must be related," Morgan said with a grin as he held out his hand. "Morgan Paxton."

"Case Randolph," Case replied, his big hand taking Morgan's.

The two men exchanged measuring looks, neither giving away much, but Raine sensed an immediate understanding between the two.

"Seen you a time or two on the tube. Always glad I wasn't where you were."

Morgan chuckled. "Trust me, my job isn't as rough as yours. Not on my worst day."

Case shrugged that off with a slight movement of his big shoulders. "Welcome home. You gonna be around for a while?"

"No!" Raine interjected a shade too quickly and much too loudly.

Morgan glanced her way, one brow cocked. "Now, honey, don't make promises you can't keep." In spite of the laconic tone to his deep voice, the expression in his eyes was dead serious.

She drew in a breath and wondered if Case would turn a blind eye to the sight of one of his neighbors braining her estranged husband with a thermos of lemonade.

"Reason I ask," Case continued, gazing thoughtfully from Raine's face to Morgan's, "Saturday night a couple of other guys and me are getting together to play a little draw poker. Six-thirty, if you're interested."

Morgan's eyes lighted. "Depends on the stakes. I'm pretty rusty."

"Nothing too painful," Case said, grinning at the notion of new blood.

"In that case, I'm in."

"Two houses east, look for the pink door that glows in the dark."

Stacy groaned and rolled her eyes. "Oh Lord, not another one." She sighed. "I was hoping to wean Boyd away from you cutthroats," she told Case with a teasing grin.

"Not a chance, sugar. MacAuley's our prime pigeon. Keeps me in cigar money."

"Funny, that's what he says about you," Stacy retorted as she bent to retrieve the raffia basket that held towels and snacks. "Grab your thongs, Tory, and let's go."

Tory looked disgruntled, but she did as she was told. "Can I come back and visit Auntie Raine after supper?"

Stacy smiled. "We'll see," she hedged before looking Morgan's way. "It was a pleasure to meet you."

"Thanks. It's always a pleasure to be welcomed home by a yard full of pretty ladies."

"Get used to it," Case said with a wry grin as he glanced down at his wife. "In a couple of weeks or so we're expecting another female."

Morgan dropped his gaze to Raine's belly. "What about us, honey? What are we expecting?"

This time there was a definite edge to his drawl, and Raine felt her face flame.

"*We* aren't expecting anything. *I'm* expecting twin boys."

Chapter 3

One hour later Prudy Randolph sat like a contented Buddha on Case's side of their big bed and watched her husband sauntering into the room wearing nothing but the towel he'd slung around his neck after his shower. His thick black hair was still damp, and his tanned skin glistened like dew-kissed bronze in the light filtering through the miniblinds.

A soft, sweet shiver went through her at the sight of the man she loved with all her heart. Even after two marriage ceremonies, one eight years before their divorce, one eight years after, she never failed to be moved by the knowledge that this man needed her in his life. She certainly needed him with an intensity so fierce, it sometimes frightened her. And every time she caught sight of the puckered scar on his abdomen, she was reminded of how close she'd come to losing him.

"Paxton seems like a stand-up guy," he said as he haphazardly swiped the thick towel over his hair.

"Mmm." Out of her loyalty to Raine, Prudy was reserving her opinion.

"Looks older in person than he does on the tube."

Prudy gave that careful thought, then decided Case was right. Raine's ex had looked pretty world-weary, as though he'd seen too many horrors and fought too many battles. Nevertheless, she refused to feel sorry for him. When Raine had needed him, he'd been chasing fame.

"He's a few years younger than you are," she said, admiring the long, clean lines of her husband's lithe body. "Forty-two or three, I think."

"Yeah? Guess that goes to show what the desert sun can do to a guy."

"Maybe. Or maybe it's guilt that put those lines in his face."

Case arched an inquisitive brow. It didn't bother him one whit to be standing there without a stitch on, while, in fact, it bothered her very much. In an extremely pleasant way, of course. Which he knew perfectly well, the rat.

"Guilt how?"

Once a detective, always a detective, she decided. "He was pretty much an absentee husband and father. He wasn't even home when their son had his accident."

"Accident?"

Prudy sighed. She wished now she'd kept her thoughts to herself. "Morgan taught his son to ski during one of his infrequent trips home. Apparently Mike wanted to impress his dad with how good he'd gotten, so one time when he was on a trip with a friend's family, he tackled a hill that was too difficult. He hit a tree and broke his neck. A massive infection set in and affected his heart."

She saw the change in Case's expression, giving her a quickly hidden glimpse of the deep vein of compassion that underlay his hard edge. An intensely kind man in the guise of a cynical cop, that was Case. Her big gruff, pussycat with the instincts and ferocity of a tiger.

"He…lingered for a week, calling for his father," she continued when he caught her staring. "Morgan was in Bosnia. By the time he got word and made it home, it was too late."

Case shook his head. "That's rough."

"From what little Raine told me, I gather she came close to a nervous breakdown after the funeral."

Prudy had been a nurse for more than half of her forty-two years, and yet she'd never been able to harden herself against the death of a child.

Case made a pass with the towel over his chest. "And Paxton? How did he handle it?"

"Raine said he just shut down. Blocked it out, and after a few weeks at home, went on with his career."

"Guess that was as good a way as any."

Prudy started to protest, then realized that Case's jaw had gone rigid the way it did when something touched him profoundly. His gaze had slid from hers, another sign that he was hiding his feelings.

"To be fair, he was locked into this contract that he couldn't break, although he offered to try if Raine insisted."

"And did she?"

"No. It was easier for her to handle things alone." She glanced at the photo that she kept on her nightstand of Case cradling Chloe against his big chest. "She said that their son was a carbon copy of Morgan. Had the same wavy blond hair and hazel eyes."

"Cute kid?"

"Apparently."

Case combed one callused hand through his hair a few times— his version of grooming. He'd grown up in an upper-class family in the San Francisco Bay area and could teach a course in embassy manners if pushed. Around home, however, he was wonderfully relaxed.

"You think Paxton's good-looking?" he asked in a throwaway tone.

"Actually, I would say that 'gorgeous' more perfectly describes Morgan Paxton," she said after a moment of feigned consideration.

His head came up as fast as a bull catching a whiff of danger, and he shot her a piercing look.

"Probably has women falling all over him."

"Probably."

"Well, hell," he muttered. "And I just invited the 'gorgeous' bastard to the house for Saturday night."

With a flick of his thick wrist, he tossed the towel toward the wicker hamper in the corner. It hit the wall behind the basket with a soft thump, and Case muttered something rude.

Prudy giggled. "I love it when you're jealous."

He shot her a disgruntled look before opening his underwear drawer. "What the hell?" he muttered, holding up a skimpy pair of bright red briefs with a look of stark horror on his dark face. "Care to tell me what this is supposed to be?"

Prudy folded her hands over her tummy and worked hard to keep from laughing. "What's it look like, Detective?"

Case's mouth twitched. "Something no real man would be caught dead wearing—unless he was working vice."

"There's this great new shop in the mall, right next to the Baby Boutique. Stacy bought Boyd a pair in black. They're real silk."

He closed his eyes and drew a long breath. "Silk," he said faintly. "Lord save me."

Prudy sat up straighter. This was going to be good, she decided with a delicious shiver of anticipation.

"Go ahead and try them on," she urged when he continued to stare down at his big fist. "Silk feels yummy against your skin."

"Not as *yummy* as other things I could name," he said, glancing over at her with a predatory grin that had her heart rate speeding.

"Behave yourself, Randolph," she ordered primly. "You heard what Luke said on my last visit. No sex until after this little darling makes her appearance."

"I heard him, the sadistic sonofagun. He actually enjoyed cutting me off." His voice was grumpy, but his eyes were hot as his gaze took in her lazy pose. So many times he'd claimed to love the way she looked with a big belly, that Prudy was beginning to believe him.

"He did have a rather devilish look in his eyes, didn't he?" she mused. "Probably because he's actually green with envy because you're a happily married man and he isn't."

"Yeah, well, this *happily married man* isn't about to parade around in silk Skivvies." He regarded the bright scrap of slinky material still clutched in one large fist as though it were a dead rat. Prudy bit her lip to keep from laughing.

"You said you read that book on pregnancy you made me buy you," she chided softly although she knew full well he had read it cover to cover. And then had started over, according to his partner, Detective Sergeant Don Petrov.

"What's that got to do with my underwear?" he demanded, suspicion darkening his blue eyes.

"It specifically said in chapter six that a pregnant woman's emotional well-being is vitally important."

"So?"

"So my emotional well-being would be greatly enhanced by the sight of my hunk of a husband parading around in red silk briefs."

Case groaned. "That's blackmail, pure and simple, Mrs. Randolph."

"It is indeed, Sergeant Randolph. Are you going to arrest me?"

"I should beat you, that's what I should do," he declared as he bent to jerk the briefs over first one muscular leg, then the other. When he tugged them over his hips, the waistband dipped a full inch below his navel and the thin silk cupped his sex with a mouth-watering snugness.

Prudy drew in a breath and let it out very slowly. Somewhere along the line, Case had picked up more than his share of sex appeal.

"Okay, look fast, because these suckers are ending up in the rag bag before the night is over," he ordered as he stood there, daring her to look, his long legs spread wide, his big hands fisted on his lean hips, the ridiculously tiny briefs a bright contrast to the burnished skin of his sinewy thighs.

Prudy smiled serenely as she let her gaze wander over her husband's broad expanse of heavily muscled chest, lingering at the triangular pelt of black-as-midnight chest hair. When they made love, she loved to bury her nose in that teasing softness, loved the way his muscles hardened when she touched the tip of her tongue to the tiny flat nipples hidden there. Her mouth went dry as she let her gaze roam lower, following the furred arrow bisecting his corded torso.

"The frontal view is quite nice," she said with a small prim nod that belied the desire rapidly building low and deep inside her. "Now I'd like to see the back, if you please, Sergeant."

Case scowled as she made a lazy circular movement with one hand. "You're really pushing this pampering stuff to the limit, sweetheart," he all but growled as he folded his brawny arms over his chest and turned his back.

Prudy was just thinking how much she loved the long, lean look of him when her gaze fell to the erratic ribbons of scar tissue just to the left of his spine. All of a sudden she couldn't breathe. The bullet that had plowed into his belly two years ago had exploded out the back, tearing flesh and spewing blood over her living room carpet. Emergency surgery, Boyd MacAuley's prodigious skill and Case's own indomitable will to survive had kept him alive. But it had been a near thing.

"Well?" Case turned to scowl at her. His feigned irritation turned to genuine alarm as he caught sight of her face.

"Prue? What's wrong?" In a wink he was kneeling beside the bed, his face tortured as he pressed one of her hands between his. "Is it time? Should I call Jarrod?"

Prudy tried to smile, but her lips were trembling too much. Case had pressed the barrel of his own .38 to his belly and pulled the trigger to keep a madman from killing her instead. She still had nightmares about that awful day.

"I… Your back. I came so close to losing y-you."

Case muttered a word that might have expressed relief or dismay. "No way, lady. You're stuck with me this time," he said as he rose, his arms already reaching for her. "Scoot over and give me room."

She did, and then next thing she knew, she was snuggled up to her husband's warm body. Safe again.

Raine inhaled the familiar scent of brewing coffee and sighed as she reached into the cupboard for a mug. Dr. Luke Jarrod had restricted her to one cup a day, and she'd already had her entire ration. The pot she was making was for Morgan.

The wall phone rang as she was trying to decide if she should offer him something to eat, and she snatched it up, grateful for the diversion.

"Lorraine, it's Father."

She smiled. Her father was a dear, but he had a tendency to be a bit of an old maid at times. "Yes, I recognized your voice," she teased gently.

"Well, of course, you did, child." Arthur Connelly sounded impatient.

Raine glanced toward the door leading to the front room. Morgan had said something about taking a quick shower after he'd retrieved his bags from her front porch. The yellow roses he'd brought her were drooping in a crystal vase in the middle of the table. Like her spirits, she decided whimsically.

"How are you feeling today?" she asked as she pulled over a chair and sat down.

"Tolerable."

"Is the new medicine helping the arthritis?"

"It's too soon to tell." He cleared his throat. "I didn't call to talk about the vagaries of my physical condition, my dear. I called to warn you."

"Warn me?"

She heard his heavy sigh. "I had a call yesterday morning from Paxton. He asked for your phone number and address."

Raine closed her eyes. "Yesterday morning?" she repeated softly.

"I wasn't sure if I should tell you. Naturally I was concerned that the news would distress you. It took me some time to weigh the pros and cons."

"Still protecting your little girl, Dad?"

"And why not?" her father retorted in irate tones. "That man wasn't a proper husband to you or a good parent to Mike."

Raine felt a kick in the vicinity of her left kidney and winced. "Dad, we've had this discussion before. It doesn't do either one of us any good."

There was a momentary pause during which Raine pictured her father scowling down at the receiver.

"Yes, well, I expect he'll try to contact you," he said stiffly. "I wanted you to be prepared."

"I appreciate the thought, but he's already here."

"The hell you say!" Her father cleared his throat again. "I beg your pardon, my dear. That man always did have an ability to make me forget my manners."

Raine sighed. "I know the feeling."

"Are you...all right?"

"I'm fine. 'Blooming,' according to my doctor."

"I'm glad to hear that, of course, but I was actually inquiring about your emotional well-being."

"It's fine, too." She stifled a sigh. "Don't worry, Dad. I'm sure Morgan has only stopped by to drop off the divorce papers."

"Don't count on it."

It was Morgan's voice that made the comment, prompting her to look toward the doorway where he stood, one shoulder propped against the jamb and his arms crossed over a wide chest now sheathed in a tight black T-shirt bearing the familiar logo of the news network.

Raine wondered if Morgan realized how shamelessly that network used his fame to its advantage, flashing his face on the television screen every night to keep the ratings up, whether he was scheduled for an appearance or not.

Glaring at her soon-to-be ex-husband, Raine said, "I've got to go, Dad."

"Go? Lorraine, wait. Shall I drive up there? I can leave within the hour."

"No need. But thanks for the thought."

"Are you sure you can handle this...development alone?"

"Perfectly sure. After all, I've been handling things alone for over ten years now. Nothing has changed."

She heard her father's distressed sigh come over the line. "Call me if you need me."

"I will," she promised before hanging up.

Sunlight slanted through the bay window looking out over the pocket herb garden that was her pride and joy. Gourmet cooking was one of her passions. Not that Morgan noticed. His preferences ran to greasy hamburgers and pork chops.

"Sounds like Arthur's still hovering."

His golden eyes were watchful, taking in more than they gave out. His jaw was shiny from a recent shave, and his shower-damp hair was slicked back from his forehead, giving him an austere look. Some of the fatigue had disappeared from his face, but his eyes were still bloodshot. Morgan never slept on planes, no matter how lengthy the flight. It was a matter of control, she suspected. An unwillingness to trust his fate to anyone else, no matter how skilled or experienced.

"You make hovering sound like a crime."

He straightened to amble toward the coffeemaker. "Do I?"

"Since Mom died, I'm all the family Dad has left."

"There is that."

Something in his voice had her wondering if he had thought himself included in the Connelly family. But of course, he had, she chided herself. Before her death five years ago, her mother had adored Morgan and considered him the son she'd never had. Her father had been more reserved toward the man he believed had callously seduced his daughter.

"I take it Arthur approves of the new man in your life?" He lifted the mug to his mouth and drank.

"What man?"

His eyes narrowed. "The father of your twin boys."

Raine felt panic run through her. She took a deep, slow

breath and felt her control steady. "Dad has never met the father."

"Ashamed of the guy, are you?"

She stiffened. Why had she thought this would go smoothly? "No, I'm not ashamed."

"What's he like?" His voice was slanted toward indifference, but the man who'd asked the question radiated pain. And...loneliness?

Her mind blanked. Surely not. The great Morgan Paxton was a confirmed loner. A man who would rather burn in hell than attend a party. A man who refused to fit his life into anyone's else's parameters.

For a moment silence built between them. She tried to look away and couldn't. The weary man lounging so casually in her kitchen was even more of a stranger, someone she didn't know.

Perhaps she'd never truly known him, she realized, just as he'd never truly known her. She'd been so young when they'd met. So willing to fall in love. So eager to be loved in return. But a frenzied attraction of one body for another wasn't love.

She would do well to remember that.

"Why are you here, Morgan?" she asked, her throat tight.

"Now that's an interesting question. One that's not quite as simple as I anticipated."

Utterly motionless, he contemplated her with that same steady gaze familiar to millions of viewers worldwide. A patient predator waiting for the prey to move first.

"Let's just say I have four months' leave coming, and I intend to take it here."

"No!"

"I left my bags in the upstairs hall. Say the word and I'll move them into the master bedroom."

She fought down an image of his nude body cradling

hers. "It doesn't bother you to sleep with a woman who's carrying another man's children?"

His eyes flashed fire. "Hell, yes, it bothers me! But not enough to walk away without a fight."

The panic that had ebbed surged again. And again, she beat it back. This was her house, her life.

"Read my lips, Morgan. *N-o.*"

His mouth firmed. "Don't worry, honey. You won't even know I'm here."

"Exactly—because you won't *be* here."

The slow smile he gave her was off center and slightly sad. The smile of a man who'd been chasing answers with such single-minded determination, he hadn't realized he'd actually been running away from himself.

"Thanks for the coffee," he said before draining his cup. Turning his back to her, he rinsed the mug carefully before upending it in the drainer. "Wake me in an hour. I'm going to take a quick nap before dinner. Don't bother to cook. We'll go out."

Raine was still sputtering when he left the room.

Chapter 4

She'd bought a new bed. A four-poster job that looked almost too fragile to support his weight. Piled against the headboard had been a half-dozen pillows in frilly cases. Fancy, feminine things that made Morgan edgy.

Is this where she'd conceived the babies now growing in her belly? he wondered, turning to his side.

The thought of her lying naked on tangled sheets, her glorious hair fanned over one of those lacy pillows, her legs spread eagerly while another man deposited his seed, made him sick to his stomach.

If this wasn't hell, it was damn close enough.

He closed his eyes and waited for the exhaustion humming in his head to override his dark thoughts. But his mind refused to settle. Instead, he kept seeing some nameless, faceless bastard making love to *his* wife.

Rage hovered just beneath the steel bands of his control, too volatile to be given freedom. Later, when he was rested, he would ask her why she'd cheated on him. Why she'd done the one thing he'd never believed possible for her to do—break her wedding vows.

He felt his back teeth grind together and consciously relaxed his jaw. Restless, he turned to his back, and then to his other side, uneasy in the strange bed.

He'd been known to fall asleep in the back of a lurching Jeep or on the floor of the equipment van taking the crew to some isolated location. It was simply a matter of discipline and concentration. Hell, he had plenty of both.

Maybe he was short on conventional education, but he wasn't ignorant. Hell no! He'd earned his GED in the army. He'd been damn proud of that piece of paper. Still carried it in his wallet as a matter of fact. While his buddies had been drinking themselves senseless in a seedy bar or trying to romance a freebie from a bar girl, he'd spent countless hours poring over a battered dictionary he'd bought in a secondhand store, patiently sounding out the words, memorizing the definitions, struggling to improve his sadly limited vocabulary.

He'd hated being ignorant, hated knowing the guys in his unit called him a stupid hillbilly. So he'd covered his pain with arrogance, slathering it on with a damn trowel. Swaggered and swore and volunteered for every dangerous, gut-busting mission. When he'd finished his tour in Vietnam, he'd volunteered to go back for another thirteen months.

He'd been as gung ho as they'd come, bent on proving himself to be as good as the next man and as single-minded about improving himself as his father had been about drinking. Now, these many years later, it was trendy to reinvent one's self, yet another fad like exotic coffee and imported cheese. Self-help gurus wrote books about it.

How to change your life in five easy steps.

Morgan released a long, weary breath. Lord, but he was tired.

Good thing he was used to the unexpected, he told himself as he eased to his back, then shoved one hand behind his head and stared up at the ceiling. Otherwise, he might have found himself damn depressed that Raine had turned to another man to help her through the grieving process.

From the glow on her face and the sexy roundness of her belly, he'd done a good job.

The bastard.

Something sharp and icy stirred inside him, like the blade of a skinning knife being slowly twisted. It wasn't a feeling he'd ever had before, so it took him a moment to realize he was flat-out jealous.

Raine was his, damn it. She'd been a virgin the first time they'd made love. His body had been the first one to breach hers. Lord, but she'd been tight and yet so wonderfully slick.

He still remembered how she'd clung to him, her eyes glazed with pleasure and her fingers kneading his shoulders like kitten claws. When she'd called his name at the moment of her first climax, he'd felt a thousand feet tall and as powerful as a king. In some mysterious way, he'd felt complete, as though something he'd lost had been restored.

Damn, but he needed to feel that again, he realized as he felt his body hardening. He'd always been a man of lusty appetites. For the food he'd missed as a half-starved kid. For excitement and acceptance. For love.

For Raine.

But first he was going to have to find a way to forgive her.

Her eyes burning with what felt suspiciously like sentimental tears, Raine stood at the doorway of her bedroom, watching Morgan sleep. Not in the guest room, as she'd directed. Oh, no, not Morgan. He'd sought out *her* bed instead, sprawling his large body across the comforter, his wealth of bronzed muscle outlined against a backdrop of deep purple softness, making her think of a languorous lion snoozing on a giant-size pillow.

A sense of yearning swept through her that set off warning bells.

Morgan. Here in her house. Her quiet, safe little world.

Peering through the gloom until her eyes adjusted, Raine could almost feel the heavy heat of him beside her, one of those thick, powerful arms slung over her waist.

Long before she could make out the details of his face, her traitorous memory conjured his visage in exact detail, tantalizing her in a way she couldn't define and resented with every fiber of her being. So what if he'd sought her bed, instead of sleeping in the guest room? So what if he resembled a tawny mountain cat too sated, or too worn-out to prowl? The fact was that he hadn't been in her bed when it had mattered, and now it was too late.

She was over him. Free. Emotionally, if not legally. Detached.

Whatever she felt for him now was purely cerebral. A faint nostalgic attachment. And maybe a little compassion that he looked older. More somber. Even sad.

The crow's-feet around his eyes had deepened, and the frown lines bracketing his expressive mouth were more pronounced. The ravages of grief, she wondered, or the natural consequence of his months in the desert?

No matter. He was still a striking man. He'd told her once that he'd gotten his coloring from his mother, his height and build from his father. Early in their marriage she'd discovered that there were no pictures of him as a child. No lovingly preserved mementos tucked into a box for safekeeping. No memories to savor and share. Perhaps that's why he'd been fanatical about taking pictures of Mike.

He'd taken roll after roll of pictures whenever he'd come

home, pictures she'd carefully tucked into a series of leather-bound scrapbooks. A record of their child's life. Eight years of memories, now lined up neatly on a shelf in the spare bedroom at the end of the hall.

A few months back, on the day she'd discovered she was pregnant again, she'd gone directly to the mall to buy an uncomplicated, but good-quality camera and two new scrapbooks, one for each of the babies tucked so snugly under her heart. In about two more months she would see their faces, feel their greedy little mouths suckling her breasts.

A wave of longing ran through her. She missed Mike so very much. His boisterous laughter, his wild shouts of happiness or dismay. The off-center smile he'd inherited from his father along with Morgan's inability to sit still for more than a few minutes at a time. The little-boy smell that was part grime, part peanut butter and always uniquely Mike.

Morgan had missed so many of the precious moments in their child's life. But then, that had been his choice, she reminded herself, hardening her heart. Just as it had been his choice to put his marriage second to his career on his list of priorities.

Now it was her turn to set the priorities. Her unborn twins came first, her need to be free of Morgan Paxton running a close second. No more part-time daddy. No more part-time husband.

She straightened her shoulders and groped desperately for her determination to feel unaffected, thinking even as she did that her wavering willpower offered precious little as armor against his masculine charisma.

A tawny mountain man, a fanciful publicist had once called him. Honey gold, his hair was thick and almost never more than finger-combed with streaks of sunlight threaded through the unruly strands, and his eyes were an amber brown that often looked golden against the deeply layered permanent tan of his angular face.

According to his bio, he'd been a raw-boned corporal in Vietnam assigned to guard a network news team when, accompanying a scouting patrol, they'd been ambushed. The reporter had been shot in midsentence, and while Morgan worked frantically to stanch the blood pouring from the man's severed artery, the camera had continued to roll.

When the patrol had returned to base, the cameraman had sent his film stateside, and Morgan's heroism had been shown in millions of homes that next night. A few days later another newsman had tracked him down for an interview, one of those inane "how did you feel when?" types. In this case, Morgan had been bluntly honest. He'd felt like hell watching men die. Though his language had been uncultured by educated standards, his innate integrity and decency had shone through, tapping into the psyche of the "common man." For all his rawness and awkwardness, Morgan had that precious intangible known as presence. In addition, the camera had loved his wild good looks, just as she did. *Seductive* was the only word to describe them, and viewers across the country had succumbed.

The most important viewer that night had been a network executive, Francis P. Weinhard, a revered member of an acclaimed group of journalists who'd emerged from WWII to remake broadcast news.

A man who'd started his career by sweeping the studio floor, he'd seen potential in Morgan and when Morgan's enlistment was up, Weinhard had offered himself as a mentor and teacher. Morgan had never had anyone believe in him before. He'd idolized Weinhard, more for his gruff kindness and faith than for his fame.

Weinhard had been relentless in his demands and teachings, drilling Morgan for endless hours on speech and diction and syntax. With his mentor's help, Morgan had acquired an air of confidence and assurance, yet there'd still been enough left of that impassioned, rough-edged soldier to captivate the viewers.

He'd started small, but it hadn't been long before he'd moved to Los Angeles, and then New York. After that, it had been straight to the top.

A shooting star.

He was still the best TV reporter she'd ever seen.

Sighing, Raine glanced at the clock. She'd fixed steaks and a salad. She should wake him so that he could eat before she threw him out.

For all his years of traveling, Morgan invariably suffered from severe jet lag for a few days after a flight, no matter what remedy he'd tried. The only thing that worked was sleep. She knew from experience that if she woke him now, he would be groggy and disoriented and irritable at the precise instant she needed him to be rational and receptive. No, she would let him sleep. And then, when he was awake and alert, she would order him out of her house. For good, this time.

Morgan woke up stiff and sore, his senses annoyingly dull. His mouth tasted foul, and his head felt twice its normal size. For a moment he wondered why he was coming off of a two-day drunk, then realized it was just his usual jet-lag hangover. From the angle of the sunlight filtering through the skinny wooden blinds, he estimated the time to be early morning.

He yawned, then glanced at his watch. How many times had he changed the time on this trip? Six or seven? He'd lost track. He was, however, meticulous in always making sure his watch was accurate, so he knew it was 7:35, Pacific Daylight Time.

He was back in the good old U.S. of A. In Raine's cream-colored bedroom with its wild accents of regal color on the walls and furniture. In her bed with one of those fat coverlets she liked so much.

He turned his head to look for her, knowing even as he did that she wasn't in the room. He would know if she were. The tension riding his spine would be gone, and he would feel lazy and content. Settled.

Her scent was there, however—that roses-in-summer perfume she loved. He felt his body stirring and allowed himself a frustrated groan. This was definitely not the time to remember the soft, supple skin beneath the erotic scent. Or the lazy mornings he'd spent tasting every inch.

With a muffled groan, he pushed himself to a sitting position, then waited for his head to clear before getting to his feet. He needed a bathroom first and then coffee. A gallon would do for starters, he decided as he paused at the door to the hall to get his bearings.

The house was quiet, the sounds from beyond the outer walls muffled and indistinct. The blessed aroma of strong coffee drifted toward him from the direction of the kitchen. He heard water running. He felt a momentary disorientation before his gaze settled on the closed door across the hall.

His head still felt thick and dull as he opened the door and walked in. A cloud of steam enveloped him in a swirl of warmth, obscuring his vision. Quickly he closed the door, then turned toward the glass-enclosed shower. Through the mist he saw the pink outline of Raine's back, the plump white mounds of her lush bottom, the gracefully tapering slope of her spine.

He felt a momentary surge of emotion, the soft, dangerous kind that he hated. The kind that made a strong man weak. After spending half his life in one war zone or another, he knew better than most that a weak man was a dead man. But a surge of sexual heat flooding a man's loins, now that was an emotion he could handle. Even seek.

It took only an instant to strip, another to open the shower door.

Raine turned quickly, her eyes huge as she backed into the tiled wall behind her. "Morgan, for heaven's sake—"

"Oh no, honey. This is definitely for *my* sake."

The stall was standard issue, but given his size and her protruding belly, it was a close fit. He felt the warmth of the spray on his face and the scald of desire running over his skin. Lord, but she was magnificent. A fertility goddess come to life.

"Don't," she murmured, putting out a hand to keep him at bay.

Afraid to push for more, he touched her face with his fingertips, a mere whisper of a caress before letting his hand fall away. He felt his muscles coil, ready to drag her against him. Eighteen long, endless, lonely months compressed into a stark, clawing moment of need. He let the hunger take hold, hot talons in his flesh, before summoning the will to beat it down.

Timing, he told himself. He was supposed to be a master of it. It was all in knowing when to be patient, and when to push.

"Turn around," he ordered with a patented Morgan Paxton grin that came harder than it should. "I'll wash your back."

He saw the surprise come into her eyes, followed by a flash of confusion that had him smiling inside. He rubbed his itchy palm against his belly and took another loop around his impatience.

"No thank you, I can manage," she said with stiff dignity that was spoiled somewhat by the ridiculous pink puffy thing in her hand that was presently mashed against his shoulder.

"Didn't say you couldn't."

He cupped her shoulders lightly and nudged her into a

little turn. She planted her feet wide and resisted. He could have forced her, but that was neither his style nor his inclination.

Patience and persistence, he told himself with a mental sigh.

"Honey, didn't your mama ever tell you never to refuse a generous impulse?"

She frowned, drew in a breath. "Morgan, why are you doing this?" she demanded as the warm water pulsed between them, a slick transparent curtain.

"I thought that was pretty obvious, angel face. I want to be with you. Since you're in the shower, that's where I am, too."

"That's nonsense," she sputtered, sliding sideways as though intending to slip past him.

"True story," he said, blocking her escape by propping a hand against the wall.

"Uh-huh."

She moved one bare shoulder. He doubted she intended the slight movement to be provocative, but he had a sudden urge to drop a kiss on the sleek slope. Right where a little clutch of freckles spattered her collarbone.

"You don't believe me?"

She nudged her chin higher. "There's missing and then there's missing."

"What the hell is that supposed to mean?"

"It means you only miss me when it's convenient for you to miss me."

Morgan felt anger spike through the sexual hunger gripping him. Controlling it, he dropped his head and stared down at the water swirling into the drain between them.

"I gotta tell you, Raine, for an intelligent woman, you can be damned stupid sometimes."

She drew in another fast little breath. "Not stupid. Realistic."

She lifted a hand to brush a lock of brown hair away from her forehead. "It's taken me a while to stop believing in fairy tales, but losing a child helped."

He felt a hard slug of pain. Habit allowed him to absorb it without visible reaction.

"I'm willing to cut you slack for sleeping with another man, though my old man would already have been loading his shotgun. I'm even fixing to forgive you. What more do you want from me?"

"A divorce." The answer came too quickly, too forcefully.

"No."

Raine felt the numbness she'd gathered around herself like a shield begin to thin at the edges. She wasn't used to standing in a hot, wet shower stall with her tummy resembling a watermelon and a very large, very much in control naked man looming over her as though it were the most natural thing in the world. But then, Morgan was a master of the unexpected, she reminded herself. It was part of that famous style of his.

"Morgan, this is silly. I have to get to work, and you..." She let her voice trail off, aware that she had no idea what he had planned. Annoyed, she waved a hand. "You need to find yourself another place to stay."

"Sounds like you're kicking me out of my own house before I even have a chance to see it all."

"This is not your house. I used the money I made from my renovation projects to buy it. I haven't touched a penny of your money for the last eighteen months."

Emotion flared in his eyes. Unreadable, but dangerous. "Last I heard, Oregon was a community property state."

Something in his voice told her she'd just made a tactical mistake, but before she pinned that down, his big hand was already slipping between her and the slick tile.

"Morg—"

His mouth came down on hers, cutting off her protest and her breath. She felt a jolt of heat, a rush of excitement, an unnamed emotion so fierce, it frightened her. He tugged her closer until her wet belly was pressed tightly against his hair-roughened abdomen. She felt the slamming of his heart beneath hers and the arrogant demand of his arousal where it jutted hard against the juncture of her thighs.

No! her mind shouted, but her body was too busy reacting to obey. It happened quickly—a small niggling of memory that quickly bloomed into an ache to be loved. Her body yearned for his warmth, his touch, his possession. Her heart reminded her that he was her husband, her lover. The man she had promised to love and cherish forever.

His arms were so strong, his mouth so tempting. He was a big, solid, aggressive male, bronzed and callused and hard, prone to making impossible demands, unwilling to bend. All that was female in her responded with a wild joy that startled her.

She strained upward, circled his neck with her arms, awash in a longing that was stronger than reason, fiercer than self-protection. When she breathed in, the clean scent of his skin went through her like a shock wave. Familiar, comforting.

Arousing.

When her lips parted for his, she knew what he would taste like on her tongue. As her fingers caressed his slick, taut shoulder muscles, she recalled the strength of him. His skin was hot and familiar beneath her touch. Soap-drenched steam swirled with warm caressing hands around them, giving the small white cubicle a surreal enchantment.

Morgan!

He was all she remembered and more. When he was with her, her world sparkled. When he was with her…

Morgan felt her grow rigid. When she pressed her palms against his shoulders and pushed, he knew he had to let her go. Shaken, breathing hard, he lifted his head and relaxed his hold. But he couldn't make himself release her. Not yet.

"I wondered if it would feel the same when I kissed you again," he said, rubbing his palms over her wet shoulders. "Now I know. It's eighteen months better."

With a small moan, she stepped back as far as she could, her breasts heaving. Her eyes had darkened and turned drowsy with desire, stopping his heart. She wanted him. He would bet his immortal soul on it.

"I want your promise you won't do that again," she ordered, her voice thick and not quite under control.

"No promise."

Her eyes flashed. The display of temper reassured him. Anger he could handle. Even hatred. It was indifference he feared.

"Then I'll call the police and have you thrown out."

He grinned. "I love it when you flash those big brown eyes at me, Raine. Gets me hot."

"You bastard," she said, giving him a hard shove that caught him off guard. He crashed against the shower door, which flew open. Before he could catch his balance, he was sprawled on his butt on the bathroom floor. He snarled a curse that never would have made it past the network censors, then for good measure added a few more creative phrases.

"Don't you dare laugh," he warned, but it was too late. Though she had her hand clamped to her lips, her eyes were sparkling with laughter.

"Oh, my," she murmured in a choked voice. "Too bad your adoring fans can't see you now."

Morgan felt the blood race to his face where it turned his skin as blistering hot as the fire his daddy had kept burning under his big copper still.

"So much for sweeping you off your feet with my suave charm," he muttered as he picked himself up. He'd never been all that great at romancing the ladies when he'd been single. Eleven years of marriage had obviously turned him into an idiot.

"Morgan—"

"Finish your damn shower," he all but shouted at her before snatching up the clothes he'd scattered haphazardly in his haste earlier. She made him feel fifteen again and too small for his skin.

"You asked for it," she said in a voice still shaky with laughter.

"The hell I did."

The smile faded from her eyes, replaced by a sadness that shook him. "For the record, I don't want your forgiveness. Nor do I need it. My life's my own now."

"Don't bet on it, sugar." He bit off the words, then froze as they replayed in his head like a split-second tape delay. The words were his, but the voice was his father's—harsh and mean.

He closed his eyes for an instant, then spun on his heel and stalked out.

Chapter 5

Raine had always loved books—fat ones, skinny ones, old ones, new ones, fiction or nonfiction. She adored the astringent smell of the ink and the slick feel of the paper beneath her fingertips. An avid reader since the age of four, she'd moved into adulthood with a book always within easy reach, either in her purse or on her nightstand, and the passion had led her to seek a degree from Bradenton College in American Literature.

By the time she'd graduated, she'd had three unpublished novels to her credit and the reluctant knowledge that she was far better at reading a novel than writing one. Still, her love of literature remained a constant, and second in line in her list of fond wishes was to someday own a bookstore.

After Mike's death, she'd known she had to revamp her life or lose what was left of her sanity, so she'd gone home to Oregon, bought her adorable little house by the river and used the rest of the money she'd saved over the years from her renovation projects to open a small bookstore and espresso bar located in an old brick warehouse near Portland State University. In the beginning, most of the books on her shelves had come from her own library, collected during the lonely months of her marriage.

Furnished in early funk, with a generous dollop of whimsy, the While Away Bookstore had become a gathering place of sorts for a certain fringe element. Many were students going to school on a shoestring budget who "rented" used textbooks from the huge collection Raine had amassed, paying only a token amount.

Others were locals—senior citizens mostly, living on Social Security. Raine's "senior rate" was the most generous around. Fifty cents for a large latte and a quarter for a muffin she baked herself. Though she lost money every month on that part of her business, she considered herself amply repaid by the friendships she'd formed with her regulars. Many had become like family to her, especially some of the elders who claimed to have adopted her.

Normally she couldn't wait to get to work every morning. She loved the little surprises each day brought. But when she'd left the house thirty minutes after Morgan stalked out of the bathroom stark naked and furious, she'd found herself heading for her neighbor Prudy's back door instead.

For a little tea and sympathy, she'd told herself when she knocked.

It was laundry day in the Randolph household, and Raine was waiting for her last load to dry. Prudy had offered hot carob and milk, nonfat granola bars and a welcoming smile. While Chloe watched TV in the living room, the two women hung out in the kitchen, two chubby ladies in maternity smocks, their friendship an invisible halo of warmth that filled the air around them, making Prudy's cozy kitchen seem even more homey and welcoming.

* * *

Lulled by the warmth and sense of security her bond with
Prudy always gave her, Raine let down all her defenses,
entrusting her friend with the details of her disturbing joust
with Morgan earlier.

"It was awful, Prudy. Just awful. There he lay, like a
lion, sprawled on my dusty rose bathroom rug, his face
almost as pink as the cotton shag."

"From embarrassment?"

Raine sniffed. "Morgan, embarrassed? You've got to be
kidding. He was furious." She shrugged. "And maybe a
little humiliated. The mighty Pax, felled by a pregnant lady
brandishing a pink net body scrubber. I whacked him as
hard as I could. He staggered backward, lost his footing on
some of the moisturizer I'd spilled, crashed into the shower
door, and—" Raine waved her hand "—the next thing I
knew, he was making like a Playgirl centerfold on my imported tile floor."

"I hope you had a camera handy. Moments like that are
too priceless to pass up."

"A camera?" Raine blinked. "I was in the shower,
Prue." She narrowed her gaze. "You're getting a good
laugh out of this, aren't you? I came here for some sympathy, you know."

Prudy clamped a slender hand over her mouth, her green
eyes dancing.

"It isn't funny," Raine scolded.

"And then what happened?" Prudy asked, the knowing
twinkle in her eye telling Raine she knew that she was
getting a slightly edited version of the actual event.

"I washed my hair. Twice."

Prudy nodded sagely. "Of course. That makes perfect
sense."

"I *always* wash my hair when I'm upset," Raine explained. "I don't know why exactly. Just one of those peculiar customs that developed over the years. It's something

about the scent of shampoo and the cascade of warm water on my scalp. It soothes me, somehow, no matter how rattled I am.''

''I'll have to try it sometime,'' Prudy commented dryly. ''The ritual may have come in handy yesterday, in fact. Case modeled those red silk briefs I bought for him. I'm on restriction, you know, until after the baby comes. I took a shower to cool off. But shampooing my hair never occurred to me. It really works, huh?''

Raine frowned. ''You're making light of this. I shampooed because I was upset, not because I was—'' She waved her hand again. ''I'm over him, Prue. Totally. It was just unsettling, that's all, having him invade my shower like that. And then to have it end as it did, with him on my floor. Well, it got my day off to a rotten start, to say the least. When I came out of the shower, Morgan was gone. Vanished.''

''I'm sure his pride was smarting a bit,'' Prudy observed sagely. ''If knocking him on his fanny didn't do it, shampooing your hair—twice—probably did the job. A man expects more of a reaction when he pulls a stunt like that.''

Morosely Raine dunked her granola bar into the cup of hot milk she'd been staring at for the last five minutes and listened to the sound of rain spattering against the patio outside the window. In her heart of hearts, she knew Morgan had elicited all the reactions any man could have hoped for, not that she'd ever admit it to Prudy.

She'd felt his kiss all through her body. In her breasts, which had tightened and tingled. In the most intimate part of her, which had swelled with a need so hot, she'd all but begged him to touch her. To stroke and pet her, to fill her. Heat surged to her face at the memory of her body's betrayal. How could she possibly condone wanting a man she was determined to shut out of her life forever?

"Is he gone for good, or just taking a walk to cool off?" Prudy asked as she cradled her mug between her hands.

"In this rain?" Raine glanced at the window, flexing her tension-tight shoulders. "Maybe he's been in the desert so long, he doesn't know precipitation will soak him to the skin."

"Can I interpret that to mean you think he just took a walk?" Prudy asked.

"His bags were still in the hallway, so I believe I can safely assume he'll be back."

"Is that a positive or a negative?"

"Nothing about Morgan is a positive."

Raine started to take a bite of granola, only to have the sodden end break off and fall into the cup, sloshing hot liquid onto the scrubbed pine table.

"There, you see!" she declared heatedly as she hastily blotted the spill with her paper napkin. "Nothing has gone right since he showed up."

Prudy risked a cautious smile. She'd never seen her usually serene neighbor so ruffled. An interesting development, she decided, watching Raine scrub the table with short, jerky movements. There was anger there, to be sure, and impatience, making Prudy wonder if Raine were having second thoughts about the decisions she'd made over the last few months. Decisions that had both opened and closed doors.

"Believe me, I know the feeling," she said, careful to keep her expression somber. "It was the same when Case was staying here with me when his leg was in a cast. He nearly drove me over the edge a dozen times."

Raine wadded the now-sodden napkin into a tight ball before placing it to the right of her mug.

"Four nights ago he was on the tube with a sand dune behind him, talking about holy wars and terrorists, and I was thinking how tired he looked and telling myself it was none of my business. The next thing I know he just...shows up."

"Men are like that. Unpredictable." Prudy waved a hand. "It's the testosterone. Some men have more than their share."

She thought of Case and smiled inwardly. Now there was an example of unpredictability. A man who'd sworn he never wanted to be a father, then doted on his little girl so much, he'd had to buy a new wallet with more places for photos. Even his partner had taken to calling him "Daddy."

"I don't want unpredictable," Raine said with so much force, Prudy wondered if she was trying to convince both of them. "I want steady and dependable and...home every night." Raine drew a breath. "Which is one of the reasons we're getting a divorce. Our marriage is over. Kaput."

"Yes, I know."

Prudy rested her hands on her bulging tummy and waited. Raine had the look of a woman who needed to vent. Since she herself had done plenty of venting to her friends during her rocky reconciliation with Case, she figured it was only fair to put in some listening time.

Raine traced an imaginary pattern on the tabletop. Her face was pale and her eyes shadowed. The result of a restless night, Prudy suspected. She empathized.

"Believe me, it wasn't easy to walk into that attorney's office and set things in motion," Raine declared far more softly. "I cried for two days afterward."

And ached to be in Morgan's arms instead of lying alone in the bed that always seemed empty now. Until last night, when she'd stood at the doorway, watching Morgan sleep...

"I remember. Stacy and I thought you were doing a pretty good imitation of a zombie."

Raine went on as though Prudy hadn't spoken. "I *de-*

spise the very idea of divorce, but I hate continuing with a travesty of a marriage even more."

Prudy blinked. "Travesty?" she said carefully.

"I don't know what else you would call it. Morgan never really lived with us. He...visited. Just when Mike and I would be getting used to having him around again, it was time for him to leave. Most of our marriage was spent in airport lounges." Raine sighed. "Or in bed."

"Hmm, that sounds promising."

"It sounds like an *affair*, which is mostly what we had. No real sharing, no genuine communication, none of the lovely little intimacies of married life. Nothing like you have with Case or Stacy has with Boyd. Heck, we never even argued. Whatever I wanted, Morgan just said 'Fine with me, honey.'" She glowered across the table, her forehead knitting. "Honestly, Prue, he might as well have been a sailor on leave, looking for a good time."

Prudy blurted a laugh, then worked to swallow it when Raine frowned. "Pardon me, but that sounds a tad like an exaggeration."

"It's not," Raine insisted, glancing toward the living room where the sound of little-girl giggles rose over the swell of familiar theme music. Mike had adored "Sesame Street," too. He'd known the words to all of the songs by the time he'd turned three. She felt a familiar ache settle over her heart. The pain of loss was no longer paralyzing, but it was always there, waiting in the background.

"Do you still love him?" Prudy asked after a few beats of silence.

Raine shook her head. "How can I, Prue? I don't really know him."

"Hmm." Prudy blew on her drink before risking a sip. "How well did you know him when you got married?"

"I didn't."

"Aha."

"I was twenty-three years old and pregnant. He didn't want his child to be illegitimate. Neither did I."

"You could have gotten a divorce after Mike was born."

"You sound like my father."

"You're hedging."

Raine considered that for a moment, then sighed. "I hate it when you're right."

Prudy laughed. "So does Case."

The dryer buzzed, demanding immediate attention, and Prudy levered herself awkwardly to her feet. "Be right back," she said before disappearing into the utility room adjacent to the sunny yellow kitchen.

Raine took a sip and stared at the rain sheeting down the window. She doubted that Morgan had a raincoat or even an umbrella. After all he'd been in the Mideast for the past six months. Guilt washed over her as she thought about him slogging through the summer downpour.

"It's not my fault," she muttered.

Returning with a basket full of baby clothes, Prudy grinned. "Uh-oh. The man's only been home one day, and she's talking to herself. Definitely a bad sign."

Raine glanced at her watch and sighed. "I should have opened the store ten minutes ago. Mr. Arnheim will be very upset with me. He claims he can't start his day properly without a cup of low-fat hazelnut latte and two bran muffins."

"You can spare a few minutes to finish your drink," Prudy declared as she set the basket next to her chair and sat down. "Besides, if Mr. Arnheim has any sense at all, he'll wait until the monsoon slacks off before he risks going outside."

Raine wondered where Morgan had gone to get in out of the rain. A bar wasn't really his style. Besides, he rarely drank. Perhaps one of the coffee shops in the mall, she thought. After all, the man had eaten virtually nothing since he'd crossed her threshold.

"Isn't that sleeper a little small for Chloe?" she asked, watching Prudy fold a tiny garment of pink terry cloth.

"Hand-me-downs for her sister," Prudy said with a soft smile as she put the folded sleeper to one side. "I've been meaning to get these ready for the last month. I figured, since I've been having a few twinges now and then I'd better not wait much longer."

Raine narrowed her gaze. "First stages of labor?"

Prudy glanced down at her belly, her expression rueful. "Not yet, but I have a hunch this little one is going to be early."

"Has she dropped?"

"Last week. Can't you tell?"

Raine inspected Prudy's rounded contours with a critical eye. Her always colorful friend was wearing a voluminous shirt, tie-dyed in brilliant hues of orange and yellow, over turquoise shorts. Her hair was tied back with a matching orange ribbon that clashed wildly with the coppery shade.

"Do you want the truth or do you want me to lie?"

Prudy grimaced. "Lie, please! Tell me you've gotten a revelation from the universe that I'm going to have this baby soon. Like today."

"Obviously, you're ready."

"Lord, am I ever! I love being pregnant, and I'm not all that crazy about the actual birth process, but enough's enough."

Raine laughed. "Stacy says the second one's easier. I'm holding her to that big-time."

"She's right. Chloe's birth was disgustingly easy. Hardly more than a sneeze. But the first..." Her voice trailed off.

"You mean Chloe wasn't your first?" Raine asked carefully.

Prudy shook her head. "Case and I lost a child during our first marriage. A little boy. I was seven months along."

"I'm sorry."

Prudy glanced toward the living room where her daughter was now singing along with Big Bird. "Case never wanted children, and I agreed to that when we were married. But I wanted a baby so badly." She drew a breath. "I stopped taking the Pill without his knowing it. When he found out, he was furious with me. He felt betrayed, and he was right. I was dead wrong."

"Oh, Prue, how dreadful."

"When I lost the baby, I, well, I guess I considered it my punishment for lying and cheating."

"Is that why you divorced?"

Prudy nodded. "Eventually, yes. It was his choice, his decision. That's why I was so reluctant to tell him about the baby when he got me pregnant the second time."

Raine had heard the story of the Randolphs' second love affair shortly after she'd bought the house. After years of estrangement, Prudy and Case had come together as godparents to his niece's child and had ended up making love. Prudy had gotten pregnant with Chloe that night.

"You told me this baby was Case's idea."

Prudy brightened. "He claimed he didn't want Chloe to be an only child. Said that we 'onlies' are spoiled brats."

"Ha!"

Prudy nodded, then took another sip of carob-flavored milk. "I saw Morgan's face when he realized you were pregnant. For a moment he looked totally destroyed."

Raine refused to feel guilty. "I didn't ask him to come home."

"And the twins' father? I assume Morgan has asked for all the gory details."

Raine shifted uncomfortably. The babies had been unusually quiet all morning, but one of them had just given her a hard kick. A rebuke? she wondered. Or a reminder?

"He asked. I didn't say much."

"Are you sure that's wise? Legally—"

"Please!" Raine protested, holding up a hand. "Don't remind me. The last thing I need for these little guys is a clouded paternity."

"But if you're still married when they're born—"

"I won't be!"

She felt another kick and pressed her hand against her tummy in an attempt to soothe her protesting offspring.

"Morgan is just feeling a bit ruffled, that's all. Once he gets over his Neanderthal act, he'll calm down and sign the divorce papers."

"Hmm."

Raine frowned. "Don't look at me like that. I know what I'm doing."

Prudy nodded. "So you don't think he loves you enough to accept another man's children?"

"That's just it, Prue. He never loved me."

"Are you sure about that?"

Raine drew a breath. "We went to bed together on our third date." She stopped, suddenly aware that the man she was describing sounded insipid, when the truth was, Morgan had been an ardent, tenacious lover. A man who had seemed to radiate a hunger so wild, it had both thrilled and frightened her.

"He was already famous when he came to give a talk at Bradenton. I was a lowly senior, tying to figure out if I wanted to go on to grad school. I took one look at him and melted."

"Maybe the same thing happened to him."

Raine shook her head. "What love Morgan has to give has always been reserved for his work. Before he met me, it was his wife and mistress and passion all rolled into one.''

"And after you married?"

"After we married, his work still came first." She felt a wave of bitterness threatening to swamp her and did her best to fight it off. "At the end, Mike could only move his eyes. He couldn't even talk. I...sat with him and held his hand. Mostly he just slept, but now and then he would open his eyes and just stare at the door." She had to stop to clear her throat. "He was looking for his father, you see. Waiting, to say goodbye, I think."

"Oh, Raine, I'm so sorry," Prudy murmured softly as she reached across the table to touch Raine's clenched fist.

Raine nodded. "Morgan tried to get home in time. Because of that mess in Bosnia, he had trouble getting a flight. I can't blame him for that, of course."

"If you don't blame him, why are you divorcing him?"

"Because I couldn't bear the thought of another child of mine staring at a door, wishing his father would walk through it. And yet, I was desperate to have another child. It came down to a choice, and I...made an appointment at the sperm bank."

Raine glanced at the window, checking the weather. The rain seemed to have grown even heavier, pounding incessantly against the panes. If Morgan had any sense, he would be having a second cup of coffee in a nice, cozy restaurant somewhere.

"I'd better go. I have an appointment with Luke this afternoon, and a stack of mail on my desk at the store that needs tending." And a life of her own to live.

Chapter 6

Though well past sunup, it was as dark as twilight outside. A typically gloomy Oregon storm, guaranteed to rust anything metal that wasn't double coated, and even then, it was iffy.

The rain was a wet dank curtain as Raine cut across the MacAuley property toward her own, heading for the cement walk that led to her carport. Huddled into her slicker, she sloshed through puddle after puddle, congratulating herself on her wisdom in slipping on her boots this morning instead of her sneakers. Even the grass beneath her feet was sodden and slick and far more treacherous than it looked. The last thing she needed now was a fall.

She was slipping through the hedge marking the property line when she remembered the back porch light. Far too absentminded lately, she'd forgotten to turn it off three mornings in a row.

Sure enough it was still on.

She was debating whether or not to take the time to return to the house when she realized that someone was sitting on her porch. No, *slumped* on her porch, his back against the shiplap siding of the house.

"Morgan? Is that you?" Even as she called his name, she was hurrying up the walk toward the rear steps.

At first she thought he was asleep. And then she noticed the terrible pallor of his skin and the odd frown on his face. He looked sick. Or in terrible pain.

"Morgan, what's wrong? Are you hurt?"

Careful to use the handrail, she hurried up the slick steps and crouched next to him, a difficult feat given the fact that her tummy bumped her knees. She reached out a hand and touched his shoulder.

"Go away," he grated, his voice little better than a harsh rasp. His body shuddered, as though even that slight effort cost him.

"Are you hurt? Did you fall?"

His frown deepened as he opened his eyes to slits, then winced, as though even the dull light of a gray rainy day had seared his retinas.

"Why the hell don't you keep a key under the mat like most sensible people?"

If Raine hadn't been so worried, she would have laughed. "Yell at me later. Right now I want to know what's wrong so that I can help you."

"Just…open the damn door and then go away so I can die in peace."

Die? It took Raine a heart-pounding few seconds to realize he was attempting some kind of macho joke.

"I'm going to call 911. You need an ambulance."

"No!" he shouted, then groaned. "No ambulance," he ordered in a softer tone. "Only a…damned headache. Pills in my bag." He glowered at her, daring her to object.

Pills? Raine took a moment to assimilate that. In all the years she'd known Morgan, she'd never known him to take so much as an aspirin or a vitamin. Fear ran through her, sharp as a knife. Was he seriously ill? Perhaps he hadn't been joking about dying. Was that it, his reason for returning?

She stopped breathing, felt a rush of weakness, a flurry of nausea. Her head suddenly seemed filled with air. It occurred to her then that she just might be sliding toward her first-ever fainting spell. It was unthinkable. Only Victorian ladies or wimps allowed themselves to swoon.

"I… Let me…open the door," she said before hauling in a lungful of rain-scented air. Using his boulder-hard shoulder as a prop, she pushed herself to her feet, then gathered in another deep breath. The giddiness lessened, though she still felt shaky and disoriented.

"Keys," she muttered, determined to remain calm and in control.

Her key ring was in her purse, which was still hanging from her shoulder. Morgan closed his eyes while she fumbled through the vast array of necessities she always carried with her. Force of habit from the days when she'd invariably had a toddler in tow.

It seemed like an eternity before she found the ring and dealt with the locked door. She thrust it open, slung her purse onto the counter, then drew a deep breath and turned her mind to the man still slumped against her house.

He was utterly still, his thick golden lashes and brows the only spot of color in his face. His mouth was compressed in a hard line, and his brow was deeply furrowed. His jeans and T-shirt were sopping wet and clinging to the impressive contours of his long, lean form with clammy tenacity. As far as she could see from a cursory inspection, he'd packed on a few more pounds in the form of hard muscle. Heavy muscle.

She thought about giving Stacy a quick call for assistance, then decided to try it alone first. It seemed imperative to get him inside and out of his wet clothes.

"Morgan, if I help you, do you think you could stand up?"

For an instant she thought he'd passed out, and then he opened his eyes to glare up at her again.

"Dumb question," he mumbled, but without much force.

She waited, then frowned. "Uh, do you suppose you could give me an *answer* to my dumb question?"

He muttered something pithy and obscene, then gritted his teeth and lurched to his feet. He stood swaying for an instant before Raine slipped her shoulder under his arm.

He managed to take most of his own weight as she clumsily steered him through the door and into the kitchen. She paused, thinking furiously. She'd forgotten how big he was. And solid. Twice her weight at least.

The bedrooms were upstairs. She considered gravity, the strain on her back and the risk to the babies. No, she would never get him up those stairs safely.

"Plan *B*," she muttered, frowning. "Which is...what?"

The living room sofa, she decided, urging him past the butcher-block island Boyd MacAuley had built for her last summer.

"Fine, now," he muttered as he made a valiant effort to untangle himself from her. "Thanks."

"Uh-huh."

She tightened the arm she'd stretched across his wide back and directed him toward the door at the opposite end of the kitchen. He moved carefully as though made of glass. Each step precise and measured.

"To the left now, a few more steps through the hall, that's it."

His forehead was beaded with sweat and he was swearing steadily by the time she maneuvered him onto the couch and helped him to stretch out on his back. The cushions sagged under two-hundred-plus pounds of hard-packed muscle and steely sinew.

Raine took a moment to catch her breath. Her heart was racing, and her back hurt. Beneath the shelter of the slicker, one of the babies gave a hard kick.

"Okay, the pills you mentioned. Which bag are they in?" she asked, staring down at him.

"Shaving kit," he replied without opening his eyes. "Bedroom."

"I'll be right back." She turned away, then swung back to order briskly, "Don't you dare try to get up."

His mouth quirked as he opened one eye.

"Right. Another dumb remark," she muttered as she hurried toward the staircase in the front entry.

Morgan heard her footsteps pounding up the stairs and blistered the silence with a particularly foul curse in Arabic, taught to him by a rummy camel driver with a talent for creative obscenity.

The pain had hit him fast this time. A piercing splinter of hot agony in his right temple, followed by the familiar crushing sensation inside his skull. Like the sharp, hot jaws of a vise closing tighter and tighter until he wanted to scream.

Somehow he'd made it up the steep, winding path leading from the river walk to the street without passing out. With whole chunks of his vision blocked by luminescent squiggles and jagged explosions and his balance more precarious than reliable, he'd had the devil's own time finding his way back to Raine's house, only to find the place locked up tight.

Resigned to a long wait in the pouring rain, he'd made himself as comfortable as possible on the covered porch at the back, then did his best to keep the vicious pain at bay by playing mind games.

It was an old trick, discovered by accident when he was

riding in a gunship heading into combat. At that time, he'd
zoned out on detailed recitation of all the things he planned
to do in Hong Kong on leave. This time he'd started by
running down a list of all the visa stamps in his passport,
then began listing each state and its capital in alphabetical
order, starting with Alabama. Methodically, just as he'd
taught himself to master everything from basic hygiene to
the techniques of killing an opponent in hand-to-hand combat during boot camp, he'd worked his way down to Rhode
Island when Raine had interrupted him.

It had been worth the agony of opening his eyes to find
her hovering over him, an eccentric angel in an oversized
yellow rain slicker, her expression stark with concern and
worry. Even in his semiconscious state, he'd felt her compassion and caring. Damn near basked in it, but then he
was a desperate man. He'd take whatever she offered and
be thankful for it.

Lord, but she'd been determined to rescue him the same
way she'd rescued the damned dirty starling with the bro-
ken wing she'd nursed back to health during one of his
visits home. An apt comparison, he realized. Too apt. The
wretched starling had infested the house with mites.

"What's wrong?"

Until he heard her urgent question coming from above,
he hadn't realized he'd groaned aloud. Bracing himself, he
opened his eyes and looked up at her. She had removed
her slicker and looked soft and touchable in a pale yellow
shirt and corduroy slacks. Her hair was more tumbled than
styled, piled in a heap atop her head. It was a casual look
that tempted a man to mess it up even more, with his hands.

In bed.

Morgan fought a sudden longing that made the crashing
pain in his head seem little more than a twinge by comparison. He closed his eyes and prayed for oblivion.

"I found the pills, at least I think they're the ones. From

a chemist's shop in London, with all kinds of warning stickers stuck on the label?''

He managed a curt nod, which he should have known was a bad mistake. The sudden shard of molten steel splintering his brain had him sucking in hard.

Raine saw the awful strain on his face and hurt for him. She'd had bad headaches before, but nothing that had even come close to incapacitating her. As soon as she got some medicine down him, she intended to call Boyd.

"It says one or two on the label," she said, careful to keep her voice calm and quiet. "How many do—"

"Two." The answer was a mere whisper of sound, forced between a grimace of pain.

"I'll just get some water from the kitchen."

Raine squinted down at the tiny letters printed on the pill bottle's label. She'd just finished spelling out the name of the medication for Boyd MacAuley who was on the other end of the phone line.

She heard the sound of a low whistle in reply.

"That's heavy-duty stuff, Raine. It's not even available in the States. The FDA considers it experimental."

She frowned down at the multicolored labels warning against mixing the medication with just about everything— alcohol, milk, other pain medication, the operation of machinery.

"It says 'for pain.'''

"Yeah, right. Hard-core. What's wrong with your husband?''

Ex-husband, she started to say, then realized that Morgan was anything but. "He said something about a headache. That's about all I could get out of him before he drifted off."

"Hmm. Hang on a minute and let me see if I can make this stupid computer tell me anything useful."

Raine leaned against the kitchen counter and listened to the faint *tap-tap* of a computer keyboard and the sound of her own breathing. It pained her to admit it, but she was terrified. Divorcing Morgan was one thing. Thinking that she might never see him again was something else entirely.

Of course it was a silly distinction, but one that had come at her with the force of a blow in the dark. She couldn't still love the man. It wasn't logical or sensible or particulary smart.

No, she was simply feeling a normal human compassion for the father of her first child. The same as she would feel for Boyd or Case or any of her other male acquaintances.

"Still with me, Raine?"

Boyd's question gave her a start. "Still here," she blurted into the receiver.

"Says here that that particular med is prescribed for cluster headaches, among other things."

Raine frowned. "Is that like a migraine?"

"Yes, but worse. I've heard of people committing suicide because they couldn't take the pain any longer. Unlike a traditional migraine, a cluster comes in bunches, hence the name."

She wet her lips, trying to remember if Morgan had ever mentioned cluster headaches. "This is the first time I've ever seen him going through this."

"Could be a recent onset. Clusters can be triggered by an injury or severe trauma. Even prolonged stress can bring them on if the patient has a genetic predisposition or physical weakness."

Raine took a moment to think about that. "Then why didn't he have one after Mike's funeral?"

She heard the sound of a weary sigh. "Raine, I don't have the answer to that. And I'm not a neurologist, but I can recommend a couple of good ones."

"Thanks. I'll...mention that to Morgan when he wakes

up.'' She bit her lip, then straightened. ''He's sleeping now. Is there anything else I should do for him?''

''Keep him warm. Check on him periodically to see that he's breathing normally.''

''Right.''

''And one more thing. Make sure you follow the dosage instructions on that medication precisely. It's nothing to fool around with.''

''I understand.'' She gave a weary sigh of her own. ''The best-laid plans, and all that.''

Boyd chuckled. ''Yeah, ain't that the truth?''

She pressed the button to end the connection, but kept the phone tucked between her shoulder and her ear as she searched for the number of her part-time sales assistant, Ginny Burks, on the list pasted to a nearby corkboard.

''Please be available,'' she muttered as she punched out the digits.

She felt a wave of relief roll over her when Ginny came on the line and jumped at the chance to put a few more hours on her time card. All she needed was five minutes to pull on some jeans and a sweater, and she'd be on her way.

That handled, Raine stood staring out at the rain. It had slacked off slightly, but the gloomy gray storm clouds seemed to hover directly over the house.

It had been a day very like this when she and Morgan had scattered Mike's ashes over Long Island Sound. Morgan's face had been the color and texture of granite. His eyes had burned with some inner torment, and the few words he'd spoken had seemed torn from him.

We could have another child, she'd told him with tears streaming from her eyes. It was as close to begging as she could come. But Morgan had wanted to wait. To give themselves time to grieve.

Gradually she'd come to realize that, although Morgan had loved Mike and had been deeply shaken by his death, he wasn't suited by temperament or inclination to the daily grind of child rearing. Or the mundane details of a traditional marriage, for that matter.

No, Morgan was an adventurer, a thrill seeker, a man too physically and intellectually restless to settle for home and hearth, while she liked nothing more than to nest.

Two polar opposites. No wonder they hadn't had anything to say to each other after Mike was gone. No reservoir of shared trials and triumphs to bind them together. No grand plans for a dream home or a vacation cottage or a trip around the world together. Nothing had bound them but their mutual love for their child.

And sex.

Before she'd met Morgan, she'd known what sex was, but not what it was like. She'd read books about soaring experiences and lofty flights, but Morgan had been more of a primitive than a poet. With him, making love was as wild as a battle for survival, no-holds-barred and no quarter given.

Raine felt a familiar swell of sensual excitement run through her and bit down hard on a protesting moan.

"No, no, no," she muttered into the silence of her own kitchen.

If only he'd loved her as much as he'd wanted her....

But he hadn't. End of story. End of marriage.

Squaring her shoulders, she turned and hurried back to the living room. On the way, she detoured to the guest closet near the door where she kept a quilt for those times when she wanted to curl up on the sofa with a book.

Morgan was still sleeping, his one arm thrown over his eyes as though to block the light. Standing motionless, she studied the tight jeans and sodden shirt. They would have to come off, or he would be miserable.

"Shirt first," she muttered, dropping the quilt on a nearby chair.

Taking a breath, she knelt in front of the sofa and tugged the soggy shirt free of the jeans. Easing it over his chest while he was lying on his back proved impossible.

Stalling, she turned her attention to his jeans. Of course they had buttons, the slippery metal kind. Once she had those undone, she hooked her fingers beneath the waistband and pulled.

Suddenly he jerked, as though in pain. Before she could move to soothe him, he'd grabbed a handful of her hair, holding her captive.

"Morgan, let go," she said calmly. "Morgan, you're pulling my hair."

His eyes remained closed, but she could swear his fingers tightened. "Morgan, sweetheart, you have to let go of my hair."

There was no response. Nothing.

Raine sighed. Her neck was twisted at an odd angle, and her back was beginning to ache. Worse, both babies were awake and engaged in a wrestling match. According to several of the books she'd read on the subject of prenatal behavior during the last trimester, babies in the womb were very sensitive to their mother's emotions.

A calm mother produced a calm child—or so one prominent researcher had claimed. The last thing she wanted or needed was another hyperactive hellion running around. Correction. *Two* hyperactive hellions.

Not that there was much possibility of that. She was all but positive that Mike had inherited from his father his inability to settle in one spot for longer than a few moments. And since these babies had a different father, their temperaments were sure to be different, as well.

Nevertheless, she wasn't inclined to take chances.

"Morgan, my neck is hurting very badly now, so it's time for you to let go." Her tone was restrained and patient. He replied by twisting his wrist and tugging harder. She let out a squeak of pain and tried to jerk away. It didn't faze him.

Desperate situations call for desperate measures, she decided.

Taking a breath, she eased closer. *"Let me go, you big bully!"* she shouted, as close to his ear as possible.

He let out a harsh cry of pain as his body jackknifed nearly to a sitting position before he fell back again. She managed to jerk free, and his hand dropped to the floor. His lashes fluttered wildly in his pale face, but he didn't waken.

Raine realized her eyes were filled with tears, and she swiped them away from her lashes. "It was your own fault," she muttered, but she knew that wasn't quite true. Oh, hell, she thought as she slowly maneuvered to her feet. She would just cut the damn clothes off of his body and be done with it.

Twenty minutes later, out of breath and irritable, she eased his sodden jeans free of his legs and tossed them onto the floor next to the shirt she'd removed earlier. All that remained was his underwear. Dark blue briefs.

Sinking back on her heels, she paused to catch her breath. Stripping a man who was mostly sinuous muscle and heavy bone had turned out to be hard work. Especially when he hadn't so much as twitched.

It had been a novel experience, she realized, watching his face.

Empowering to the max, Ginny would no doubt call it. But then Ginny was fearless when it came to her relationships with men.

Raine was anything but. Her parents had raised her to be a lady. An ornament and an asset. A helpmeet.

It was an archaic view of the world, but then her parents had both been raised by gentle, scholarly educators. Her maternal grandfather had been an expert on Regency En-

gland. On her tenth birthday, her mother had given her a
leather-bound collection of Jane Austen's works. A tacit
lesson in proper behavior. Raine cringed now to think of
the romantic notions she'd had spinning in her head when
she'd met Morgan.

Not once in their married life had she ever felt in charge
in the bedroom. Or anywhere else where he'd taken a notion to make love to her. He'd been the one to undress her.
The one to set the pace. To assume control. She doubted
he would allow her to take charge.

Still, the thought seemed to shimmer in her mind. Of
Morgan quivering under her touch as she'd once quivered
under his. Mindless with hunger. Helpless.

She realized she was holding her breath and let it out in
one slow jagged stream as she leaned forward. The heat of
his body enveloped her as she slipped the tip of the scissors
between the hard-packed muscle of one thigh and the sturdy
blue cotton.

He frowned as the cold scissors touched his skin, and
she froze. Then slowly she cut away the cloth, baring the
lighter skin of his groin to view. The thatch of thick hair
framing his shaft was darker, a rich honey gold, and as
wiry as the hair on his chest was soft.

She felt her breathing change and realized she was becoming aroused. Biting her lip, she quickly snipped him
completely free of the underwear and tugged the scrap of
blue from beneath his heavy buttocks.

He was beautiful. A classically magnificent statue fash-
ioned from warm, vibrant flesh and densely layered muscle
roped with steely sinew. It was the body of a warrior,
crafted for strength and endurance.

Raine felt tears springing to her eyes and frowned. How
she had loved this man, she thought, shaking her head.

She cupped her hands over her belly and closed her eyes.
Once, just once, she wished Morgan loved her enough to

give up his precious control to her. To put her first. To give what she would never again ask of him.

But that was a dream and a fantasy, and she'd had enough of both.

Chapter 7

She had merely intended to close her eyes for a moment to rest them. The next thing she knew she was being jerked out of a sound sleep. After a momentary disorientation, she realized that Morgan was thrashing around on the narrow sofa, muttering incoherently.

She sat up so quickly, she felt light-headed and had to grab the arms of the armchair where she sat to keep from overbalancing. As she waited for the room to stop its giddy spin, she kept her gaze fixed on Morgan as though somehow the sight of him anchored her.

The quilt she'd ever so gently tucked around him from his big feet to his stubborn chin was now a jumble of color bunched at his navel, with one end trailing to the floor. One big hand was clenched tightly around a wad of the material, as though he'd gotten too hot and jerked the cover away from his chest.

His breathing was labored, as if he'd been running, and his facial muscles were taut, giving him the look of a man trapped in a some horrible maze with monsters around every corner and with no way out. A quick look at her watch told her that a little less than four hours had passed since he'd fallen into a drugged sleep.

The room was brighter. To the west the sky was still crowded with clouds, but a sliver of blue was threatening to push them aside. Finally! Something was going right, she thought as she cast her gaze in Morgan's direction again.

The muttering had stopped and his breathing had eased slightly. His face was flushed now, instead of deathly pale, but it was an odd sort of flush. Like a swath of dusky red swabbed over his cheekbones with a broad brush and ragged at the edges.

Mike had looked that way sometimes when he'd been running a fever.

Frowning, she eased to the edge of the seat, then used the arms to push herself to a standing position. Thirty extra pounds of babies, most of it sticking out ahead of her like the softly rounded prow of a ship made graceful movement impossible.

Instead of kneeling by the sofa, she sat on the heavy oak coffee table, wincing when it creaked ominously under her weight. Ever so gently, so as not to wake him, she pressed her wrist to his forehead, testing for heat. His skin was warm, but not overly so. It was also faintly damp. Not clammy, per se, but close enough to give her pause. Still, anything was better than that awful ghostly pallor.

Tomorrow she would do some browsing through the While Away shelves, she decided, watching his big chest rise and fall in jerky movements. She was pretty certain she'd taken in a medical encyclopedia in trade at the end of the semester. A heavy, impressive tome with tiny print and thin pages, if she recalled correctly. With all those pages it was sure to have a section on headaches.

Just to make sure Morgan was truly all right now, she sat there a few more minutes, then realized she was hungry. And no wonder. Her usual lunchtime had come and gone. The babies were probably fuming at their mama's lack of concern for their welfare. Smiling faintly, she pressed a gentle hand to her tummy. What would it feel like to nurse two babies at once? Or was that possible? She was still pondering that with a sense of wonder when Morgan suddenly turned his head and cried out.

"No...*no!*"

He drew one leg up, then let it drop. He flung out an arm and his clenched fist hit her breast so hard, she gasped. Instinctively she grabbed his hand and held it fast between both of hers. His hand went slack, then tightened, gripping with an almost crushing strength.

She winced, but refused to pull away. Something told her that at this precise moment, he needed the touch of a human hand.

"Morgan, it's all right," she crooned in the same voice she'd once used to soothe away their son's bad dreams. "You're fine. You're safe."

He drew his sun-bleached brows together, and his lashes fluttered, but remained closed. He seemed to hold his breath for a dangerously long time, then slowly expelled the air.

Where was he? she wondered. In Vietnam? Or one of the other war zones that seemed to draw him with such unremitting power? He'd had nightmares before. Gristly, bloody reruns of scenes he'd witnessed firsthand.

The downside of the job, he'd told her, laughing off her concern.

But this was different.

Suddenly his fingers dug into her flesh. His body tensed until the tendons and sinews stood out in stark relief under the sun-gilded skin.

"No!" he shouted. Pleaded. "Take me, not him."

"Morgan, wake—"

"Oh, God, Mike! Not Mike. Not my son."

Shaking, Raine pressed his hand against her breast and leaned forward. "Morgan, listen to me," she said in a quiet, though urgent tone. "It's over. All over. Let it go."

He drew in a harsh breath and tossed his head from side to side. He flinched, as though from some inner blow. Cried out. Tears ran down his face and dropped from his jaw to his chest. Raine realized that her own cheeks were wet.

"Morgan, wake up," she whispered, hating to see him suffering so. "You have to wake up."

Suddenly the phone rang, startling her into crying out. He stiffened, then opened his eyes and looked around wildly, his pupils huge and unfocused. The phone rang again, and he bolted upright, nearly jerking her from her precarious perch.

In the den she heard the muffled sound of her own voice as the answering machine played the greeting message. After the sound of a beep, a deeper voice spoke briefly, followed by another beep.

Morgan shuddered and drew another breath. He turned his head to look at her. Recognition glimmered in the wide circles of his pupils, followed by a look she read as shame. The flush that stained the hard curve of his cheekbones seemed to deepen.

"Dammit, Raine, I told you to let me die in peace," he grated in a hoarse voice as he lifted a hand to scrub away the tears.

"Not in my house," she shot back, her heart racing beneath the big hand still pressed to her breast.

A corner of his mouth curled, and some of the shame left his eyes. "You're the one who dragged me inside."

"I had to. It's an image thing." Her voice was only slightly shaky, but inside she was Jell-O. "Only tidy people are allowed to live in this neighborhood."

"Yeah?" His tone was cautious.

She nodded. "I admit, I did think about digging a hole and dumping you in it, but I had on clean clothes, and besides, I couldn't remember where I'd left my garden shovel."

"A definite handicap when one is digging deep."

"Very true."

He wasn't actually laughing, but the laugh lines at the corners of his eyes had deepened, and the expression in the dark depths had altered. A small victory, she thought with quiet satisfaction. She didn't blame him for Mike's death, and she didn't want him blaming himself. It had been an accident. A tragic one to be sure, but an accident nonetheless.

"How's your head?" she asked quietly.

"Still hurts, but the worst of it is gone."

"How long have you been having these headaches?"

He shrugged his unscarred shoulder. "They started when I was a kid. After my mama went shopping and never came back. Went away when I left home."

"They came back after Mike died, didn't they?"

His lashes flickered, the one sign of emotion he'd never been able to fully control. "Yeah, they came back."

"I'm sorry."

"I was, too, but now..." He suddenly grinned, layering amusement over the shame still lingering in his golden eyes. He did that often, she realized. Forcing an emotion he could control over one he couldn't.

"I never really believed that old adage about black clouds and silver linings until now." He shifted his gaze to her chest—and the hand she was still cradling between her breasts. "This particular silver lining is hard to beat."

She stiffened and tried to release him, only to find herself held fast. "Let go, Morgan. I need to check my answering machine."

"Later." He drew a breath, then eased his long legs over the side of the couch. Face-to-face, now, knee to knee, he watched her with those lion's eyes. "I can feel your babies rousting around beneath my hand," he said with a quiet awe.

The sudden change of subject caught her off guard. "The boys have this teamwork thing going," she said, smiling at the thought. "One stays up all day to hassle me while the other sleeps, and vice versa."

He lifted his brows. It was a look of utter enchantment, but with a distinctly masculine edge. She refused to be charmed.

"Yeah? Well, the day team's got a kick like an old mule we had once. Meanest jackass in two counties. Used to have to whack him a good one across the nose with a big old hunk of firewood just to—"

"—get his attention? I know, I've heard that joke before."

"Joke?" He heaved an exaggerated sigh. "Hell's fire, honey, that weren't no joke. That old reprobate took more bites outta my backside than a passel of skeeters."

"Oh, yeah? How come there aren't any bite mark scars on your backside?"

"Sure there are. Wanna see?"

Raine felt her face heating again. "You're impossible, you know that."

"But lovable?" His deep voice gave the question a playful inflection, but the look in his eyes was dead serious.

"I'll grant you likable, as, of course, all media stars are required to be," she said, not even trying for lightness.

Something flickered in his eyes, only to be blinked away. His mouth firmed as he withdrew his hand. She felt a moment of terrible loss before realizing how ridiculous that was. How could she lose what she'd never had?

"You knew how I earned my living when you agreed to

marry me," he said, his voice suddenly steely. "You said you understood how it had to be."

It was more difficult than it should have been to keep her gaze steady on his. "I thought I did. And then I had a baby." She took a breath. "Everything changes when you have a child's needs to consider. I didn't know that when it was just you and me."

His jaw turned hard as though he'd clenched his teeth. "I thought we were doing all right." His tone was tightly defensive, with just a hint of sadness thrown in.

"Admit it, Morgan. You never would have asked me to marry you if I hadn't gotten pregnant."

"How can I admit what I don't know, Raine?" He shifted, then winced, reminding her that even though the worst of his headache had passed, he was still hurting. "I will admit I never saw myself growing old as a happily married man, but then, I never saw myself growing old, period. Never wanted to get old—until I met you."

She glanced down. "Sounds like I spoiled your plans."

"No, you *changed* them." His voice was gruff, drawing her gaze to his eyes. They were dark with some inner turmoil. "There's a difference."

"Perhaps there is."

She wanted to ask him why he still wore his wedding ring. She wanted to ask him a lot of things. It surprised her that she still had unanswered questions, surprised her more that she was still valiantly trying to know him better at a time when she was working very hard to move him out of her life. She was beginning to suspect she had more unresolved issues than she'd expected. But then, perhaps that was true with all divorcing couples.

"What?"

She answered his question with a blank look. "You looked like you were wrestling alligators. Maybe I can lend a hand."

She smiled at the colloquial analogy. Morgan was almost as well-known for his unusual language as he was for his dazzling grin.

"It's nothing."

"Uh-huh. It's something. You only wrinkle your nose when something's bugging you."

Once again he seemed to be teasing her, but the air seemed to crackle around them with tension. When was the last time he'd pushed her for more than the most impersonal confidences? Her mind stretched back years, to those shimmering days after they'd met when every word spoken between them was precious and every touch magic.

"Did you love me when we were married?" The question was out before she had sense enough to stem it.

His gaze narrowed, sharpened, and she sensed a sudden stillness in him. "If I told you I did, would you still want to divorce me?"

She respected him too much to give a fast answer. Instead, she took a moment to sit quietly and consider. Did a man in love with a woman who was carrying his child leave her two days after the ceremony? Perhaps, if he'd signed a contract and was too honorable to break it. But what about the promise he'd made her to be home in time for Mike's birth? The baby hadn't been early. Morgan had been late. Just as he'd always been late.

Or not there at all.

Not there when Mike, at six, had come down with chicken pox *and* measles at the same time. Not there a few months later when Mike had gone running through the house with a straw in his mouth and tripped over feet that had grown too large too fast, sending the straw into the back of his mouth with enough force to sever a tonsil. His pediatrician had kept him in the hospital overnight and she'd stayed awake the entire time, watching him to make sure he wouldn't suffocate. And he hadn't been there when

Mike had begged her to let him go skiing with a friend and his family....

"No, it wouldn't change my mind." Suddenly worn-out, she got to her feet and offered him a tired smile. "You must be famished. I'll fix you some bacon and eggs."

Morgan watched her go, his mood dark. Famished, hell! He was also ticked off, big-time.

As always, when he was angry or frustrated or horny, he needed a challenge to bleed off the wild energy slamming around inside him. Something impossible was preferable, like the daunting task of making a sorry-assed hick into a silk purse, to mangle a metaphor.

At the moment he'd settle for damn near anything that would distract him.

He brooded on that for a moment, then decided that getting himself into the bathroom without falling on his face seemed a good place to start.

Holding his head still, he tossed off the homey quilt, only to realize he was stark naked. Since he didn't remember disrobing, he had to conclude that Raine had done the honors. Right down to and including his shorts.

"Well, hell, and I missed it," he grated, cursing whatever ancestor had passed down the flawed gene that opened him up to a foul headache every time he let himself get too tired or too stressed.

It took some effort and a few selected Lebanese profanities to get himself on his feet and headed toward the stairs at a careful enough pace. As always, when he was caught in the aftereffects of the medication, his senses were almost unbearably heightened. Colors seemed more vivid, more defined, none more so than the rich burgundy of the huge cushy sofa. And the bright hues swirling over the area rug in front of the tiled fireplace seemed to pulsate with light and texture. Beneath his bare feet the slate-colored carpet felt inches deep and as warm as sun-kissed sand. He could hear the sound of his heart thudding in his chest and the swish of blood moving through his veins.

He paused at the bottom of the stairs, soaking in the warmth of the sun streaming through the two long narrow windows bracketing the front door. A sense of euphoria pulsed inside him, drug fueled and dangerous. Nothing he'd ever experienced before in his life came close to getting him as high—not even the rotgut acid from his daddy's still. Nothing with the exception of making love to Raine.

He expanded his chest slowly, drawing in the scent of her lingering in the air. Roses and soap and woman. A nice combination, he decided as he slowly began the ascent to the second story.

The banister was slick and warm under his palm as he pulled himself upward. Unyielding and hard.

Raine had been soft and pliant, an eager kitten twining herself around him until the rhythm of their beating hearts entrained, two becoming almost as one.

With her, he had felt all-powerful, a genius and a blue blood. When he was a part of Raine, he was no longer a mongrel with dubious parentage.

She was his light. His warmth. His soul.

A man could live a lifetime on the memories of one night with her, he thought as he gained the landing and turned toward the jumble of luggage stacked along the wall.

If a man were content to live only in his head.

He wasn't.

Morgan came downstairs forty minutes later, feeling almost human again. A shower and shave had done a lot to clear the cobwebs from his drug-fuzzed brain, and the skull-splitting ache in his head had subsided to a dull throbbing. Maybe he'd get lucky this time and escape a repeat performance. It happened that way sometimes.

He found Raine in the kitchen, sitting at the table with

the morning paper in front of her and a nearly empty glass of orange juice at her elbow. His mouth watered at the tantalizing aroma of freshly brewed coffee.

There weren't many things about the Mideast he cared to import to the U.S., but their strong, wonderfully bitter coffee was at the top of that short list.

"Help yourself," she said when she caught him eyeing the pot.

"Thanks." She'd already laid out a mug for him, along with the sugar bowl and a spoon.

"How about you?" he asked as he poured.

"I've had mine, thanks."

"Have another." He spooned sugar into his cup, then stirred.

"My doctor won't let me. One cup a day's my limit."

Morgan groaned at the thought. "What about decaf?" Unleaded was better than nothing, he supposed.

"Luke says no. Even the trace of caffeine might be bad for the babies."

Morgan carried his mug to the chair opposite hers and sat down. She hesitated, then folded her paper and put it aside.

"Your color's better," she said after a brief but intense scrutiny.

"Sorry to put you out."

"You didn't."

He lifted one brow at that, and she grinned briefly. "Not much, anyway."

Eyes narrowed in concentration, he took a greedy sip, then sighed mightily. "I'm not sure I could survive without caffeine. Giving up smoking was enough of a sacrifice in the interest of health."

Raine glanced at the stove. Too hungry to be polite, she'd already wolfed down two pieces of toast slathered with peanut butter. Enough to take the edge off her appetite, but not her jumpy mood.

"I thought I'd make Spanish omelettes."

"Sounds great. I've always loved your Spanish omelettes, honey."

"I've never made one for you before."

"You're sure?"

"I'm sure."

He grinned. "Something to look forward to, then." He cupped both big hands around the mug, his wedding ring clinking against the china. Hers was in her safety-deposit box, put there on the day she'd found out she was pregnant by another man.

"There was a message on my machine for you from someone named Joel Bronstein. He wants you to call. He left a number and said it was urgent."

Morgan frowned. "Everything's urgent with Bronstein. He was born in a panic."

"I recognized the number but not the name. He must be new at the network."

"Been with us about two years. He took Greg Lamont's job when Greg was promoted." He took another sip, then swiped his tongue over his lower lip to mop up a drop that remained. Raine felt suddenly breathless.

"I, uh, always liked Greg, even though he was a real pain sometimes, especially when he was trying to get you to cut your leave short for one reason or another. I'm glad he finally got the recognition he craved."

He leaned back, his gaze on hers. His eyes were still shadowed, and he looked far more worn than he should.

"I said he got a promotion, not recognition."

"How is it possible to get one without the other?"

A wicked smile came into his eyes. "By marrying the chairman's daughter."

"Not Cindy Margolis?"

"One and the same."

Raine finished her juice and tried to ignore the tantalizing aroma of coffee wafting her way from Morgan's cup. Prudy had warned her about Luke's dictum against coffee. She hadn't realized just how serious a deprivation it would prove to be.

"How many husbands does that make for Cindy?"

"Four. I think."

Bert Margolis's daughter was sleek, blond and utterly spoiled. She was also as oversexed as an alley cat. "And which one were you slated to be. Two or three?"

"Two. I turned down that offer and several others she made me." The expression in his eyes was suddenly cold and flat. "I never cheated on you. Not once."

Unbidden, her gaze dropped to the big hand still wrapped around his coffee mug. To the wide gleaming band on the third finger.

She'd been told by the wife of one of Morgan's colleagues to find a way to get a glimpse of the skin beneath that ring. *If it's as tanned as the rest of his hand, watch out. He's cheating on you.*

"I know you didn't," she said with quiet sincerity. "Just as I know you must have received a great many similar offers."

He dismissed that with a shrug. "You, on the other hand, have obviously said yes to at least one such offer. And not, my dear wife, to your husband." He suddenly got to his feet, startling her. "I'm going to return Bronstein's call, and then you and I are going to have one of those frank talks you always liked so much."

Chapter 8

Raine put down her fork and sat back. She'd eaten the entire omelette, three rashers of bacon and a grapefruit half without tasting a thing. Across from her Morgan had worked his way through a meal twice the size of hers without saying a word. He'd also gone through two thirds of a pot of coffee, taking it black this time.

When he, too, was finished, he pushed away his plate, leaned back and folded his arms over that monstrous chest. Outside, the storm was rapidly clearing. Inside, it seemed about to begin.

"Okay, who is he?" he demanded.

She allowed herself a small sigh. She refused to be forced onto the defensive. She'd tried to play fair with Morgan, whether he believed it or not. And done all she could to spare him pain.

"First, I want you to know that I have absolutely no obligation to tell you anything at all about this pregnancy," she said with feigned calm. "According to my attorney—"

"Screw your attorney. I want a name." The mountain twang was back in his voice, stronger than she'd ever heard it. The harsh consonants and badly distorted vowels added an element of dark menace to his already dangerous persona.

She knew enough about the life in the hills where he'd grown up to know it had been a stark, sterile existence. A throwback to an earlier, more primitive time. From the few things he'd said over the years, she'd come to realize that it had also been perilous, especially for outsiders. He'd been his daddy's lookout, he'd told her once. An *armed* lookout—and a deadly accurate shot. His father had whipped him until he could hit the notch of a tree ten out of ten tries.

At the time he'd told her about the "training of a mountain sharpshooter," she hadn't thought him capable of shooting an innocent intruder. Now, however, she could see him striding silently through the densely forested hills, rifle in hand, ready and willing to defend his own. She wasn't certain she liked the image, but she couldn't seem to get it out of her head.

"I can't give you a name, Morgan," she said quietly in spite of the flurry of nerves in the pit of her stomach.

He narrowed his gaze to slits, and his mouth compressed. She felt the force of his will, the strength of his personality reach across the table to envelop her.

"If I have to, I'll get it myself. I'd rather you tell me."

"Why?"

The question seemed to throw him, but only for an instant. "Why the hell do you think? So I can make him an offer he can't refuse."

Because she was genuinely frightened, she tried for a light touch. "C'mon, Morgan, that's sounds like some kind of threat."

"No threat. I'll flat-out take the guy apart if he doesn't agree to get out of your life and stay out."

Raine gaped at him. "That's...ridiculous."

He lifted a brow. "Is it? I think not."

"But...but you've already admitted you don't love me."

Violence flared in his eyes, as hot as a flame, before it went out. "You're mine, Raine. You've always been mine." He leaned forward, his palms flat on the table. "Are you going to give me his name, or do I have to start making calls?"

She was cornered. She knew it, and so did he. Morgan never made threats he didn't intend to back up. His reputation as a man of his word was part of his carefully guarded credibility with sources and targets alike.

Sure, she could stall him for a few weeks, but in the end, he would win. And she would be worn-out from nerves and anxiety and anger. Serenity at all costs, she told herself. Her boys needed calm to develop calm personalities. Besides, once Morgan knew the truth, he would lose interest in the hunt and fold his tent.

"I can't give you his name because I don't know his name," she said with perfect truth.

"You expect me to believe you slept with a guy without knowing his name?" He shook his head. "Honey, you're selling as hard as you can, but I ain't buyin'."

"Hear me out before you start threatening me again," she ordered, raising her voice slightly.

"I'm listening."

Raine took a breath and wet her lips. It wasn't enough. She reached for her water glass and drained it.

"I don't know if you remember or not, but I had some complications with Mike's birth."

He looked impatient. "A prolapsed uterus. Your obstetrician said you might have trouble conceiving again."

She acknowledged that with a brief smile. How could

she have forgotten that awesome memory of his? Once Morgan heard or read something, it was with him forever.

"Exactly." She cleared her throat. "Over the years it's become progressively worse. This year, when I went in for my annual exam, Luke Jarrod—he's the obstetrician who delivered both Prudy's and Stacy's babies—told me that a hysterectomy was inevitable."

His face paled. "You're talking major surgery, right?"

She nodded. "Luke also told me that if I wanted to have another child, I had to conceive immediately. The weight of the baby would anchor the uterus long enough for the baby to grow safely to term. Then, when I delivered, Luke would also remove my womb."

He shoveled his hand through his hair, his expression grim. The sickly pallor of pain hadn't completely faded, and the lines bracketing his mouth seemed to have deepened.

"Sounds risky."

"Luke assured me it wasn't." Even if it had been, she would have taken the risk.

"Easy for him to say," he muttered, glaring at her.

"True." She swallowed, trying to decide how much to tell him. "I had to do a lot of thinking and soul-searching in a hurry. Was I ready for another child? Could I love him or her as much as I'd loved Mike? Would I be dishonoring Mike's memory if I gave birth so soon after his death?" She drew a breath. "It was a difficult decision to make. In the end I realized I wanted another baby more than anything else in the world."

"So you went out and got yourself pregnant by the first guy who got a hard-on in your presence? Is that what you're telling me?"

She refused to cringe at the crude description. "Not exactly, but in essence, yes."

Funny how simple and straightforward and unemotional

it all sounded when it had been anything but. In fact, she had all but made herself sick agonizing.

"Hell, honey, if all you wanted was stud service with a smile, why didn't you call me?" He sounded almost bored, as though the question were asked out of idle curiosity, nothing more. Something told her that the more casual he became, the greater the danger.

"Because you were part of that soul-searching," she told him quietly. "Or rather, our marriage was."

He was very still. "Go on."

Her back was beginning to ache and she shifted position. It helped somewhat, but the dull throb remained. "I knew you didn't want any more children."

He scowled. "I didn't say that."

"But that's what you meant, wasn't it? When you said the time wasn't right to have another baby?"

"Yeah, that's what I meant," he conceded grudgingly. "But not because I don't like kids. Or…or because I resented Mike."

"But I did want another child. Desperately."

"I would have—"

"Forced yourself to rise to the occasion?" When he looked ashamed, she smiled sadly. "You're right. That's exactly what it would have been. A concession on your part. A gift to make me happy."

"You make it sound like there's something wrong with that." His steely control slipped. "I'm your husband, damn it."

"Yes, but a baby should be a joy to both parents. Equally loved and wanted."

"Sure—in the best of all possible worlds. Which this definitely ain't."

Raine drew a breath. "There was another reason," she said more softly.

In some secret way, he seemed to brace himself. "Which is?" he demanded in an equally soft tone.

"I wanted this child to have stability in his life. A solid sense of security."

He looked puzzled. "So?"

Raine stood and gathered the plates. The sudden movement made her queasy for a moment. She swallowed, and the sour feeling passed.

"Think about it, Morgan," she advised as she carried plates and silverware to the sink, returning with the coffeepot in hand. "Remember the first few times you came home after Mike was old enough to know there was someone new in his little world? Remember how he was afraid of you because he didn't know who you were?"

For an instant, he looked hurt. "He was just a little squirt."

"Little squirts are capable of recognizing the important people in their lives. It's called bonding."

She refilled his cup, then put the pot on the table and sat down. For once, both babies seemed to be resting. How long would that last? she wondered. So far the record was twenty minutes.

"Are you telling me my son and I never bonded?" His tone was belligerent, his jaw hard.

"No, but it took a long time, and according to the books I read on child psychology—"

Morgan offered his opinion on such books in his usual blunt and pithy fashion. "Mike was a good kid. He understood how things had to be."

His voice was sharp and shaded toward angry. She knew him well enough to know that his true feelings were often buried inside that anger. Feelings that he had consistently refused to share with her. Feelings that only surfaced in his dreams where no one else could intrude.

"Yes, he understood, but that didn't stop him from mop-ing around for weeks after you left. Or later, when he got older, acting out.''

"Acting out? What the hell is that supposed to mean?''

"It means he tried to ease the pain of losing you again by misbehaving.''

"He didn't *lose* me, dammit. I went back to work, just like a father's supposed to.''

"You weren't home every night, and he wanted you to be. To a child, that's tantamount to a loss—or abandonment.''

"Hell, my old man was home every night, and it didn't seem all that positive to me.''

"The circumstances were vastly different, as you well know.''

He stared at her as though he'd never seen her before. "Is that how you feel, too, Raine? Abandoned?''

"Sometimes,'' she admitted softly.

Morgan felt a need to lash out, but made himself back off. She was being honest with him, which was as much a sacred trust as his wedding vows. Only a man who had been lied to by the best and the worst of the world's power players knew just how precious and valuable a commodity honesty truly was. Raine's openness was one of the things he'd found irresistible from the first.

"How many times did you sleep with this guy before he got you pregnant?'' It hurt him to ask the question, but he had to know.

"I was artificially inseminated three times.''

Morgan was rarely at a loss for words. Sometimes the ones he chose were inappropriate, far too often they were obscene, but he couldn't remember a time when he hadn't been able to come up with something. Even when his daddy had switched him raw for being a smart-ass, he'd managed to have the last word. But now he simply sat there and stared at the shuttered look on Raine's face, unable to utter one damned word.

"Are you all right?" she asked softly when the silence turned so brittle, it all but crackled.

"No, how the hell could I be all right?" he managed to get out. "I just found out my wife would rather have a stranger's baby than mine."

Her eyes turned bright with hurt. "It's not like that, and you know it."

"Isn't it?"

He knew he wasn't really bleeding inside. Suddenly he wished he were. Anything was better than the feeling of utter emptiness. As though from a distance he realized that Raine was beginning to look alarmed.

"You wanted the truth," she reminded him.

"Yes. Thank you for that at least."

He took a long slow breath and began reciting the Hebraic alphabet. The heaviness in his head began taking on sizzling edges, and he ground his teeth. He realized he was clenching his fists and slowly relaxed his fingers.

The first slice of pain wasn't bad. The second would have taken him to his knees if he'd been standing. He waited for it to ease off, then managed to push back his chair.

"Excuse me, please," he said as he very carefully got to his feet. A phosphorescent arrow shot across his field of vision. He heard her call his name, saw her leap to her feet. There was a pulsating halo of light around her. A shimmer of vivid red, and then...nothing.

Seated behind the cluttered desk of his small office off the wing of emergency room cubicles, Dr. Boyd MacAuley flipped to a clean page in the folder bearing Morgan Paxton's name and continued scribbling, filling the paper with his own version of shorthand as the Saudi Arabian physician on the other end of the overseas call read from Morgan's medical record.

"How long ago was that?" he asked when the man paused to take a breath.

"One moment, please, Doctor, while I check the chart," Dr. Habib requested in his precise Etonian accent. "Ah, yes, here we are. January of this year."

Boyd frowned, very aware that Raine was watching him intently from her seat across the desk. "And you say he made a full recovery?"

"According to this, yes. As I said, my colleague, Dr. Rashid, actually treated Mr. Paxton and this other man, Stebbins. At the request of the U.S. consulate general."

Boyd shifted his gaze to Raine's worried face and smiled. "Thanks very much for the information, Doctor," he said into the receiver. "I appreciate your cooperation."

"Not at all, Doctor," Habib replied with clipped courtesy.

After another exchange of formal pleasantries, Boyd replaced the receiver in the cradle and let himself slump back into his chair. He'd put in two hectic days in a row and he was beat. He longed for a shower, a cold beer and a long, lazy session in bed with Stacy. Only for Raine would he have hung around to wait for the call he'd placed earlier to be returned.

"Looks like the guy you called in New York—what was his name?" He lifted a brow.

"Joel Bronstein," she supplied impatiently.

"Yeah. Looks like Bronstein was right. Paxton and his producer picked up a spore all right, something exotic that's indigenous to an isolated area in the Middle East."

Raine seemed to have difficulty swallowing. "Is...is it fatal?"

Boyd gave her a smile guaranteed to reassure the most confirmed pessimist. Or so Prudy had told him once.

"Not if it's treated quickly, which, in this case, it was. Apparently, the network takes very good care of its own. Brought in a chopper as soon as Paxton and this other guy showed signs of illness. Took them to the Royal Saudi Hospital at Riyadh. Kept them there two weeks before giving them both a clean bill of health. Other than the headaches you and I discussed yesterday and a low level of iron in his blood—probably the result of overwork—the man is fine. Or will be, once he surfaces again."

Disbelief clouded her eyes, and he braced himself. Stacy and her friends had a way of pushing a man to the wall when they wanted something.

"Boyd, he passed out cold in the middle of my kitchen floor." She drew a fast little breath. She was wound tight and was exhausted at the same time. Luke Jarrod would have his head if he didn't convince her to rest.

"You should have seen him. One minute he was getting up from the table and the next... God, he went over like a felled oak."

"A combination of the drug he'd taken earlier, jet lag and a fairly intense case of fatigue. Plus the fact that he'd been hit with another headache."

"How do you know that?"

He wondered when she'd slept last. He wouldn't ask, not yet. "He told me when he came to for a few minutes in the ER."

"He was in pain?"

"Yeah." He hesitated, wondering just how much to tell her. "Pain" was a mild term for the agony he'd seen in Paxton's eyes. Cluster headaches weren't serious in and of themselves, but the cumulative effect of recurring agony over a long period had proved too much for some patients to endure.

"We gave him a good-sized jolt of morphine and sent him back to sleep. It was about all we could do."

"So you're telling me he's fine, right?"

"Other than the headache which he just has to sleep off." He pushed back his chair and stood. "Which is exactly what I'm prescribing for you, neighbor. Eight solid, uninterrupted hours of sleep."

He came around the desk to offer her a hand, which she accepted with a wan smile. "These days I count it a victory if the boys allow me four," she said as he tugged her to her feet.

"I can prescribe something mild that won't hurt the babies."

She shook her head. "I'll be fine."

Boyd decided he didn't like the faint tremor in her voice. "Tell you what, I'm heading home myself in a few minutes. Why don't you let me drive you? You can leave your car in the lot. Pick it up tomorrow."

"No, I don't like to be without transportation these days. Just in case. It's silly, I know, but it makes me feel more secure to know I could get myself to the hospital if I had to."

"Sure, okay. We'll leave my car here and take yours. Stace can drop me off in the morning."

"That's really very kind of you, but—"

"Nothing to it, neighbor. Just give me a minute to check on a couple of patients."

"Thanks. I admit I'm feeling a little frayed at the edges."

Raine let him drop his arm over her shoulder and steer her toward the door. Boyd had been a tower of strength from the moment she'd placed a frantic call to the hospital while the 911 paramedics were loading Morgan into an ambulance.

Outside, in the corridor, a huge red-haired man with Popeye arms and an orderly's blue badge pinned to his white tunic approached, pushing an elderly man in a wheelchair.

"Hiya, Doc," the orderly said with a grin. "How're those pretty gals of yours?"

"Blooming," Boyd replied. "And Stace says to thank you for sending her your fudge recipe. It was an instant favorite."

"No problem, Doc," he said as he passed.

It was well past the dinner hour, and the bustling air Raine had noticed earlier had eased off. She hated hospitals. Too many memories of Mike's last hours on earth were wrapped up with hospital sounds and hospital smells. Morgan had come running down a corridor very much like this one the night Mike died, his jaw bristling with a two-day beard and his eyes haunted and bloodshot.

He'd been nearly torn apart to discover he'd arrived too late.

Raine couldn't quite suppress a shiver, drawing Boyd's sympathetic gaze. "Cold?"

She offered him a tired smile. "No, a memory I can't seem to lose."

"For what it's worth, the worst of it fades with time." His voice was gentle, his eyes sad.

Raine knew that he'd lost his first wife and child in an auto accident a few years before he'd met and married Stacy, and that the grief he'd suffered as a result of his loss had driven him from medicine for a time.

"He was such a great kid." She squared her shoulders. "He would have made a wonderful big brother."

Boyd acknowledged that with a nod. "How much longer before you get a peek at the two you're busy brewing?"

"Ten weeks, give or take a few days. Luke keeps warning me that twins are early more often than not."

"Don't tell Prudy. According to Case, she's all but pacing the floor in the hope the activity will bring on labor."

"Yes, I know. She has great hopes for next Wednesday."

They turned the corner toward the patient rooms lining the first-floor corridor. "Why Wednesday?"

"Full moon. Prudy swears the pull of the moon's gravity brings on labor if a woman is anywhere close to her time."

Boyd laughed. "She's more right than wrong about that. Full moon time is always busier than usual in all the wards. The ER is always jammed when the moon is full. We get a lot of regulars then. 'Moonies' we call them."

He stopped at an open door and looked down at her. A quick glance at the number affixed to the wall told her that Morgan was one of the patients Boyd intended to "check on."

"Can I see him?" she asked.

"I don't see why not." He stepped back to let her precede him.

While Boyd paused just inside the door to remove the chart from the holder on the wall, she tiptoed to the side of the bed and looked down at the man sleeping there.

His face was nearly as pale as it had been when she'd dragged him in out of the rain. His hair, too, was wet and sticking to his forehead in golden ringlets. Not from the rain this time, but his own sweat.

He was frowning in his sleep, and tension was stamped on his angular features as though with a heavy hand. Only the long thick lashes resting on his hard cheekbones showed a hint of softness to counterbalance his unrelenting masculinity.

Oh, Morgan, she thought, fighting a mix of emotions. Why did you have to come back now? When I'd just gotten everything in perfect order?

Biting her lip, she reached out a hand to brush the damp hair away from his brow. His skin was warm to the touch, and she allowed her fingertips to linger just a little longer. She had missed him so. She had a feeling she would always miss him.

Steeling herself, she withdrew her hand and stepped away from the bed. "I'll wait for you outside," she told Boyd as she went past him.

A few minutes later he emerged from the room and closed the door. "He's in good shape," he said when she met his gaze.

Too tired to reply, she nodded.

He slipped an arm around her waist and headed back down the now-empty corridor toward the elevators. "You're still crazy about the guy, aren't you?" he said quietly.

"Yes, but I'm getting over it."

"Why?"

She didn't pretend to misunderstand. "Because every time he leaves me, he takes a little piece of me with him. Sooner or later there wouldn't be anything left."

"So ask him not to leave."

Raine drew a weary breath. "I can't. I gave him my word when we were married that that was the one thing I would never ask of him."

"You want him to make that decision on his own, is that it?"

Raine nodded. "But I know he never will. Which is why I *will* stop loving him."

I will, she repeated silently. Sooner or later.

Chapter 9

Morgan opened his eyes to find the doctor from the emergency room standing next to the bed, watching him. He recognized the face, but to his dismay, couldn't dredge up a name.

The man was blond, about his size, wearing jeans and a sports shirt under his starched white coat, the kind of ruggedly boyish guy women tended to mother—or seduce—depending on their age. Morgan figured him to be younger by a few years, and from the lazy look of contentment in the guy's eyes, a whole lot happier than he was with the way his life was going.

"Morning." He winced at the raspy quality of his own voice. He couldn't remember swallowing his regular pills, but the sluggish aftereffect of a powerful painkiller was all too familiar. It made him feel stupid and slow. "Or is it afternoon?"

"Split the difference and make it a little past noon."

Moving only his eyes, he checked the window behind

the respectable spread of the other man's shoulders. The sun was shining, and the sky was a hazy shade of blue. The color reminded him of a paler, more insipid version of Raine's front door.

The scene in the kitchen came crashing back to taunt him. Artificial insemination. Son of a bitch. The very thought had his temper humming and his gut tightening. It was humiliating and insulting. And it hurt like hell.

"Today is…Wednesday?" he guessed, returning his gaze to his visitor's face.

"Yep. You damn near slept around the clock."

"I figured."

Morgan took a testing breath and realized he'd survived another round with most everything intact. "Which one of us was doing the talkin' that woke me up?"

"You." The doctor grinned. "Have to say I didn't recognize the language, but I have a feeling you were blistering the air pretty good."

"You might say that," he owned. "Doesn't seem to help much, but it's gotten to be a habit."

The doctor held out a hand almost as large as his own. "I'm Boyd MacAuley. We met yesterday, in case you don't remember."

Morgan grinned as he shook the doctor's hand. "I have a vague recollection."

"How do you feel?"

The subtle shift in the doc's tone told him it was a serious question, so he gave it serious consideration before answering. It took a moment to run down an inventory of an assortment of aches and twinges, another to translate sensory impressions into a recognizable pattern.

"Like I want to rerun the tape and do some heavy editing."

The doc looked thoughtful. "Sounds reasonable. Which part do you want to cut out?"

"The part where I made a fool of myself, which is pretty much everything after I got out of the damn taxi in front of the lady's house."

"That bad, huh?"

"Worse."

Morgan fumbled with the controls for the bed until he found the one that raised the head. Someone turned on the TV in the next room. A phone rang in another. Familiar hospital sounds. He had to get out, and fast—before he started remembering too much.

"My memory's fuzzy, but I have a bad feeling I lost a lot of ground with a certain exasperating female."

"Women have a knack of making a guy feel that way, even when it's not true."

Holding his breath, he turned his head slightly and was relieved when the dull throbbing didn't shatter into piercing pain.

"You sound married."

MacAuley nodded. "Almost five years now. You met my wife on the day you arrived."

Morgan thought back. "Dark hair, world-class smile?"

A smile dawned in the medic's gray eyes. Morgan read pride and love there and fought a hard stab of envy.

"That's my Stacy. She's…special."

"By my count you have two daughters, right? Tory and…Shelby?"

"Right." MacAuley shifted, lifted a brow. "That's some memory you've got there."

"A mixed blessing."

"Expect that's true about a lot of talents."

Morgan felt some of the cobwebs unsticking in his brain. He knew from past experience that it would take him a good day to snap back to normal. Longer, if this headache wasn't done with him.

"You got any objections to me getting the hell out of

here today?'' he asked with only a slight edge of demand in his tone.

"Not a one, although I would advise you take life slow and easy for the next week or so. Get as much rest as you can, soak up some sun. Tank down a steak or two."

"No problem. I can do that."

MacAuley narrowed his gaze. An easy man to like, Morgan decided, but not an easy man to fool.

"According to the Saudi doc with the upper-class accent who gave me a rundown on your stay in Riyadh, you were strongly encouraged to take a long rest before going back to work. Instead, you were on the air the day after you were released."

"Goes with the territory. A man in my business is only as good as his next scoop."

MacAuley frowned, giving Morgan a glimpse of the tough, no-nonsense professional under the lazy grin and casual clothes. Not a man to cross without a damn good reason.

"Raine had no idea you'd even been sick."

It was Morgan's turn to frown. "You told her?"

"Not exactly. She heard it first from some guy she called in New York. Fella by the name of Bronstein."

Morgan grunted. "My boss."

"He's the one who told her about the bug you picked up overseas and your recent stint in the hospital."

"Man always did have a big mouth. Just can't resist blabbing everything he knows. Probably one of the reasons he's behind a desk instead of working in the field."

MacAuley flexed his shoulders. Someone laughed in the hall outside the open door.

"She was scared. You hit the floor pretty hard."

Morgan winced. That explained the sore elbow. "Guess she thinks I'm pretty much a wimp."

"That's a question you'll have to ask her. I took her home and put her to bed."

Morgan tensed. "Is that right?"

MacAuley's mouth twitched. "Metaphorically speaking."

"Uh-huh." For the sake of his sanity, he forced himself to accept MacAuley at his word.

"Guess you know most of the doctors in town," he probed as MacAuley pulled a stethoscope from the pocket of his white coat.

"By reputation, if not by sight. Why?"

The doctor lifted a brow as he slipped the end piece of the stethoscope into the neckline of Morgan's hospital gown. Damn thing was cold as an ice cube. Morgan figured it was MacAuley's version of revenge.

"You know an obstetrician by the name of Jarrod?"

MacAuley checked his watch as he listened to Morgan's heart, counting off beats. Finished, he pulled the earpieces free and straightened.

"I know him," he said as he wound the stethoscope into a tidy package and slipped it back into his pocket. "He's my wife's ob-gyn."

"Raine's, too."

"Yes, I know." MacAuley met his gaze steadily, his expression somber. A dead-end street for information. Morgan cursed the idiot who'd invented professional ethics, even as his respect for the other man increased a few more notches.

"You got any idea where I can find this Jarrod?"

MacAuley's beeper went off just as he started to answer. He plucked it from his belt, checked the number on the readout, then sighed as he replaced the small device.

"Forgot about a staff meeting," he said by way of explanation. "Guess the chief of staff finally got around to taking names."

Morgan grinned. "Better you than me. I'm not big on meetings."

MacAuley grinned. "I'll sign your release papers on my way out."

"Much obliged."

The doctor started for the door, then paused and turned back. "If you plan on sitting in for a few hands at Case Randolph's on Saturday night, you'll probably run into Luke Jarrod sitting across the table from you. He's a regular."

Chloe Randolph dropped the tomato seedling into the freshly dug hole, then plopped her chubby bottom down next to it and grinned.

"Dere," she said with great satisfaction.

Raine couldn't help grinning back. The little dickens was covered with dirt from her soft terry-cloth sun hat to her bare toes. Chloe was in little-girl heaven.

"Now that's what I call a terrific planting job, kiddo."

"'Wiffic'," Chloe echoed, eyes gleaming beneath the hat's drooping brim.

"Now, the next thing we do is pat the dirt around the little plant's roots nice and gentle."

Raine took the little darling's plump little hand and pressed her fingers into the loose warm soil.

"Like this, okay?"

"'Kay." Chloe patted exuberantly, leaving tiny handprints in the bed.

Grinning, Raine gently extracted the last seedling from the pony pack before putting the pack aside.

"Ready for the next one?" she asked her eager little farmer.

Chloe nodded and held out her hands.

"Keep your thumbs together and make a kind of bowl out of your hands," Raine instructed as she handed over the tiny plant. "That's good, sweetie. Give me a minute to dig another hole."

Raine scooted backward and picked up her trowel. After two years of pampering, the soil in her herb garden was rich and crumbly, a dream to work. She'd already planted cherry tomatoes. Now it was time for the big juicy beefsteak kind. Her mouth was watering already. Sometime during her fifth month she'd developed a craving for tomatoes. She ate them whole, like apples.

"Okay, let's put the plant in its new home."

"'Kay."

Her brow knitted in concentration, Chloe slowly conveyed the seedling to a spot directly over the hole, then glanced up. At Raine's nod, she opened her hands and let the baby tomato plant drop.

"Another perfect job, Chloe! I swear, you're just about the best garden assistant I've ever had."

"Hey, I thought you told me I was the best."

Raine stiffened at the sound of Morgan's distinctively deep voice. Glancing up, she saw him standing a few feet away, his booted feet braced wide, his hands fisted on his hips. His hair had been combed by the wind or his fingers—or both—and he needed a shave.

He looked anything but rich and famous, she thought. More like reckless and impatient and just a little jaded. She felt a flutter in her stomach and a pain in her chest.

The man was a heartbreaker when he was rumpled.

"What are you doing here?"

She lifted a hand to shade her eyes. It annoyed her that she hadn't heard the sound of the gate opening and closing.

He heaved a sigh. "Funny thing, all the way home I had this image of my wife running into my arms and kissin' me breathless the minute I arrived."

Raine refused to remember all the times she'd done just that. "How are you feeling?"

"Tired of that question."

He sauntered forward until his shadow touched them, then went down on his haunches. The soft, well-used jeans sheathing his legs strained at the seams as his thigh muscles bulged. Raine clamped her teeth together and ignored the tug of purely physical interest that ran through her.

"Hiya, Chloe. I sure do like that hat." He reached out to touch a long finger to the brim and Chloe giggled.

"Hat," she repeated proudly. "Chwoe's hat."

"You bet. A real stunner."

Morgan looked smitten. Raine felt something tear inside her. It was next to impossible to resist the man when he let his guard down to reveal the softer side of his hard edge.

"Chloe's mommy is taking a nap, so we decided to get some sun," Raine explained with a grin for the goggle-eyed little girl. "Right, sweetie?"

"Uh-huh."

Morgan shifted his gaze Raine's way. His pupils were still slightly dilated, and he looked tired.

"Where's *your* sunbonnet, Mrs. Paxton?"

She frowned at the use of the name she was determined to shed. "Inside. I hadn't planned to be out long."

She knew she sounded stiff and unfriendly. She told herself it was necessary. Morgan had already shown her just how easily he could get under her guard.

Chloe used Raine's shoulder as a prop while getting to her feet, then toddled off toward her little yellow tricycle parked at the edge of the sidewalk. Raine dropped her trowel into her carrying tray, then tugged off her gloves and stowed them neatly away next to the trowel.

She started to rise, only to have Morgan loop a long arm around her waist and lift her effortlessly to her feet.

"Thank you," she said in that prim little voice that made her cringe inside.

"I used to picture you in your garden," he said, watching her. "With your hair tumbling over your shoulders and a smear of dirt on your chin."

Reaching out, he brushed the ball of his thumb over her jawline. She felt something quicken inside. Her heart speeded. It was simply an adrenaline rush, she told herself. An involuntary reaction of her nervous system to the proximity of the male of the species.

A very large, highly intense, utterly ruthless male.

"Morgan, don't," she said in a strained voice. "It's over."

"So you keep saying."

She looked into his eyes, surprised by the unusually deep resonance of his voice. "This isn't easy for me."

His eyes crinkled, but the smile remained unborn. "Good. The harder it is to divorce me, the better."

He lifted a hand to capture a corkscrew curl blowing across her face. His mouth quirked as he rubbed the long strand of hair between his thumb and forefinger.

"I've made my share of mistakes in this marriage. More than my share, which is why I'm willing to deal."

It took Raine a moment to realize what he was saying. "Deal?"

He tucked the errant curl behind her ear, then settled his hand lightly on her shoulder. She felt the skin beneath her shirt begin to tingle. She'd always loved his hands. So gentle in spite of the hardened ridge of calluses. So arousing against her skin when they made love. Large blunt hands that would forever mark his humble origins. She'd had to go to three jewelry stores before she found a wedding band large enough to fit him.

"You want a divorce, I'll give you a divorce. But only after those babies presently kicking up a storm in your belly are delivered safely."

He took a half step closer. She felt the heat of his body and the tightly lashed-down tension of his restraint. She told herself not to look at his mouth, but found she couldn't look anywhere else. He had firm lips, well-defined. Oddly sensual when he smiled, intimidating when he frowned. His teeth were large and white and intriguingly irregular. But it was the shallow dimple that winked in one tanned cheek that had always enchanted her most.

"I don't need your permission to divorce you, Morgan."

She tried to make her voice firm. It came out oddly breathless. She shifted her gaze to his eyes and saw that his were molten gold and very intense.

"No, but you need my *cooperation* to ensure it doesn't drag through the courts for a lot of expensive years."

He ran a fingertip down her cheek, and she shivered. It would be so easy to step into his arms, so easy to give in to the longing to try again. To somehow start fresh.

"I should check on Chloe," she murmured.

"I see her. She's rocketin' that trike up the sidewalk like she's on the last lap of the Indy 500." His gaze shifted to her mouth, and his own firmed.

"Don't," she whispered, but his mouth was already settling over hers.

Her body refused to grow rigid. Her arms refused to push him away. Instead, she arched upward, her arms already encircling his neck. His lips were both firm and gentle. Persuasive and demanding. And so wonderfully familiar. She tasted toothpaste and coffee and marveled at the erotic impact of so mundane a combination.

It was just as she remembered—the heat of his hard body, the feel of his big hand splayed against the small of her back, urging her closer, the warm, sweet demand of his mouth moving over hers. Nipping, tasting, molding to hers for a long, hot kiss.

Sensation swamped her. Pleasure, excitement, a heady joy. And need. So much need. Her head whirled and spun, as she met the demand of his mouth with a demand of her own.

He groaned, then shifted until he could ease one long leg between hers. Moisture pooled between her thighs as she felt his thigh rub the most sensitive part of her. She moaned, and he moved closer until she was riding his thigh.

Pleasure shot through her, so strong, she caught her breath. *More.* She wanted more. Needed more.

She needed him. His strength. His heat. His courage.

When he lifted his mouth from hers, she started to protest, only to have her words turn to a moan as he skimmed his mouth over her throat. Eagerly she tilted her head to give him freer access, and the scent of soap drifted over her. His morning beard rubbing her skin was a delicious contrast, an erotic reminder of the primitive part of him that lay just beneath the surface.

She arched closer, her fingers digging for purchase in the hard musculature padding his wide shoulders. Then his mouth was exploring her ear, his teeth teasing and tugging before he whispered something she couldn't understand.

Later she would ask about the words. All that mattered now was the desire building in her. With an incoherent murmur, she framed his face with her hands and dragged his mouth back to hers.

Morgan felt something rip inside him, like the last link on a painful chain. He hadn't known until this instant just how much he needed to know she still wanted him. At least sexually.

A start, he told himself as a wild painful pleasure bucked and raged inside him, desperate for release. His cheek grazed hers as he kissed one side of her face and then the other. He was desperate for the taste of her. The feel of her in his arms.

No one had ever wanted him the way Raine had wanted him. No one had turned to warm, sweet fire in his arms, her body trembling under his touch. She was balm for a lifetime of hurt, nectar to sooth a parched soul. Life to warm the icy hollows in his heart.

He felt his control edging away. It had been so long. So damn long. Needing more, he tangled his fist in her hair and smelled sunshine. He skimmed his palm over the graceful curve of her spine until he could palm the lush roundness of her bottom.

His body throbbed, so ready he feared he would burst.

Inside. He had to get them both inside the house where—

Water hit him full in the face, and he jerked back. Raine cried out, her fingers digging into his forearms for balance as he steadied her.

"Chloe, you little devil," she shouted, water dripping from her chin.

Hopping up and down in glee, Chloe giggled happily as she waved the hose nozzle in wild circles, soaking them both. Her short little legs were already dotted with mud from the puddle at her feet.

Laughing and groaning at the same time, Morgan stepped between their assailant and Raine, blocking the spray. The water plastered his shirt to his belly, and he gasped.

And he thought little girls were supposed to be timid.

He ducked his head and went in low, managing to grab the hose before Chloe caught him in the face again. Drenched and dripping, he followed the hose to the spigot, and twisted it nearly to off. Then, with the water running slowly, he splashed enough on Chloe's fat little legs to send her squealing to Raine for protection.

"Don't come to me, you traitor," Raine teased as she scooped Chloe into her arms for a smacking kiss. Chloe squealed and wrapped her arms around Raine's neck.

Raine's face was flushed and her hair was a tumbled

mess, wet in spots, flyaway in others. The spray had drenched the front of her shirt and it clung to her breasts and ripe belly, sending a jolt of pure need racing through him. Still partially aroused, he sucked in a breath, then shook his head.

"Randolph owes me big-time for this," he muttered, only to have Raine burst out laughing.

It wasn't exactly the way he would have chosen to end their backyard romp, he decided as he cut off the water, but it wasn't half-bad. In fact, it was pretty damn good.

Chapter 10

"**I** swear, Pax, I didn't have a choice. Your wife can be damned persuasive when she wants something." Joel Bronstein's clipped New York speech sounded tinny coming over the phone line to Morgan's ear.

"You didn't have to give her my entire medical history."

Bronstein's sigh was long-suffering. "I didn't. I just gave her bare bones, I swear."

"Oh, yeah? What'd you leave out?"

"The part where they told us you had the highest fever ever recorded in a living patient in the whole damn sand-ridden country. And if packing you in ice didn't work, you were a dead man."

"Bull. Someone read the damn thermometer wrong, that's all."

"Guess they were wrong when they warned you not to catch the same thing again."

"Right."

He drew a tired breath and cast a gaze around the cozy, book-lined room. He felt at home here. Welcomed. It was the one room in Raine's various houses that always stayed fundamentally the same.

"Look, Joel, about that other thing you called about yesterday—"

"It's all arranged." Morgan heard the excitement in his boss's voice and bit of a sigh. "As soon as you get here—"

"I'm on leave."

"But—"

"Stow it, Joel. Get somebody else to meet with Josefa."

"She wants you."

Morgan stared down at the glossy surface of Raine's desk and rubbed two fingers over the dull ache in one temple. "The last time I dealt with that woman she had me running down one false lead after another for six rotten months. Damn near made me crazy."

"Yeah, well, she's got the hots for you. She wanted to keep you around."

"Uh-huh. Exactly my point. I'm not interested in being some kind of toy boy. Get someone else to play her little game."

He heard his boss inhale. "She's hinting about a new hard-line fundamentalist group that's emerging, one that intends to start taking hostages again."

Morgan felt a familiar tension seize the back of his neck. "That's nothing new, Joel. I've been hearing rumors like that since Desert Storm."

"Stebbins says she swears it's good info. And that she'll only give you the particulars."

"What particulars?" he asked warily.

"Names, affiliations, the so-called 'manifesto' they're planning to release after they've snatched the hostages."

A spasm of coughing had Bronstein gasping for breath. The last time Morgan was in New York for contract negotiations, Joel had never been without a cigarette smoldering between his nicotine-stained fingers.

"Sorry," Bronstein muttered before clearing his throat. "According to Stebbins, Josefa's hinting about high-profile types as hostages."

Morgan frowned. Was it possible? He thought back over five years of dealing with his mercurial Lebanese informant. In the beginning she'd given him some good solid leads, but recently he'd been doing little more than chasing dead ends.

"Look, I can't leave now. Have Stebbins explain to her that I'm stuck in the States. Pay her for the info if you have to. She likes emeralds. Claims they match her eyes."

"You sure you can't get away early?"

Morgan let his gaze rove the shelves, seeing familiar titles mixed with new ones. "Damn sure."

"Hmm. How about this? Split your sabbatical into two parts. I could maybe get you a few extra weeks as a payback for your sacrifice."

His gaze halted at a photo of Mike he'd never seen before. Mike was wearing the ski sweater Morgan had sent him, posing next to the new skis Morgan had given him for Christmas that last year. Racing skis.

Designed for an expert skier, not an overconfident kid.

Cool, Dad! Just like yours. When can we hit the slopes so's I can try them out?

They'd planned the trip, but never taken it. Things had heated up on a story he'd been tracking, and he'd left several weeks before they'd been scheduled to leave. That had been the last time he'd seen his son. His last words to the boy had been a promise to take him skiing the next time he got home.

Morgan closed his eyes and tried to erase the memory of Raine's drawn face at Mike's funeral. It didn't work. It never worked.

"Get someone else," he told his boss in a flat tone.

"Pax—"

"No."

Bronstein cleared his throat. When he spoke again, Morgan heard the subtle change in his tone. It was his hardball voice. "If I have to, I'll take this upstairs to the guys in the penthouse."

"Covering your ass, Joel?"

"Damn straight, Paxton. You have a responsibility to this network."

Morgan took a deep slow breath and felt some of the pounding in his head ease. "In 117 days I have a responsibility to the network. Until then, I'm off the clock."

He hung up before Bronstein started screaming.

"Is that dirt I see in your ear, Chloe Randolph?" Towel poised, Prudy pretended shock, and her daughter chortled.

"Chloe aw wet!"

"I'll say." Prudy dried her daughter's legs, tickling each fat little foot in turn while Chloe's bare bottom squirmed on the kitchen counter. "Your daddy never should have taught you how to turn on the faucet. Not until you were in college, anyway."

Chloe grinned and pointed a stubby finger toward the table where Raine was sitting, nursing a glass of orange juice.

"Auntie Waine aw wet, too."

Prudy shot Raine an amused look. "So I see."

"We were doing fine until Morgan showed up," Raine said with a sigh. Her cheeks were still warm, and her chin tingled where his beard had rubbed. She could still hear his laughter as she'd anchored Chloe on her hip and stalked off toward the Randolphs' house.

"Morgan started the water fight?" Prudy sounded confused, and far too amused.

Raine scowled. "Indirectly."

Prudy slipped a clean shirt over her daughter's head and helped Chloe find the arm holes. "I'm surprised Boyd let him go home so soon."

"I doubt Boyd had much say in the matter."

Prudy looked up. "Now why does that sound familiar?"

"Because your husband is just as bullheaded and impossible to handle as my—as Morgan."

Glumly, she watched while Prudy helped Chloe into clean panties and dry shorts. The two females Case liked to call his "ladies" were so much alike. The same delicate bone structure, the same fiery hair, identical green-colored eyes. But Chloe's square little chin had come directly from her father as had the widow's peak.

Raine bit her lip as she tried to imagine the combination of features her twins had inherited. Her dark hair or the lighter hair of the donor? His hazel eyes or her brown ones?

Mike had gotten Morgan's light hair and golden eyes. Her contribution had come in the form of a button nose and an inability to carry a tune. Mike had had her feet, too. Short and wide. An interesting combination.

Morgan wasn't the father of the babies she carried now, but it wouldn't surprise her if they resembled him. She hadn't deliberately set out to select a donor whose physical characteristics replicated Morgan's. Only after she'd filled out the form had she realized what she'd done. It had been too late then. And even if it hadn't been, she wasn't sure she would have changed her mind.

"Okay, tootles, time for milk and cookies, and then I want you to take a teensy nap before Daddy gets home."

Raine laughed. "Poor Chloe. That's a real good-news/bad-news scenario."

Prudy lifted her daughter off the counter and helped her climb into her youth chair. "I started out determined not to resort to bribery to motivate my child. I intended to use logic and reason and infinite patience. That lasted about seven months. Now I use bribery every chance I get.'' She scooted chair and child close to the table, then bent to drop a kiss on Chloe's curly topknot.

"Cookies," Chloe demanded, slapping both hands on the table.

"Such a patient child," Prudy muttered as she took two peanut-butter cookies from a large ceramic jar on the counter. She was about to replace the lid, then shrugged and took two more.

"Want some?" she asked when she caught Raine watching her.

"Yes, but I'm being strong this week."

Prudy laughed as she returned to the table. "I'm not."

"More," Chloe demanded when her mother placed two fat cookies on a napkin in front of her.

"After dinner, sweetie," her mother told her before fetching milk and two cups.

"So you're going to let him stay?" Prudy asked, pouring Chloe's milk.

"Short of getting a restraining order and having the cops throw him out, I don't know how I can keep him from it."

Prudy watched while Chloe lifted the plastic cup to her mouth and drank. Satisfied that her daughter was in one of her neater moods, she returned the milk to the fridge, then sat down and reached for a cookie.

"You know that if he stays, he'll want to make love with you," she said quietly.

Raine couldn't quite suppress the funny little thrill that winked through her at the thought. "That would be a mistake."

"Probably." Prudy bit into a cookie, her gaze still on Raine's face.

Raine took an impatient breath. "There's no 'probably'

about it, Prue. That's how I ended up married to Morgan in the first place.''

"Fortunately, that's not a risk this time, since you're already married—and definitely pregnant.''

"You sound as though you *want* me to become involved with the wrong man again.''

"Sweetie, you're already involved.''

"That's the point. I'm trying to become *uninvolved.* No one but my attorney seems to be taking my side.''

Prudy crunched another cookie between her teeth. Her expression was sublime.

"What does that tell you?''

"It tells me that the legendary Morgan Paxton charisma is alive and well on Mill Works Ridge. And after only three days.''

She wasn't surprised, of course. The man had a magic about him. Some indefinable magnetism. Or maybe it was simply an abundance of testosterone. Whatever. Bottom line, she'd been half in love with Morgan by the time he'd finished giving a two-hour talk. A talk that she hadn't even planned to attend. Somehow she'd found herself swept into the lecture hall after showing him the way.

"Yoo-hoo, anyone home?'' Without waiting for a reply, Stacy opened the screen door and walked in, carrying a sleepy-eyed Shelby on her hip.

"Hi, Stace,'' Prudy chirped, waving her in. "Join the party.''

"What's the occasion?''

"Raine has decided to have an affair with her husband.''

Raine shot Prudy a look dripping with reproach. "I certainly haven't decided any such thing, and you know it.''

Stacy glanced from one to the other, then grinned. "This sounds promising.'' She carried Shelby to the cupboard and took out a cup.

"Careful, Stace," Prudy warned with a grin. "She thinks we're ganging up on her."

"You are!" Raine told her.

"Sounds like you two need a totally objective third party to mediate. I volunteer." Stacy put the glass on the table, pulled out a chair and sat down with Shelby on her lap. "I have exactly forty-seven minutes before Tory gets home from her play date at Lance's house, so talk fast."

The two little girls jabbered greetings to one another before Chloe offered her mother a crafty look.

"Shelby wants cookies, Mama."

"That's my little opportunist," Prudy muttered as she got up to fetch the cookie jar. Raine noticed that she pressed one hand to her lower back and frowned.

"Prue, are you sure you're not having pains?"

"Nope, just little warning twinges. I had them for two solid weeks before I delivered Chloe." She set the jar in front of Stacy before carefully easing onto the chair she'd just vacated. "And don't try to change the subject, Raine Paxton."

"I wasn't aware that there was a subject to change," Raine bluffed.

Prudy and Stacy exchanged knowing looks. "Prickly, isn't she?" Stacy remarked airily.

"A mere hormonal imbalance," Raine maintained.

"I'll say," Prudy said, nodding sagely. "I don't know about you, Stace, but I detected a definite spark between our neighbor and her estranged husband the other day."

Stacy handed her daughter a cookie, then reached for the juice pitcher. "I noticed the same thing. In fact, I told Boyd that there'd been enough sexual electricity rocketing around in our neighbor's backyard to light the entire north end."

"Excuse me," Raine said archly. "It's getting so deep in here, I think I need to fetch my boots."

Stacy took a sip of juice before offering some to her

daughter. "How is our illustrious visitor feeling?" she asked, her expression suddenly serious.

"As domineering as ever," Raine muttered. "And wet. Chloe turned the hose on us while we were, um, discussing his departure date."

Stacy laughed. "Oh, my."

"'Oh, my' is right." She started to take a drink, then realized her glass was empty and reached for the pitcher. "Actually, I should be grateful to the little darling. I strongly suspect I was about to do something I would have regretted."

"Aha, I knew it!" Prudy crowed. "You're still in love with him."

It was on the tip of Raine's tongue to deny it. Then she realized that she would be lying. "Did I ever tell you how much I hate it when you're right?" she muttered with a sigh. "And don't think this changes anything, because it doesn't."

"So have an affair with him," Prudy said matter-of-factly. "Enjoy yourself. Risk free."

"Which is saying a lot in this day and age," Stacy chimed in. "What with AIDS and...stop squirming, lamb."

"Down," Shelby demanded, kicking her feet.

"Okay?" Stacy asked, directing an inquiring look Prudy's way.

"Sure. Do me a favor and help Chloe get down, too."

Stacy set her daughter on the floor, then got up to help Chloe. "Play nice, you two," she called as the two little girls sprinted for Chloe's bedroom and the bulging toy box.

Stacy settled back in her chair and offered Raine a smile. "Don't you want to sleep with the guy?"

"No!" She sighed. "Yes."

"Then do it."

"We did," Prudy added, winking at Stacy. "And look how happy we are."

Raine looked from one to the other. Both had faced the
pain of loss and hurt. Both had been divorced. Prudy from
the man she eventually remarried. Stacy from a policeman
who had developed an incurable psychosis after he'd been
injured in the line of duty. Both had found the courage to
love again.

"There's one difference," she said as she slowly got to
her feet.

"What's that?" Stacy asked, her brows knitting.

Raine offered her a bittersweet smile. "Your men stayed
with you. Mine always leaves."

Prudy looked at Stacy. Stacy looked at Prudy. Neither
said a word.

How could they?

Raine was sweating by the time she reached her own
place. According to the thermometer affixed to the post
holding up the porch roof, it was a scorching ninety degrees. In the shade.

Inside the house, it felt about ten degrees cooler, and she
sighed with relief. When she'd renovated the old house,
she'd installed central heat and air as a matter of course,
but she preferred her air fresh whenever possible.

Morgan was just coming out of the utility room when
she walked into the kitchen and closed the screen door behind her. His long legs were sheathed in clean, dry jeans.
His feet and his chest were bare. He stopped when he saw
her, and glowered at her.

"Uh-oh," she said when she saw what he had in his
hands. It was the remnants of the T-shirt she'd cut from
his body.

"This just happens to be my favorite shirt." He looked
pained. "Correction, this *was* my favorite shirt. Now it's a
rag."

She felt her lips twitch. "I, um, forgot it was special. I'm sorry."

"Care to tell me what happened, Mrs. Paxton?" He was frowning, but his voice seemed to soften over her name.

"You were soaking wet and starting to shiver, and I couldn't get you to move. I had to do something, so I just...cut it off of you, like they do in the hospital emergency room."

His brow furrowed. In most areas of his life, Morgan was remarkably dispassionate and logical. When it came to his clothes, however, he had a tendency to be a tad eccentric. He had his favorites, which were as sacred to him as holy relics are to religious zealots. It was one of the things that Raine had found most endearing during those times when he was home.

"Frank Weinhard gave me this shirt when I signed my first network contract," he said in a tone dripping with accusation. "It was still in great shape."

Raine's jaw dropped. "Are we talking about the same shirt here? The one with the frayed neckline and a giant hole in the front?"

"I didn't say it was perfect." He sounded offended.

"Just that it was in great shape?"

"That's what I said."

She came closer for a better look. Dry now and a mass of wrinkles, the old shirt was even worse than she remembered. Extending a finger, she poked at one of the faded letters. She knew it was a *B*, but to the uninformed, it could be any of four or five other letters.

"Yes, I can see it's in a pristine state. And such a lovely color of drab, faded gray."

His mouth quirked. "I admit it's seen a little wear."

"Now that is an understatement if I've ever heard one."

A sheepish look came over his face. "I guess you think it's pretty dumb, getting all worked up over a shirt."

"I think it's called sublimation." She lifted a hand to touch the shirt, then let it drop. "Maybe it can be mended."

"Can it, Raine? Or is it too late?" His husky whisper seemed to thrum all the way through her. Suddenly he was no longer talking about a ruined shirt.

"I don't know," she admitted, shaking inside. "Maybe I'm afraid to find out."

He lifted a hand to smooth the same stray curl behind her ear. She shivered, and his mouth slanted.

"Maybe I am, too."

She drew a shaky breath. "I've never known you to be afraid of anything."

His lashes flickered. "You're not supposed to know."

"Why not?"

"Bad for my image."

There it was, that teasing grin designed to charm. Or was it to keep others from probing too deeply?

"I didn't marry an image, Morgan."

The look that whisked across his hard features was poignantly sad. "No, we both know you married the father of your child."

"Because I loved you."

He held himself very still while his gaze probed the depths of her eyes. She wondered if he would reach for her. When he didn't, she realized she was disappointed.

"And now?" he asked very quietly after a long moment of silence.

"Now I'm confused and muddled and...pregnant."

His eyes crinkled. "Which came first?"

"The pregnant part," she admitted. "The confusion and muddle arrived at just about the same time you did."

"Funny, that's when it hit me, too."

Raine found herself laughing. "This isn't funny," she said, biting her lip. "You're supposed to be furious with me, and I'm supposed to be totally impervious to your charm.''

"Is that right?'' He draped the tattered shirt around her neck like a towel and gripped both ends.

"We'll only end up hurting one another."

"That's one possibility. Way I see it, there's another."

"Which is?"

He edged closer. Close enough for her to feel the heat of his bare chest. Close enough to see the tiny needle marks in his shoulder from sutures placed there years ago by an army surgeon.

"I could turn out to be a terrific househusband. Indispensable, even. So indispensable you'd end up keeping me."

"You mean like a pet?"

His mouth rose at one aggressive corner. "Sorta, yeah. Provided I get to warm your feet at night."

He slowly drew the soft cotton shirt back and forth across the sensitive nape of her neck. Tiny shivers ran through her, part pleasure, part anticipation.

"I...don't think that would be a good idea."

"Sounds to me like you're afraid," he taunted gently, his gaze fixed now on her mouth. "The question is? Of whom? Me or yourself?"

She felt him tug on the ends of the shirt, drawing her closer. She knew she should resist. Any second now she would. Even as his head was descending, even as her eyes were fluttering closed as though beyond her control, she told herself to step back.

He touched his mouth to hers in a brief kiss. A mere whisper no longer than a breath. "Don't be afraid, honey."

She watched his mouth, enthralled by the sensuality of movement, the provocative creasing of his cheek. The flash of strong white teeth.

"I'm as chubby as a blimp."

It seemed vitally important for him to und... could he want her when she carried another man's chi...

"Not chubby. Blooming. As round and ripe as a peach fixin' to fall from a tree."

She managed a shaky laugh. "You've become a poet."

His eyes crinkled. "Nah, I must've read that somewhere."

"You're always reading." She realized she was spouting nonsense. Stalling for time.

"Not always. Sometimes I'm sleeping. And sometimes I'm daydreaming about making love to my wife."

His tone was both wistful and amused, with an undercurrent of sensuous promise. She felt a thrill run through her, followed immediately by the cold water of panic. Perhaps that was the reason she flinched when he let one end of the shirt fall to her breast and lifted his hand toward her face.

"Easy, sweetheart. I just need to touch you, that's all."

"Why?"

His mouth firmed. "Silly question."

His fingers skimmed her cheek as he traced the sweep of her cheekbones. With the ball of his thumb, he followed the line of her lips. It was a tactile seduction, all the more arousing because she sensed the control he was exerting to go slowly.

"So soft and sweet," he murmured, his voice very deep. "Such a pretty mouth." She felt his breath on her face, tinged with toothpaste.

His lips seemed to hover over hers for an eternity. Mesmerized, she let her eyes drift closed. An instant later his mouth found hers. She felt a jolt, a spread of warmth, a small catch of excitement in her throat as he rubbed her mouth with his. She remained perfectly still as emotion fluttered through her. The glint in his eyes had promised

giving her slow and gentle. A

felt the tautness draining from her
made slow nibbling motions. When
lip between his teeth, she uttered a
protest. When she felt his tongue touch
protest became a moan of pleasure.

He withdrew. Took a breath, then found her mouth again.
It was a deliberate mating, utterly sexual, yet layered in
complexity. He kissed her again and again, setting his own
rhythm, slow and lazy, a symphony of constraint. Each time
his mouth pressed hers, she felt more heat, more need. Each
time his mouth withdrew, she moaned, bringing his mouth
to hers again.

Each kiss took her deeper.

Each time, his lips were parted more, making him both
aggressor and supplicant. She responded by opening her
own lips in invitation.

He shifted, lithe as the cat he resembled, perfectly co-
ordinated. He tilted his head to one side, fitted his mouth
to hers. He skimmed his palms over her bare arms in a
slow caress that warmed her flesh and heated her blood.

She snuggled closer, her belly pressed to his. Between
them the babies shifted and settled, eliciting a sound from
him halfway between a laugh and a groan. His arms closed
around her, drawing her into a powerfully intimate em-
brace.

His toes tangled with hers where they peeked from the
straps of her sandals. His large palms cupped her buttocks,
drawing her even more snugly to him.

Something crested inside her, spilling over into pleasure.
She needed. Wanted. No longer content to be passive, she
put her arms around his neck and arched upward. She heard
a growl of approval rumble in his bare chest, even as he
slipped his tongue into her open mouth.

She felt exultant, alive.

It was heaven being held like this. How she loved feeling defenseless against his overpowering masculinity! Soaring, she gloried in the tightly coiled strength of the well-muscled arms holding her so securely. She basked in the feel of his hardness against her yielding softness.

The hard ridge of his arousal emphasized the elemental difference in their bodies. The demand of his mouth epitomized the contrast in their natures. His tongue was wicked and daring, making love to her mouth with each darting stroke. She felt her body opening, softening. Moisture gathered between her legs.

As though sensing her response, he changed the tempo of his seduction. His tongue was disciplined now. Controlled. Stroking into her mouth with slow deliberation.

She imagined him laving her body with those same slow strokes, and her breasts tingled. Another moan escaped her as she imagined the feel of his tongue on her stomach, on her thighs. Imagined a gently insistent intrusion into her body. A hot rush of demand.

She tensed and dug her fingers into his neck. Some semblance of sanity rose above the sensual bombardment, and she managed to wrench her mouth from his. Panting, she dropped her head to his chest and waited for the wild surge of need to pass.

"Please, Raine," he grated, his breath fanning the top of her head. "I need you."

Morgan felt the words being torn from him almost against his will, and winced. What had started as a prelude to seduction had escalated into a hunger so powerful, it frightened him.

Schooling himself to patience, he drew back and used his fist to nudge her chin higher until he could see her face. Her cheeks were flushed, her lips rosy and kiss swollen.

Her eyes were closed, her brow furrowed. A pulse as wild as his own beat in the fragile hollow of her throat.

He felt a rush of tenderness as fierce as his physical need. Because he couldn't help himself, he kissed her again, praying she wouldn't pull away. When she responded by opening her mouth, he nearly shouted his happiness aloud.

Instead, he murmured her name before kissing her again. Harder this time. She stayed with him, her fingers burrowing into his hair, opening and closing in delicious little spasms that tugged on his scalp and whetted his appetite.

His hands roamed the supple curve of her back. The soft cotton shirt was still warm from the sun and felt soft against his fingertips. But not as soft as her skin would feel. Or as satisfying.

The tail of her shirt was loose, allowing easy access to the warm skin it covered, yet he hesitated. Once he'd felt the silk of her flesh, he doubted he would have the strength to stop before he was buried deep inside her.

He drew back before it was too late, and the jolt of disappointment he felt nearly overrode his control. Her lashes fluttered, then lifted, and her drowsy gaze found his.

"Honey, we have to stop," he whispered, his voice thick with unslaked desire.

"Stop?" She sounded dazed. And...annoyed? He felt a rush of hope.

"It's been too long. I'm about to bust."

She choked back a laugh. "I withdraw my previous remarks. You're not a poet."

He felt a rush of tenderness. "At least give me credit for trying to be a gentleman."

As she looked at him through hazy dark eyes, he cursed himself for being a fool. Yet, there was too much at stake to risk a mistake now.

Timing was everything.

At the moment his felt lousy.

"Maybe I don't want you to be a gentleman," she whispered, her gaze searching his.

He inhaled sharply. His control became even more precarious. "Careful, honey. I'm not in the mood for teasing."

Raine drew a shaky breath. She'd forgotten how meticulous Morgan had always been about their relationship. No games. No coy pretenses. Everything up-front and honest.

"I'm...not teasing," she made herself admit.

His expression turned fierce, his eyes molten. "Tell me you want me," he demanded.

"I...want you."

He closed his eyes for a long moment, his face stiff with need and something more. Something riveting.

"In that case, honey, hang on tight."

With one powerful, tightly controlled movement of muscle and sinew, he scooped her into his arms and headed for the bedroom.

Chapter 11

He kissed her hard before setting her gently on her feet. It seemed to drain the last of his control. His expression was fierce, his muscles taut as he ripped open the button fly of his jeans. He dipped the other hand beneath her shirt and jerked her shorts over her hips, letting them fall to the floor.

Even as she was stepping free of the puddled cotton, his mouth was finding hers in a hungry kiss. Gone was the gentle wooing, the tender persuasion. The self-imposed moderation. Her mouth opened to his demand, allowing his tongue to enter.

Raine moaned, her senses quivering, brought to full life by the stroking of his hands and the sweet persistence of his kisses. Whatever doubts and reservations remained concerning the wisdom of making love to this man seemed irrelevant. All that mattered was the all-consuming heat of his passion.

He pulled back, his face taut with his need, his eyes

smoldering, his arms corded as he slowly eased her shirt above her waist.

"Lift your arms for me, baby," he ordered, his voice thick.

She obeyed, poised on the knife edge of embarrassment. He'd never seen her in full-blown pregnancy, never made love to her when her belly was distended and her breasts were swollen.

Impatiently he tossed away the shirt, then dealt swiftly with the plain cotton bra. Her breasts spilled free, engorged now by need as much as her advancing condition. She waited as he stood unmoving, staring down at her. Gradually, like the bloom of shame, she felt heat rising from between her breasts. Suddenly miserable and uncertain, she bit her lip and tried to edge backward.

"Sweet heaven, but you're magnificent," he said, his voice rough with reverence. "My sexy fertility goddess."

His manhood sprang free of his shorts, his arousal heavy and throbbing through the open fly of his jeans. Raine swallowed, feeling her body warm and soften, eager to receive his. She had forgotten how large he was. How powerfully male.

She lifted her gaze to his, her cheeks flaming.

Seeing the drowsy desire in her eyes drove Morgan to the brink. He fought for control. He had to touch her. Now.

But suddenly he was afraid. What if it was too soon? What if he wanted her too much to be gentle?

He felt awkward and ungainly, a peasant yearning for a queen. The ignorant son of a moonshiner with rough hands and the finesse of a mule.

"Raine, baby, I…" He swallowed, tried again. "Tell me if I'm hurting you."

"Oh, Morgan," she whispered, her voice vibrating with the same need he felt pulsing in his loins.

Gently, his hands trembling, he reached out to palm her

breasts. She swayed, bringing her hands up to brace against his shoulders. Her eyes closed, and her lips parted on a sigh.

He lifted the fullness of one breast, then the other and watched the emotions playing over her face. With his thumbs, he teased the dark nipples until they were hot, hard nubs. It was beautiful to watch her body responding. He was wildly aroused, yet humbled by the openness of her acceptance.

"Honey, I can't...wait much longer," he grated, his painfully engorged body clamoring for an end to the exquisite torture.

Raine heard the strain in his voice and arched closer. He took her in his arms and held her fiercely, his body shuddering. Her hands closed around his neck as she rubbed her aching nipples against the crisp hair on his chest. He groaned, and buried his face in her hair. She felt the steely strength of muscle beneath the warm, taut skin of his neck, sensed the power in the broad shoulders. His hand cupped her buttocks, pulling her hard against the straining hardness of his arousal. She felt spurts of pleasure inside, like tiny sparks.

"That feels so good," she murmured softly. "So good."

He groaned, then suddenly lifted her.

"Straddle me, honey. Let me feel your heat."

Arching upward, she clung tighter, felt his arousal probing for the warmth behind her thin panties. At the same moment he moved backward toward the bed.

Still holding her securely, he slowly sat down, his hard shaft pressed against the delta of her thighs.

"Ah, that's so...nice," he managed in a breathless tone of raw desire. His thighs bunched hard under hers as he drew up a hand to wet one finger.

"Easy, sweetheart," he begged as he slipped his fingers beneath the lace of her panties. When he found the tiny bud hidden between her legs, she cried out, her body already contracting around his fingers.

Her eyes sprang open and she looked into his eyes as pleasure coursed through her in fast, shimmering waves. With a groan, he withdrew his hand, only to use it to push aside the barrier of her panties.

His face was a mask of strain as he slowly pushed into her, his shaft as hot and slick as sun-kissed marble. Holding her now with both hands against her buttocks, he eased closer until he was fully seated inside her.

She felt his thigh muscles quivering as he dropped his head to her shoulder and held himself very still. When he had himself under control again, he began to move, drawing back with a slowness that was nearly unbearable.

Her body reacted like quicksilver, growing moist and tense again as the pleasure built. She squirmed against him, wringing a groan from his throat as he suddenly thrust hard again. She shivered, then dug her fingers into his neck.

Small delicious shivers ran through her, one after another. Unable to help herself she arched her back and pressed closer. A sob escaped her as the small shivers gathered into a rush of feeling. She was sliding toward a precipice, going faster and faster. And then she was falling.

She felt Morgan go rigid, then thrust once more. He cried out, his voice hoarse and exultant. She sagged against him, her cheek resting on his shoulder and her lips pressed against his neck. His skin was hot and wonderfully damp. She loved the feel of him when he was still slick and fevered from lovemaking.

His arms tightened and he held her close as her body still trembled. Closing her eyes, she rested against him, her body sated and heavy with a glorious lassitude. Gradually her breathing slowed, gentling as his gentled.

For a long time neither moved. His body remained in

hers, no longer hard, but still filling her. She felt content. Willing to remain this way forever.

Then slowly, he began rubbing her back with long, even strokes. "Little tiger," he murmured, his voice very deep. "So wild."

She smiled. "I look like I've swallowed a watermelon, and yet I feel so wanton."

"You're wonderful." He moved, forcing her to lift her head and open her eyes. His face was suddenly taut again, his eyes intense. "I nearly lost it when I thought you'd been with another man."

Raine reached up to touch his face. "There's been no one else but you."

"Really?" He sounded both gruff and hopeful.

"Really."

The tight lines around his mouth relaxed and went from a fierce frown to a lazy grin. "Well, all right, then. That's settled."

"What's settled?"

His face stilled. "Us. You and me. We're a couple again, right?"

She longed to tell him yes. To commit herself to him again without reservation. But she was determined to go slowly this time.

The emotional distance she'd felt after Mike's death was lessening, but it was still there. A shield against the impulsive part of her nature that only seemed to surface when Morgan was around.

"I need a shower," she murmured, trying to ease herself free.

His mouth firmed, and his arms tightened.

"Oh, no, you don't. You stay right where you are until we get this thrashed out."

"Uh, it's, um, difficult to be logical when I can feel you, um, stirring inside me."

He frowned. "Try."

She sighed. So much for a graceful retreat. But then, Morgan was anything but reticent when it came to getting what he wanted. Hadn't he fought tremendous odds all of his life, winning more often than not?

"We made love, Morgan, but that's all that happened. Nothing's changed."

"Like hell. You wanted me. I could feel it."

"Yes, I wanted you. I've always wanted you. But that doesn't change the reality of our situation. We have different goals. Diametrically opposed goals."

He narrowed his gaze. "Opposed how, specifically?"

"I want stability and permanence and a normal life. You know, a nine-to-five, Sundays-at-the-park kind of future. You want—no, you *crave*—change and excitement." She drew a breath. "You're a thrill seeker, Morgan. One of those people who was born with a need to test himself against the highest mountain or the steepest cliff or...or the most dangerous story. You can't change, and I can't survive in a part-time marriage."

She pressed her hands against his heavily padded shoulders and pushed. This time he let her slip off his lap. "It's not your fault that you're the way you are, any more than it's my fault that I no longer want to arrange my life around yours."

His expression was remote, his eyes cool and assessing as he studied her face. Finally, he nodded. "That's spelling it out clear enough." His grin flashed briefly. "And mostly in words of one syllable that even a thickheaded guy like me can understand."

"No...hard feelings?" she asked quietly, holding her breath.

"Nope."

She waited, but he remained silent. If he was upset, nothing showed on his face but the remnants of the fatigue he'd brought with him from the Middle East.

"Well, fine. Good."

She glanced down at her shirt and thought about bending to pick it up. And then she remembered her body didn't bend in the middle these days. Turning her back, she padded to the bird's-eye maple highboy that had been her mother's. Opening one drawer, then another, she gathered a change of clothes.

She turned back to find he'd shucked his jeans and was in the act of kicking them aside. Glancing up, he grinned. "Race you to the shower."

"Pardon?"

"I've got this hankering to see what else you can do with that pink puffy thing besides using it to slam me out of the stall."

He sauntered toward her, unapologetically naked, two hundred plus pounds of hard-edged male. Though no longer aroused, he was still powerfully sexy. A man of physical power and strong character, with a magnificently formed body.

Raine resisted an urge to back up. "If you stay here for the next four months, we'll have to set some ground rules."

"Ground rules?" He looked uncomfortable.

"It's the only way."

"It is?"

He was close enough now that she could feel the heat of his body. She told herself to ignore the fact that they were standing belly to belly, having a serious discussion while neither of them had on a stitch of clothing. Under other circumstances, she would have been convulsed by laughter.

"Yes, of course. It doesn't make sense for us to just pretend this is a normal situation."

His mouth quirked, as though he, too, realized the absurdity of this confrontation. "It doesn't?"

She shook her head. "I admit the idea of an affair is very appealing to me, especially now when I'm, well, not exactly at my best."

"Couldn't prove it by me."

"Yes, well, that's certainly a point in your favor."

Something changed in his eyes. It was a small shift, a subtle narrowing. A suggestion of ice over turbulent water. She fought off a shiver.

"I didn't realize you were keeping a tally," he said without inflection.

Because he was far too close to the truth, she frowned. "I'm not. I was being ironic."

"Ah, irony. Not my best subject."

"Then we're agreed? We sleep together while you're here, for as long as my doctor says it's okay. And then, when the babies are safely born and you've fulfilled your, um, mission, we'll part without regrets."

"Whatever you want, honey. It's your call all the way."

The lazy drawl was back in his voice, a soft slurring of consonants and liquid vowels. It was the voice he used when he was relaxed. Or on the air. She told herself she'd only imagined the flicker of hurt that had crossed his face.

"You pay your bills. I pay mine."

"Fine."

"We'll split the cost of the food."

"Okay."

"And you'll sign a statement relinquishing all rights of custody?"

Something dangerous flashed between the thick lashes. But his voice, when he answered was mild. "If that makes you feel more comfortable, sure."

Just that easy, he renounced the children she was carrying. She should be pleased. Relieved. In fact, she was. Of course, she was, she told herself as she put out her hand.

"Shake on it?" she asked with a small grin.

"Oh, I think we can do better than that."

He gripped her shoulders and pulled her toward him. His kiss was possessive and profoundly intimate, his hand stroking her fanny as his tongue darted and stroked. Just when she felt herself starting to melt, he lifted his head. A hard flush rose over his cheekbones as he slipped a hand behind her neck to press her face against his neck. With a sigh, he bent his head over hers, and held her, his arm a steel band against her back. He held her close, rocking them back and forth gently for several silent moments before he lifted his head and stepped back.

"Now, about that shower..." he drawled, his grin devilish.

"Pax, they mean business this time."

Morgan sat back in Raine's delicate desk chair and rubbed at the dull ache in one temple. "This time?" he jeered into the receiver. "You mean they were only kidding two years ago when they threatened me with a breach-of-contract lawsuit if I extended my emergency leave?"

On the other end of the phone line, his agent let out a long, heavy sigh. Paul Slotsky was an ex-NFL lineman with a calculator for a brain and the determination of a bull in full charge. The deals he'd cut for Morgan during the past twenty years had made them both rich.

"Give me a break, Pax, okay? Can the sarcasm and just listen while I try to save both your career and your butt."

"First irony and now sarcasm. Hell, I am comin' up in the world." When he'd left the hills with thirteen dollars in his jeans and a savage need to survive burning in his gut, he'd never heard either word.

"Jeez, you are in a rotten mood this morning." There was a pause. When Slotsky spoke again, his voice was subtly altered. "Look, I know this divorce thing hit you hard, especially coming so soon after Mike's death, but—"

"No divorce," Morgan grated through a tight jaw. "And that's personal. We're talking about Bronstein and his gestapo tactics."

"It's in the contract, Pax. They have a right to your time."

"Under certain specific conditions. Placating a neurotic source with an itch doesn't even come close to making the list."

"Bronstein claims she's got solid information."

"Then let Bronstein wine and dine Josefa. I'm on leave."

He closed his eyes and listened to the muffled sound of an exercise video Raine had playing in the living room. It was a yoga tape, mostly stretching, she'd assured him, her brow puckered into that earnest look of concentration he'd always loved. She claimed the babies liked the slow and easy movements better than the traditional prenatal exercises she'd practiced earlier in her pregnancy.

"Pax, be reasonable. How long can it take to check out her story? A week? Two at the most. If it's true, you'll come home a hero, with a sure Pulitzer nomination in your pocket and a pot of network goodwill to carry into our next contract negotiations."

"Screw goodwill. I gave Raine my word."

This time the pause was longer. He had a feeling he wasn't going to like what Slotsky was working up his nerve to say.

"Three years ago, when you scrawled your name to the bottom of that contract, you agreed to the terms. Which means you also gave the network your word."

Morgan muttered a foul oath that had Slotsky chuckling. "So you'll call Bronstein and tell him your flight number to Beirut?"

"Get stuffed, Slotsky."

"Okay, *I'll* call him."

"The hell you will. I haven't even been home a week, and already he's hassling me."

"Technically, you've been on leave for two weeks. The network doesn't care about travel problems."

Morgan waited out a wave of hot fury before speaking again. "Look, Paul. If I really thought there was even a tiny possibility Josefa had solid stuff this time, I'd already be on a plane. But she's been floating talk about this off-the-wall plot for years. I spent a lot of valuable time checking it out, only to come up with zilch."

Morgan could almost see his burly agent's scowl. "Okay, you win. I'll invite Bronstein to an obscenely expensive lunch—on you, by the way—and ply him with martinis and bull. It's worked before. Who knows? We might get lucky."

Morgan told himself to relax. "Thanks, buddy. I appreciate it."

"Don't thank me yet, Pax. We might both end up on the wrong end of this one, and I, for one, am not ready to give up the life-style to which you have accustomed me."

Morgan snorted. "What's the worst they can do? Fire me?"

"Exactly, and throw in a lot of ugly talk about your lack of loyalty, et cetera. It could—no, it's *sure* to—get ugly."

"So?"

"So your entire history will be spread all over the tube for weeks. All the old rumors about your mother's disappearance and your father's, shall we say, less-than-exemplary life-style."

"I can handle it."

"Sure you can. But what about Raine?"

Morgan scowled. He'd never lied to her about his past. Not once. But he'd been deliberately vague about the details. Some things were better left buried.

"Raine's no snob. She'll understand."

"I'm not talking about understanding. I'm talking about a mother who lost a child in the not-too-distant past. How do you think she'll feel when she sees Mike's funeral replayed over and over again?"

Morgan winced. The pain in his head sharpened. His hand tightened around the receiver as his gaze went to the photograph of Mike on the bookshelf across the room. It hurt to see the bright look of eagerness in his son's eyes. The total trust in the goodness of life. Morgan knew better.

"Handle it, Paul. I don't care how many concessions you have to make."

Slotsky cleared his throat. "This might cost you your reputation, Pax. Hell, it might even cost you your career."

Morgan felt the blade of icy fear slice into his gut. He *was* his career. An image on the screen that he'd invented. Without it, he was just another pretty face without substance. An ignorant pretender one mistake away from the gutter.

From the other room he heard a crescendo of music, followed by silence. The video was over. While it was rewinding, Raine would take a shower and get ready to go downtown to that little hole-in-the-wall bookstore she loved so much.

He felt himself smiling as he remembered the feel of her soapy skin beneath his hands as he scrubbed her back. He felt his body stir, and the pain in his head ease.

"Handle it, Slotsky," he said into the receiver before hanging up. He felt the need to take a shower.

Chapter 12

Morgan was feeling almost normal by Saturday night. Since Raine was planning an evening out with Stacy and Prudy, he was looking forward to an evening of poker.

The sun had still been a brilliant ball hanging over the river when he'd escorted Raine to the Randolphs' back door. Stacy and Prudy had greeted him with warm hugs and inquiries into the state of his health. He'd barely gotten out an answer before Prudy was introducing him to the two men in the group he hadn't already met.

Detective Sergeant Don Petrov and Dr. Luke Jarrod.

It seemed that Petrov was Case's longtime partner, a craggy middle-aged bear of a man with a lived-in face, unusual green eyes and a look of quiet integrity about him. Morgan liked him immediately.

He was more inclined to reserve his opinion about Dr. Jarrod. Morgan had never met a medic quite like him. Given the man's rangy toughness and weathered face, Morgan would have pegged him for a far different career. A rancher, maybe. Or another cop. Even as he shook the man's hand, he'd sensed that Jarrod was dealing with his own reservations about one Morgan Paxton. Something about the look in the man's intelligent gray eyes had Morgan wondering what Raine had said about her absentee husband.

"Now you boys play nice-nice," Prudy had said as she dropped a kiss on her husband's thick black hair. "No biting in the clinches."

Case Randolph had colored fiercely, but his eyes had been soft as he gruffly ordered his energetic little wife to be careful.

After warning Morgan not to let down his guard around the Mill Works Ridge cardsharps, the three women with the impatient little girls departed.

Morgan stifled a pang of jealousy that Raine merely lifted a hand in farewell instead of kissing him goodbye in front of the others. Since they'd made love, she'd been as jumpy as a snake-bit hound dog. He'd been walking on damn eggshells for two days, trying not to spook her, but his patience was beginning to thin.

"Don't worry, Paxton," Case said with a raised brow. "We'll take it easy on you first time out. Right, guys?"

"Damn straight," MacAuley muttered, his grin reminding Morgan of a sheep-stealing wolf he'd shot once.

Jarrod merely nodded as he reached for a handful of peanuts.

"Yeah," Petrov grated, sounding very much as though he'd been swallowing briers. "We only pick you clean after we get to know you better."

The big man grinned as he shuffled the cards. From the look of the expert moves he was putting on the pasteboards, Morgan had a feeling he was in for a an old-fashioned ass kicking.

An hour into the game Morgan was trying to recall the exact amount of the credit on his Visa card. He was a decent enough player, but his skills were rusty. It didn't help that he kept wishing he was home in bed with Raine, making slow, delicious love to her rotund body.

"Did you ever wonder what they do on their so-called 'ladies night out'?" Case Randolph asked around the cigar clenched between his teeth.

"Some, but I figured it was best not to know," Mac-Auley replied as he took his turn dealing. He had an impressive stack of chips in front of him and a satisfied gleam in his eyes. "I figure a man has to retain some illusions about his woman."

"Illusions, hell," Case's burly partner scoffed, his big hands already arranging his cards. "You married guys are purely pathetic, letting those little ladies of yours lead you around by big old rings in your noses." He glanced across the table at their host. "Especially you, Randolph. It's downright embarrassing to be in your presence when some misguided fool asks about your family."

Case cocked a thick black eyebrow. "You guys ever notice how green my partner's complexion has gotten since Prudy and I got married again?"

Luke Jarrod snorted a laugh. "Hell, Case, Petrov's skin has always had a peculiar cast to it. I figure it comes from living on cigars and coffee instead of real food."

"Don't forget all that beer the man guzzles," Boyd chimed in with a pointed look at the long-necked bottle at the big man's elbow.

"Nectar of the gods, son," Petrov retorted, throwing down two cards. "What about you, Paxton? Is it true you have to go without booze over in those Mideast countries?"

Morgan discarded three cards before glancing up. "Mostly, yeah, though liquor is available in the foreign compounds and the embassies. Especially the French."

"Seems to me they ought to pay you extra. Sort of like depravation rations."

Morgan picked up the cards MacAuley had shot him and grinned. Three pretty ladies to go with a pair of twos.

"I'll mention that to the chairman next time I'm in New York."

Randolph eyed the soft drink in front of Morgan thoughtfully. "Doesn't look to be much of a problem for you."

"Nope."

Petrov drew a cigar from his shirt pocket and peeled off the cellophane. "Not much of a drinker?"

"Not since I was young and dumb." He felt his stomach twist as bad memories threatened the barriers he'd been piling around them for years. "My old man made a living selling 'shine. Had me too much of it one time too many and damn near died. Doc Smiley said I was lucky I hadn't fried my brain permanently." He grinned. "'Course, there are those who claim I did."

"I know the feeling," MacAuley muttered. "My brother and I used to pickle our gray cells on a regular basis before my grandmother found out and darn near skinned us raw."

"Pikers. Letting piddling little old reasons keep you from having fun."

Petrov fired up his cigar and puffed contentedly as he studied his hand. His expression revealed damn little.

"I'm in," Petrov declared, tossing in his two chip ante. Randolph did the same. "Me, too."

MacAuley frowned at his cards, then shrugged and tossed in a couple of chips. "What the hell?"

"Too rich for me," Jarrod muttered, folding his hand. "All this talk about boozin' has me real thirsty. Since I'm not on call and none of my ladies are in labor, I think I'll get me a beer." He got to his feet. "Bring anyone somethin' from the kitchen?"

"More chips," Randolph muttered without bothering to lift his gaze from his cards.

The betting held another round. When it was his call, Morgan glanced at his full house. His first shot at taking a decent pot all night. With a inner sigh of regret, he folded. Priorities, he reminded himself.

While the betting went around again, he got up and stretched, then followed Jarrod to the kitchen. The lanky doctor had just pulled a beer from the fridge and was shutting the door when Morgan entered.

"Thought I'd get the chips," Morgan said offhand.

"On the counter."

Jarrod twisted the top from the bottle and tossed it into the trash basket by the fridge. Instead of returning to the game, he leaned against the counter. "Heard you paid Port Gen a visit a few days back."

Morgan ambled toward the counter. He wasn't hungry, but he tore open the bag of chips and tossed a couple in his mouth.

"Port Gen?" he asked, crunching on chips.

"What those of us on staff call our beloved Portland General Hospital."

Morgan lifted a brow. The world got small in these parts, it seemed. "Raine panicked and called 911. Guess they figured they had to justify the trip, so they kept me overnight."

Jarrod tipped the bottle to his mouth and took a swig. "You feeling recovered?"

"Pretty much." Morgan took a breath. It was now or never, he figured. "You mind clarifying a few things for me while we've got some time?"

Jarrod glanced at the swinging door leading to the living room and the game. "Guess that depends on what 'things' you have in mind."

Morgan couldn't fault the man's caution. He had enough of that himself when it came to questions from strangers.

"Raine said you're going to perform a hysterectomy after the babies are born."

"That's the plan, yes."

"So, no more babies?"

"No more babies."

Jarrod's voice softened, as though he sensed Morgan's inner turmoil. It hurt to realize that Mike would be his only child. He'd always figured they would have another. Eventually.

"But so far she's fine?"

Jarrod nodded. "Indications are she'll have a normal delivery."

"And she's due September second?"

"Give or take a few weeks."

Morgan glanced at the small calendar affixed to the fridge door by a heart-shaped magnet.

"Two weeks after Mike's birthday," he said as though to himself.

Jarrod took another sip of beer. He didn't seem to be in any hurry to return to the game. Morgan waited. Sometimes it was the questions a man *didn't* ask that elicited the most valuable information.

"There is one thing that concerns me," Jarrod admitted finally. "Guess it wouldn't be a violation of professional ethics to mention it. You still being her legal husband."

Morgan felt a clutching in his stomach and eased in a careful breath. "I'm listening."

"Raine thinks she's stronger than she is. Emotionally, I mean. On the surface she seems fiercely independent and perfectly confident. A nineties woman—or so she keeps reminding me."

Morgan focused intently. It felt strange to be discussing his wife with another man, even if that man was her doctor.

But then, he rarely talked about Raine. He'd made it one of inviolate rules to always keep his personal life separate from his work.

"And beneath the surface?"

Jarrod frowned. "Something tells me she's terrified of losing these babies. And if she does, she knows that she won't have a chance to get pregnant again."

Terrified?

That wasn't a word Morgan ever thought to use in connection with Raine. She'd always seemed so calm and serene. His rock. It shook him to realize how much comfort he'd drawn from simply knowing she would be there, waiting for him if he needed her.

Had he ever told her how important she'd been to him? Somehow he doubted it. And who was her rock? Not him, that much was certain. The list of his sins was growing daily. It wasn't a thought he cared to dwell on all that much. But he knew he would, late at night when he had trouble sleeping.

"Losing Mike was…rough on her."

Morgan shifted, suddenly uncomfortable. As always, when thoughts of his son pressed too close, he redirected his thoughts to a subject that he could pin down, information he could analyze.

"This artificial insemination… I assume the donors go through some kind of a screening process."

"Several. The sperm bank we use is very stringent about quality control."

"About these donors… How does a woman select one?"

Wariness flashed in Jarrod's eyes. "Maybe you'd be more comfortable asking Raine these questions."

Morgan felt heat splotch his cheeks. The bastard wasn't making this easy. But then, why should he?

"I'm asking you."

Jarrod took his own sweet time, downing another long

swallow of brew, then studying the label while Morgan considered gutting the man.

"The donors are listed by physical characteristics, ethnic history and educational background," Jarrod said at last. "No one with a history of chronic disease or a family predisposition for genetic defects is accepted."

"Provided the guy tells the truth."

Jarrod considered him steadily. "Very true." He hesitated, then added, "Many of the donors are medical students who need the money. Not that doctors have better genes, you understand, but they're willing."

"Not to mention handy."

Jarrod's mouth twitched. "Right."

Morgan was beginning to regret the impulse that had led him to follow Raine's doctor into the Randolphs' kitchen, yet he couldn't make himself walk away. "What about paternity rights?"

"Waived." Jarrod shifted.

Morgan considered that. "And the identity of both parties?"

"Totally protected."

Morgan grabbed another handful of chips. He popped them into his mouth and thought back over the stories he'd covered. In every case, he'd found a way past so-called unbreachable safeguards.

"But not impossible to uncover?"

Jarrod narrowed his gaze. He was suddenly all business. "Are you thinking of doing some investigative work?"

"Would you, if it were your wife carrying another guy's kids?"

Morgan met Jarrod's gaze and felt himself being measured. From the look on his face, he hadn't climbed very high on the doctor's list of admirable people.

"Not if I was gonna get on a plane in a few months," Jarrod said finally.

"You think I'm a gold-plated bastard, don't you?"

A glint of something resembling sympathy appeared in the doctor's eyes. "I think you're a man who took too many things for granted. Maybe because Raine allowed it. Maybe even encouraged it. And because you didn't know what a treasure you had, you lost it." Jarrod narrowed his gaze. "But then, I think you're beginning to realize that."

Morgan saluted that with a nod. "You're dead right, Jarrod. With the exception of one thing. I'm still here, and the divorce papers are still unsigned. Which, in my book means I still have a chance."

"A chance for what, Paxton? To hurt her again?"

"No, damn it. To make it up to her. To show her that I—" Morgan broke off and forced a careless grin. "What the hell? Guess we'd better get back to the game."

He grabbed the chips and headed for the door. He had one hand on the panel, ready to push it open, when Jarrod called his name.

"Yeah?" he replied, looking back.

"If you're not prepared to go the distance this time, it would be better for Raine if you left now."

"Now?"

"Yeah. Planes fly twenty-four hours these days. But then, I'm not telling you something you don't already know, am I?"

Morgan felt sick. "Thanks for the information—and the advice. I'll give it some thought."

He returned to the game. He lost every pot.

It was just past nine when Morgan kicked back in his chair and watched Raine standing at the stove, stirring carob powder into a pan of milk. She was concentrating carefully, her brow furrowed and her expression absorbed.

The hot chocolate had been her idea. A comfortable end to the evening.

Another marital ritual about to be born? He felt a moment of uneasiness before he pushed it away.

"So, where'd you ladies disappear to tonight?"

"River View Mall."

She glanced his way. Her nose was shiny and her hair mussed. He thought she looked amazingly sexy. He felt a punch of desire and had to take a breath before he was steady again.

"You took those little hellions shopping?" He tried to imagine the chaos that could be caused by three rambunctious little girls. It was beyond him. "I salute your courage."

Grinning, she blew a stray lock of curling hair away from her mouth. He felt his own mouth soften. He could kiss her for hours and not get enough. He shifted, tried to ignore the sudden heaviness in his body. He wondered how she would react if he suggested they skip the hot drink and go directly to bed.

"Actually, we went to a Disney movie," she said finally, her voice just shy of saucy.

"No shopping?"

Her expression became impish. "Well, while we were there…"

"I knew it. Put six females in a mall and shopping happens. It's an immutable law of nature."

"Now that's a ridiculous statement if I ever heard one."

"Uh-huh."

He crossed his arms over his chest and let his gaze roam freely over the slim line of her back and the taut muscles of her fanny. Even pregnant, she looked tiny and delicate. The tug to haul her off to the bedroom and explore every inch of her glorious body was strong enough to make his heart skip a few beats. Patience, he reminded himself.

"What did you buy me?" he asked when he caught her sneaking an uneasy peek in his direction.

"Now, that's a typical male. Only thinking of himself."

Though her words were teasing, they were far too reminiscent of his recent conversation with Jarrod. He cleared his throat.

"Tell me what kind of man you want me to be, then." He kept his tone light, but he'd never meant anything more.

She gave the hot milk a final stirring, then put down the spoon. "I'm not asking you to change," she said as she turned off the burner. "I've never asked you to change."

"Maybe you should have."

"And have you resent me more than you already did? No thanks." She poured milk into two mugs, then set the pan in the sink.

"I didn't...don't resent you," he said as she set one mug in front of him, the other on the place mat opposite.

"Really? I always had the feeling that you did."

Raine pulled out her chair and lowered herself onto the seat. Pain like the sudden twist of hard fingers ran through her back and she winced.

Alarm shot into Morgan's eyes, and he straightened, sending the front legs of the old oak chair thudding against the tile.

"What's wrong?" he demanded, his voice sharp.

"Nothing major. Ginny and I took inventory today. I guess I was on my feet more than usual."

He frowned. "If you needed help, why didn't you ask me to pitch in? Hell, all I did today was hang around here and read."

"Morgan, don't fuss. I'm fine."

"Men don't fuss."

"No? What do you call it when a man exhibits undue anxiety about a trifle?"

"I call it what it is—taking care of his wife, whether she likes it or not."

Though he had himself under rigid control, he looked

like a man who would much rather be dodging bullets in some international hot spot than sitting in her quiet kitchen drinking hot milk. But then, it had been five days since his arrival, most of it spent flat on his back or unconscious. That was a long stretch of inactivity for a man as restless as Morgan.

No wonder he'd been strangely withdrawn since they'd returned home, she decided as she lifted her mug to her lips and blew on the steaming contents. Probably wondering how to tell her he was leaving sooner than he'd planned. An emergency assignment, perhaps. Or an order from the network brass. He'd used both before.

She told herself she was prepared for him to go.

"I like your hair piled up in that prim little knot," he said, watching her over the rim of his mug. "Makes a man want to pull out all the pins so he can watch it tumble down."

She saw the banked fire in his eyes and felt a stir. He wanted her, blimp belly and all. It was a heady sensation, one she hadn't felt in a very long time. Because she wasn't sure what to say, she lifted the mug to her lips and took a cautious sip. He dropped his gaze to her mouth, and the fire in his eyes grew hot enough to singe. Somehow she stopped herself from sliding her tongue along her lower lip to cool it.

"So, uh, how much did you lose tonight?"

Her voice was calm enough, but she felt jittery inside. It was the same feeling she'd gotten as a kid at the amusement park, right before the roller coaster started its downward plunge.

Amusement drifted over his hard features, and he lifted a brow. "I don't remember telling you I lost."

She inhaled the exotic aroma of carob. It was a mistake. The fast little jolt of pleasure made her think of Morgan's hard, hot body sliding into hers. She felt her cheeks growing hot and took another sip.

"You didn't say you won," she said with a smug little smile. "Ergo, you must have lost."

Surprise glinted for only a split second in his eyes, reminding her of the incredible mastery he had over his emotions. It was a skill she envied and sometimes coveted, especially at a time like this when she was feeling more than a little hot and bothered inside.

"You're right, Ms. Smarty-Pants. I came away busted."

"Uh-oh, sounds like we're dealing with a bruised ego here."

"Bruised, hell. Stomped into the ground is more like it."

He offered her a disgruntled look. It occurred to her that she liked him best when he was laughing at himself.

"Drink your carob. It does wonders for stomped-on egos."

"I know something a lot better."

"No way. Nothing's better."

His smile was slow and easy, and her heart raced. "Finish up, darlin', and then I'll commence proving you wrong."

Chapter 13

It was ridiculous to be embarrassed, Raine told herself as she slipped out of her sandals. Morgan knew her body as well as she did. He'd seen her naked countless times before.

"Something wrong, honey?"

He'd already stripped off his shirt. The glow from the lamp on the dresser picked up the gleam of desire in his eyes. His arousal was already straining to be freed from his jeans.

"I think I forgot to turn on the back porch light," she said, glancing toward the bedroom door. "I... It's an unspoken rule that we all keep our lights burning at night."

"No problem. I'll take care of it."

"But—" He smothered her protest with a hard kiss that was over far too soon.

"Keep that on account. I'll be right back."

Quickly, before she could talk herself out of it, she shimmied out of her maternity slacks and swept off her shirt. Her breasts were already tingling as she removed her bra and stepped out of her panties. She heard his footsteps on the hardwood floor in the living room as she jerked open the closet door to remove the thin cotton nightshirt hanging on a hook inside. She'd just smoothed it over her head when he reappeared.

"Hey, no fair," he said when he caught sight of her. "I need to look at you."

She drew an unsteady breath. "You *are* looking at me."

He looked thoughtful for a moment, then frowned. "Are you afraid of me, Raine?"

"Of course not." No, she was afraid of the power he wielded with just one of those lopsided grins.

"I've never pushed a woman farther than she wanted to go. Even if I wanted to, which I don't, a long line of Paxton women would come down from heaven and wale the tar outta me."

He was both serious and teasing. To cover a painful memory, she suspected. His mother had been the only softness in his childhood. His only source of love. It hurt to imagine what life must have been like for him after she'd disappeared.

"I've never been afraid of you," she repeated, sensing a need in him for reassurance.

"Good. Because I would hate it if you were."

"I know."

He ambled closer, his bare chest gleaming like well-rubbed bronze in the diffused light from the lamp. Her breath hitching, she waited for the slow, rolling sensation that always came when he touched her. Though he stopped just short of arms' length away, his big callused hands remained at his side,

"Maybe this is just your subtle way of warning me off?" His drawl was silken, yet with enough roughness to suggest the rumbling purr of a big cat.

"If I wanted to warn you off, I wouldn't have agreed to

have an affair with you." She grinned. "As for subtle, I doubt there's a subtle bone in your body."

He considered that with a frown hovering over his brow. "I think I've just been insulted," he said finally, looking annoyed.

"Complimented," she corrected with a laugh. "You're too straight-arrow to be devious."

"Now I *know* I've been insulted."

She blinked, suddenly confused. "You're upset because I think you have integrity?"

"Hell, yes, woman," he all but growled as he closed the distance between them. "No self-respecting journalist wants to think of himself as one of the good guys."

"He doesn't?"

"No indeed. Haven't you been paying attention to the conventional wisdom? We're slimeballs. Opportunists. Blood-sucking vampires who'll drain their grandmothers dry for a story."

Raine stifled a giggle. "Surely not?"

He nodded solemnly. "Sleazoids, scum, pusillanimous purveyors of falsehoods. Left-wing agitators."

It seemed perfectly natural for him to cup her shoulders with his big warm palms. At his touch, some of the tension clawing her spine drained away.

"I can see now why you'd hate being lumped in with those 'good guys' you mentioned," she assured him earnestly. "And I apologize for calling you a straight arrow."

"Thank you."

He skimmed his palms down her arms, then linked his arms at the small of her back. She stiffened slightly, waiting for him to pull her closer. Instead, he simply stood there, holding her loosely.

She drew a breath. The faint aroma of cigar smoke clung to his skin. It should be repugnant to a dedicated nonsmoker like her, she decided, but it wasn't. Perhaps because it was so intensely masculine, so blatantly aggressive. In her mind she could see him in riding breeches and shiny boots, urging a blooded stallion over a high fence, his tousled hair golden in the sunshine, his rich laughter rolling over the green hills.

It was impossible to resist a smile. According to Morgan's sketchy description of his background, there wasn't an ounce of blue blood in his veins. Just the opposite. In fact, he wasn't all that certain his parents had ever married. And they'd certainly lived a crude life, yet, there was something about the way he carried himself that suggested an aristocratic upbringing. The man who considered himself an ignorant hillbilly was really a gentleman at heart.

"Hey, where'd you go, honey?" His voice was soft, with amusement curling the edges.

"Regency England," she murmured. "Or maybe the antebellum South."

"Uh-huh."

She burst out laughing. "Don't look so alarmed. It's the hormones. Luke said I might have odd moments now and then."

Something changed. She wasn't sure why or what, but she felt it. And it scared her.

"Luke?" he said in a flat tone.

"Luke Jarrod. My obstetrician. You met him tonight."

The arms that encircled her suddenly seemed stronger somehow. More rigid. "Sounds like he's more than that."

"Well, yes. He's a friend, too. Just like Boyd is a friend. And Case." She took a breath. "Prudy's the one who recommended I make an appointment to see him when I started having problems."

"And he's the one who recommended the insemination bit?"

"No, actually Prudy mentioned it first, and then I talked to Luke—"

He bit off a curse that had her eyebrows ⬚⬚⬚⬚ felt a jolt of anger, followed almost instantly by an ⬚⬚⬚ desire to hug the man. In all the years of their marriage she'd never once glimpsed this obviously volatile side to his nature.

"I don't believe this," she declared in soft wonder. "You're jealous of my doctor."

"Bull. I'm protecting my interest."

She saw determination in his eyes and desire and something else, something she didn't know how to read.

"But I'm divorcing you," she protested.

"Trying to divorce me. I'm fighting it."

"Why?"

"Because we're good together. I understand you. You understand me. And we're dynamite in bed. What more could you want in a marriage?"

She burst out laughing, but the feeling inside her was more sad than amused. "A lot more, as a matter of fact. Like love and companionship and sharing."

His mouth quirked. "Hey, I'm here, you're here, and there's a nice big bed just a few feet away. Perfect for love and companionship. And definitely made for sharing."

"Sex. You're talking about sex."

His grin was endearingly lopsided. "Yeah, guess I am at that."

"It's just a chemical reaction. A physical creation of nature. My father used to lecture me about it all the time."

"With charts, too?"

She laughed. "No. He didn't go that far."

"Thank the Lord for that, anyway."

"You disagree?"

He raised a brow. "Me, disagree with the professor? Besides, there ain't nothin' wrong with physical, darlin'," he drawled, slipping his arms around her once more. "In fact, it's damned good, when done right."

...eyes, giving her a glimpse of ...ost man who was reaching out. ...s and unhealed wounds. She felt a ...A softening. A need to hold him. And ...unt lashes swept down, and his mouth ...man who needed so desperately disappeared, repl... ...y a rogue with a naughty gleam in his eyes instead ... shadows.

She felt a shiver. A surrender. Desperate longing.

"And I suppose you think you know how to do it right?" she whispered thickly.

"Maybe not, but I'm a fast learner." He brought his mouth closer to hers, and a shiver of anticipation ran through her. "All I need are a few pointers along the way."

He touched his mouth to hers in a sweet and tender kiss that sent warmth all the way to her toes. Lazily, as though time was irrelevant, he nudged her mouth open with his tongue, then found hers. Tips touching, he kept the kiss gentle, even as she felt his breathing quicken. He ended the kiss too soon, and she fought a wave of disappointment.

"You like that?" he asked, his mouth still only inches away.

"Very much," she admitted, her arms automatically encircling his neck. His skin was warm, his body solid. Unable to resist, she lowered her head to the swirl of golden chest hair and touched her tongue to one tiny flat nipple.

He groaned and stiffened at the same time. Beneath his skin, hard muscle spasmed involuntarily, beyond his control. Raine decided she liked having power over this man, if only physically.

"Sorry. Did I hurt you?" she teased, before tasting him again.

He sucked in air. She felt a rush of purely carnal satisfaction.

"No, you didn't hurt me, little witch."

"Good, because I wouldn't want to hurt you."

She ran her hands over his chest, using just the short, rounded tips of her nails. When she trailed her touch lower, to the corrugated wall of his belly, he let out a low groan. At the same time he grabbed her wrists, imprisoning her with hard fingers.

"You're enjoying this," he growled, his eyes golden.

She pretended to think that over. "Yes, I think I am at that," she admitted after a moment. "I like the idea of being in charge for a change."

Morgan saw the fire in her brown eyes and felt a fast jolt of satisfaction. Anything was better than the painful vulnerability he'd sensed in her earlier.

"Who says you're in charge?" He kept his voice gruff. The triumph he saw in her eyes told him it was the right slant to take.

"You do."

"Yeah? Well, who's holding who here?" he challenged, directing a pointed look at the spot where his hands manacled hers against his chest. Though she was tanned, his skin was shades darker, the result of a lifetime spent under the open sky.

"But if I weren't in charge, why would you be so determined to take control?" she countered with a look he could only call smug.

"I'm the guy here. That's my job."

"Nonsense."

Her lips curved, and he had to fight a need to trace that sweet smile with his tongue. Instead, he rubbed his thumbs over the thin skin of her wrists and felt the fast surge of blood through her veins. His body grew harder.

"Admit it, honey. You wouldn't like a wimpy lover."

She rubbed her belly against his like a cat with an itch. He swallowed. Tried to concentrate. Reminded himself that he was in charge.

"There's a difference between being wimpy and being sensitive," she murmured, splaying her manacled hands against his chest.

He felt the scrape of her nails against his skin, like kitten claws. His train of thought veered off into a more erotic track, and he had to fight to concentrate.

"Difference?" he demanded gruffly. "What difference?"

"A sensitive man realizes that a woman sometimes likes to take the lead."

"Guess that depends on where his woman is fixin' to take him," he said with a grin.

"Let me go, and I'll show you."

Morgan felt a prickle of wariness, akin to the hot tingle of warning that had saved his sorry ass more than once in the past. He braced inwardly, ready to defend himself from some unnamed threat, then relaxed his grip.

"Well, hell, my mama didn't raise no coward. Why not?"

Surprise glittered in her eyes for an instant before a darker, richer emotion took over. He felt an edge of anticipation like a jolt of adrenaline.

"Lie down," she ordered, her face turning a delicate pink as she darted a glance at the bed behind him. His arousal grew more insistent.

"Which way? Front or back?"

The blush on her cheeks grew deeper. "On your back."

Her eyes sparkled as her tongue made a nervous pass over her lower lip. He nearly groaned.

"Whatever you say, honey."

He backed up slowly, his gaze on hers. He was beginning to like this game. In fact, he was getting turned on so fast, he wasn't sure how long he could last before he had to take over again.

"Under the covers?" he asked when he felt the hard edge of the mattress against his shins.

"On top, so you can feel the satin against your skin."

She advanced slowly, her unfettered breasts swaying beneath the cotton shirt. Her nipples looked like hard little buds poking at the thin material, and his mouth went dry. She wanted him.

Praying he wouldn't burst before she finished with him, he stretched out on top of the shiny comforter. The satin slipped easily beneath his bare shoulders as he crossed his arms under his head and grinned up at her.

"Okay, woman. Have your way with me."

She drew her eyebrows together and regarded him intently. "I suggest you take this very seriously, Mr. Paxton," she warned, tapping one small bare foot. "Otherwise, I shall be forced to be severe with you."

"Severe?" He thought about that. "Sounds kinky."

Her soft, pale mouth twitched at the corners, sending another jolt of hunger racing through him.

"Don't move," she ordered, glancing at his legs. He was still wearing his jeans and briefs. Nothing else.

"No, ma'am."

She took a slow, deep breath, and her breasts swayed. He swallowed. She'd always been beautiful to him, but now, in the full bloom of pregnancy, she was magnificent. A woman in all of her intended glory.

"First we have to get rid of these sorry-looking jeans," she murmured, reaching for his fly.

"Watch it, woman. These suckers have been with me a long time."

"Obviously."

Her fingers were busy with the metal buttons, and he held his breath. Suddenly she slipped her fingers beneath the waistband and tugged, and the air trapped in his lungs came out a rush of harsh sound.

"Am I hurting you?" she asked, grinning down at him. "Shall I stop?"

He gritted his teeth and glared at her. "Stop and I'll never forgive you," he muttered.

She choked out a laugh, and it was like a rare gift.

"Step two," she said, tugging his jeans lower. The backs of her fingers skimmed over the skin of his lower abdomen, and he groaned.

"Lift your hips," she ordered.

He obeyed.

"Higher."

With one last tug, she had his jeans off and on the floor. Looking down the length of his body, he saw his arousal straining to be free of his tight briefs and wondered just how far human skin could stretch before it burst.

"Uh, honey, maybe you'd best let me...ah." He closed his eyes on a wave of hot pleasure when she slowly, deftly freed him from the confines of his underwear. He took a few deep breaths, struggling to regain some measure of control.

Her hands were soft and clever and—

"Raine, baby, don't...oh, heaven help me."

"You like that, do you?" Laughter flavored her words— the same words he'd used earlier to tease her. He started to reach for her, to drag her on top of him, but she stopped him with a hard little squeeze that had his breath leaving his body.

"Don't move, remember?" she chided, her fingers trailing the length of him. "I'm having my way with you."

Morgan couldn't help himself. He arched upward, thrusting against her hand, and she sucked in air.

"Oh, my," she whispered, her voice thick.

He swore, frustration and desire tearing at him. "Baby, I can't handle much more of this," he warned, his jaw so tight, it was difficult to force out the words.

"Soon," she murmured, staring at him with an absorbed look that was almost as arousing as the soft stroking movements of her fingers.

"Take off that shirt and let me see you," he ordered, his hands clutching at the slick comforter.

"First the briefs."

She released him and he all but growled in protest. Her hands were wonderfully warm as she slid the underwear down his legs. Nothing remained to shield him. He was naked. Vulnerable. With no place to hide and no energy to run.

"Raine." He heard his voice calling her name. Heard the throaty timbre and raspy urgency. Was it a plea or a threat? He was too dazed to know. He only knew he needed her. And she was so close.

He was about to take over when she hiked up her shirt, then knelt next to him on the bed. Then slowly, almost tentatively, she drew the shirt over her head and let it fall to the floor.

He felt a rush of emotion, a soaring need. Slowly, reverently, he lifted a hand to touch the ripe curve of her belly. Her skin was taut, yet soft, and as pale as milk. He thought he said something. He wasn't sure what.

Her smile told him that his words pleased her.

"I want you," he whispered. Or so he thought. At the moment he was lost in a haze of desire so powerful, he was half-afraid to move.

"And I want you," she murmured as she slowly straddled him. Her thighs were warm against his, sending his heart rate skyrocketing.

"Take me," he begged, so aroused, he was panting.

She did as he asked, her fingers curling around him gently as she guided him to the hot, moist spot between her thighs. It took the last measure of his control to keep from surging upward, into her.

Taking her own sweet time, she eased him into her, the soft inner folds slowly parting to admit him. He sucked in his breath and willed himself to endure. Her body adjusted inch by inch until he was fully seated. Absorbed. He released the breath he'd been holding and exulted in the feel of her body clinging to his.

"Raine, baby—"

She reached for him, her fingers curling over his shoulders. Eyes half-closed, her lips softly parted, she began to move, riding him slowly at first, then faster and faster.

Morgan could scarcely think. She looked so lovely astride him, her hair flowing back, her face flushed with passion. For him.

It was like a miracle. A precious benediction.

She wanted him. This special woman wanted him.

No one had ever wanted him like this. With this abandoned freedom. With this unconditional generosity. No one had needed him the way Raine needed him. Now. This moment.

He called her name, his voice thick with his own need, his own wonder. She smiled, even as her fingers dug deeper into his shoulders. He was hers, in her power, under her control. For the first time in his life he was lost.

She leaned closer, her belly snug against his, her breasts warm and inviting. He fought to last long enough to give her the pleasure she sought, but hot pincers of desperate need were clawing him.

"Hurry, honey," he begged, knowing he was at the edge.

He felt her body tighten around his, heard the soft little cries in her throat, and then soft rippling spasms were gripping him, urging him to let go.

He cried out, and at the same time felt the explosion of her climax. His body gave up the struggle, surging his seed into her in violent waves until he felt utterly drained.

She collapsed on top of him, her face pressed to his neck.

There was a sheen of perspiration between her breasts, and the smell of musk surrounded them. He relaxed deeply, his eyes half-open, her hair tickling his cheek.

"If this is severe, I'm all for it," he managed to murmur against her hair.

He heard her laugh, felt her hands caress his slick shoulders. "If you're a good boy, I might give you another lesson one of these days."

"Trust me, honey. I'll be good."

Morgan rubbed the small of her back with the flat of his hand. She sounded damned pleased with herself, this wife of his.

It was a start, he told himself. All he needed now was time.

The bedroom was still shrouded in soft gray velvet when Morgan awakened, his mind instantly alert and his body tensed and ready. One whiff of danger, and he would be up and moving.

But this time it wasn't danger that had jerked him awake. At least, not the kind that a man could fight with action. Raine was snoring. Soft little puffs of air that tickled his neck. He smiled into the darkness and enjoyed thinking about teasing her the next morning.

Already he was beginning to learn how to accommodate her tossing and turning next to him. When she moved, he moved. He liked the feel of her body next to his, and felt uneasy when she wasn't close.

At the moment her head was pillowed on his shoulder and her belly tucked against his side, one small hand still tangled in the hair on his chest. She'd fallen asleep playing with that hair, teasing him with her fingertips and teeth.

It pleased him to remember how cocky she'd been. And how wonderfully uninhibited. Her nightshirt was still puddled on the floor where she'd tossed it, forgotten after her enthusiastic seduction. His lady had been as lusty as any courtesan once she'd gotten over her initial embarrassment.

He'd been very thoroughly tumbled and—

Jeez, what was that?

A kick, he realized an instant later. Right in his ribs. One of the babies had gotten him good. He sucked in his breath, then let it out slowly. The kid had some power behind that little foot, all right. He'd be lucky if he didn't end up black and blue.

Raine sighed, and he waited for her to waken. Instead, she smiled in her sleep as though taking pleasure in her son's muscle.

Her son. But not his.

Damn.

He'd opened a door tonight. It was as though he were poised on an important threshold. Behind him were a lot of years—some good, some lousy, a lifetime of decisions he couldn't change. Sacrifices that had seemed necessary at the time seemed foolish to him now.

Ahead was...what?

A real home where his clothes hung next to Raine's and he didn't have to stop to get his bearings when he stumbled out of bed in the middle of the night to use the bathroom?

A feeling of belonging? Of permanence and warmth?

Love?

He closed his eyes and let that thought settle. It scared him to think that it might actually be possible.

A home. Twin sons. Raine.

The thought shimmered in his head like a brilliant dream. A fantasy just beyond his reach. His stomach twisted, and he felt a rush of soul-deep longing.

It would take some doing. He knew that full well. Raine could be stubborn. But so could he.

If she wanted solid and dependable, that's what he'd give her. If she wanted trustworthy, that's what he'd be. Maybe she didn't love him as much as she had once, but he'd never once doubted her belief in his integrity. Hadn't she told him tonight that he was one of the good guys?

Hell, yes. Maybe it wasn't all he craved, but it was a start. A man could do anything when he had the respect of a woman like Raine.

He'd be the best damn husband in the state of... Where the hell was he? Oregon? Yeah, right.

The best husband in the whole damn state of Oregon.

"Count on it," he whispered into her soft little ear. She murmured something and snuggled closer. He felt an odd niggling in the back of his mind. *If you leave, you lose,* a voice taunted. *Think about that when you're feeling so damned pleased with yourself, hotshot.*

The room was suddenly ice-cold.

Chapter 14

He woke her with a kiss that tasted like coffee—and a smugly masculine smile that had her feeling deliciously warm all the way to her toes. He was apparently fresh from a shower and a shave, and the bare skin of his arms and chest smelled like her shower moisturizer. Had he used the pink scrubber? she wondered, grinning to herself.

Bemused and as relaxed as any woman could be seven months into pregnancy, Raine blinked up at him from the nest of covers and yawned.

She'd slept soundly all night long. A luxury these days.

And, she realized with a sense of wonder, she'd slept late.

It was well past dawn, her usual time to wake. Sunshine slanted through the thin slats, casting stripes of golden droplets on the dark silk of the duvet. The bad-tempered Steller's jay that lived in her giant Photinia bush was already setting up a ruckus. The air was already warm in the bedroom, holding the promise of another hot day.

"Mornin', sugar. How're you and the gang feelin'?" Morgan asked as he bent closer to prop a pillow behind her back.

"It's too soon to tell," she mumbled as he helped her sit up.

His eyes crinkled as he retrieved the mug he must have set on the night table when he came in. "Would coffee help?"

"Immensely."

"Careful, it's hot," he warned as he turned the mug so that she could grasp the handle.

"Hot or cold, it's coffee."

She inhaled the rich aroma of the steam and sighed in greedy pleasure. He watched as she took a careful sip, then cocked one eyebrow. Morgan had never made her coffee before. She'd always been up first on his visits, eager to make him feel welcome. It was a new experience to have him pampering her.

"Too strong?"

It was sludge. "It's perfect," she told him with a grin. "Just the way I like it."

"You take it black, right?"

Only when she ran out of milk—and she never ran out of milk. "Yes, black."

Actually, it wasn't bad, she decided as she took another sip. She stretched her legs, feeling them slide over the warm sheets. Her body was slightly stiff from the rigors of their lovemaking. And delightfully sensitized.

"Sore?" he asked, watching her carefully. Looking for signs of regret? she wondered.

"A little," she admitted. "I'm not used to so much...exercise."

He sat down on the side of the bed and grinned. "You look very pleased with yourself, wife."

He ran a finger over the curve of her jaw, his touch gentle

in spite of the calluses on his skin. Unable to stop herself, she leaned into his touch. He flattened his hand against her cheek and used his thumb to caress her mouth.

"Are you planning a safari?" she teased, directing a pointed look at his khaki shorts. Made of rugged twill, they had pockets everywhere, and fitted his hips with a satisfying snugness. His legs were long and densely muscled under soft hair bleached to pale gold by the sun.

His mouth slanted as she rubbed two fingers over his thigh. "Yep. To the nearest bakery—as soon as I get your car keys and directions."

"Ah, the mighty hunter, always prepared."

She took another sip, and he watched the cup all the way to her lips. It pleased her to see the way his eyes darkened and his breathing changed.

"You want bagels or Danish?" he asked when she swallowed.

"Danish."

She watched him over the rim of her cup while her fingers traced lazy swirls over the hard, warm muscle below the hem of his shorts. When she pushed her fingertips beneath the heavy material, his gaze narrowed.

"And the directions?"

She heard tension in his voice now. It was a heady feeling to realize just how easily she could affect him.

"Take Mill Works to Greenleaf. Turn left, seven blocks down on the right. Heavenly Daze Bakery and Deli." She pushed her fingers higher against his thigh, and he sucked in hard.

"My car keys are in my purse."

His eyes were the color of heated bronze. "Where's your purse?"

"Over there." She shifted her gaze to the right. Her soft gray suede bag hung from an old brass hat rack, along with a backpack and her robe.

"Anything else you need?"

She arched her eyebrows. "What do you have in mind?"

His mouth twitched. "You'd be surprised."

She forced herself to take another sip. A growing excitement made it difficult to concentrate. She wanted to feel him filling her again. It astonished her to realize how much the balance of power had shifted between them. Funny how much difference an impending divorce made, she thought.

"I like surprises."

Was that sultry purr really her voice? She inhaled slowly, watching the amusement gathering in his eyes. She saw doubt there, too, and wariness. Emotions she'd never seen in him before. But it was the slow bloom of heat in his dark pupils that had her breath catching.

"You're actin' mighty bold for a lady sittin' there without a stitch on under that sheet you got pulled up to that stubborn chin of yours," he murmured gently as he took the cup from her hand.

"Hey, that's my coffee," she protested in a voice too breathless to sting.

Instead of answering, he set the mug on the table with careful precision, then reached for her. When his mouth found hers, his eyes were already closing, the lashes twin crescents of dusty gold against his tanned cheekbones.

Pleasure jolted though her the instant she felt his lips. She felt a curl of heat and a rush of need. But when she reached up to link her arms around his neck, he drew back.

"My turn to be severe with you, my sweet little tease," he murmured, his eyes glittering with desire.

"Aha."

He removed her arms from his neck and placed them palms down on the bed, then held them there. "I need you, Raine. More than I should."

"Show me." Her throat felt thick.

"Yes, ma'am." His mouth was soft at first, then more

insistent as he made a thorough exploration of her lips, her throat, the sensitive skin below her ears.

His teeth were insistent and eager as he drew her earlobe into his mouth, then took small nipping bites. She gasped, unaware until now of the exquisite sensitivity of that part of her anatomy.

Desperate, she slipped her hands from beneath his and grasped his shoulders. Once again, he drew her arms to her sides, refusing to let her hurry him. He was in control, yet it seemed as though it was her needs driving him, her soft moans guiding him. Her pleasure that was paramount, even though he was powerfully aroused. The hard ridge straining against the fly of his shorts was proof of that. Yet, when she moved to touch him, he restrained her.

"I know now why our ancestors thought of pregnant women as goddesses," he murmured, sliding one hand over her swollen belly. She moaned at the pure bliss of his hard palm rubbing her taut skin.

"Beautiful, beautiful Raine."

He pushed the sheet to her waist, exposing her breasts. When his fingers touched her breasts, she pushed against his hands, driven by pulses of pleasure and need. Her skin burned. Her nipples ached. His fingers were deft, arousing her to the point of frenzy before moving on to another spot, another ache.

"Please," she whispered, desperate to feel the hard length of him entering her.

"Soon," he whispered before fastening his mouth over one breast. He suckled gently at first, then with an urgency that sent fire arrowing into her. When he shifted to the other breast, she cried out in frustration and joy, her hands escaping his to thread with desperate need into his thick golden hair.

Tiny pinpricks of pleasure and pain assaulted her nipple, and she writhed uncontrollably. She fought to escape his grip, desperate to free him from the prison of cloth separating them.

He sucked in hard when her fingers brushed his rigid flesh, and his cheeks turned a dusky red.

"Not yet," he grated, his harsh tone matching the tension in his face.

Morgan fought his own raging hunger, taming it by sheer will as he feasted on her mouth, the fullness of her breasts, the hard nipples. When she was moaning steadily, he began lapping her with his tongue, determined to taste every salty, slick inch of her.

For her, he told himself. Her pleasure.

But part of him knew he was deliberately branding her with his hands and his mouth and tongue. Claiming her the only way he knew how. Imprinting himself on her so thoroughly, she wouldn't be able to go through with the divorce.

Maybe he wasn't as smart or as cultured or as pedigreed as other men she knew or might know, but no man who breathed could want her more. Or be more determined to make her happy.

"Morgan, please, please. I need you. I need you." Her desperate little cries threatened his control. He took a moment to shore it up, then, blood pounding, he eased her down onto the mattress. She shuddered as he lowered his head to kiss the most intimate part of her.

He found her hot and damp, and the knowledge that she was ready for him both thrilled and humbled him. Using his fingers and his lips, he worshiped her until she was writhing beneath him.

Raine was mindless, carried on a wild, surging wave. Her breath swooshed from her as she crested, shuddering, gasping. Her hands opened and closed, tugging at his hair. He didn't stop. The pleasure went on and on. She felt the muscles of her legs quivering, but she was powerless to stop the shaking.

The blood swam in Morgan's head as he felt the rake of her nails against his scalp. He felt her dissolve again, her urgent cries filling him with a wild happiness. He'd never known this depth of desire, not even with her. It was magic. It was holy.

Touching her only with his mouth, he rid himself of his shorts and briefs, kicking them aside. His arousal sprang free, harder than he would have thought possible.

"Hurry, Morgan," she pleaded, her voice a hot gasp.

Straddling her, he lifted her hips and felt her heat beckoning him closer. Teeth gritted against the need to plunge into her with one hard thrust, he exerted every ounce of his will to enter slowly.

Her body closed around him, hot and ready. His vision blurred, and his head pounded. And then she was crying his name.

He seated himself fully and felt himself explode into her in wave after wave until he was empty and sated.

It took him a moment to realize she was crying. Guilt tore into him, and he wanted to die.

Careful not to weigh her down, he eased up her body until he could take her in his arms. Sobs racked her and tears ran down her flushed cheeks.

"Baby, I'm sorry," he whispered brokenly. "God, I'm sorry. Don't cry. I didn't mean to make you cry. Don't hate me for wanting you too much to go slow."

She stopped him with the touch of two fingers against his mouth. "I love you, you idiot," she murmured, laughing and crying at the same time. "I tried so hard to stop, but I can't."

He let out a heartfelt sigh that seemed to come from deep inside him. "Thank heaven for small favors," he murmured, kissing her temple.

Raine wondered if she would ever be able to move again. Her bones seemed to have dissolved sometime between the first and fourth orgasm.

"This is serious, Morgan. How can I divorce a man I love?"

"You can't."

He sounded so cocksure. So confident, as though all their problems had been swept away. She knew better. Admitting her love to herself and to him had only made them more complex.

"But your job…"

She felt him tense. "I'll make it right, Raine."

"And the babies? They'd have your name if we stayed together, but they can't have your blood."

"We'll work it out," he said gruffly. "I promise."

Tears pricked her eyes again as she nodded. When they dripped onto his chest, she licked them away. And was surprised to find they tasted bitter.

It was the fourth Sunday that Morgan had spent in Oregon. The full moon had come and gone. So had the Fourth of July, celebrated on Mill Works Ridge with fireworks and a block party barbecue. Raine was three weeks into her eighth month, and Prudy was still pregnant.

The entire neighborhood was jumpy. Stacy checked on her twice a day, sometimes more. As the resident medical expert Boyd worked overtime soothing anxious females and reassuring his fellow males. Still, Case's normally sanguine mood was beginning to fray at the edges. According to Don Petrov, every time the phone rang at work, Case all but leapt for the receiver. In addition, he'd taken to wearing an extra beeper, in case one failed.

Sweltering in the heat, Raine sat in the shadiest part of the Randolphs' backyard, idly petting the butterscotch cat snoozing in her lap and watched Case and Morgan standing in the center of an amazing array of colorful pipes, swings and gleaming steel hardware, arguing about the proper way to put together Chloe's new jungle gym.

It was the first time she'd ever seen Morgan doing anything remotely mechanical, and she was fascinated by the aggressive way he was approaching the task. It was all a matter of following directions, he'd declared several times, the thick instruction booklet clasped firmly in one large hand.

Case seemed equally confident. His method seemed more centered in intuition. And good old common sense.

"Just like a cop," Prudy muttered, fidgeting restlessly in the chair next to Raine's. "Case doesn't believe in the empirical method."

Dressed in one of Case's old tank tops and a pair of cerise maternity shorts, Prudy looked hot and tired and rumpled. After a brief, but intense argument, she had finally convinced her daughter to settle in for a nap.

"Case is just anxious. He'll be fine as soon as you deliver."

"*If* I deliver," Prudy grumbled, rubbing her swollen belly. "I was almost two weeks early with Chloe. Now I'm two weeks late—at least. This little one is just being coy."

Raine offered her a look of genuine sympathy. With each day that passed, she was learning more and more about the disadvantages of carrying two babies in a space designed for one.

"I thought you were going to talk to Luke about inducing labor."

Prudy grimaced. "I did. He's 'considering' it."

"When do you see him again?"

Prudy glanced down at her grossly distended belly. "Can't be too soon for me," she said with a long-suffering sigh.

Raine laughed. "Let me rephrase that. When's your next appointment?"

"Tomorrow. Case is taking the day off to go with me."

Prudy's gaze rested on her husband's tanned back. Both he and Morgan had stripped off their shirts shortly after bolting together the first few parts of the complicated apparatus. Case was wearing cutoff jeans. Morgan sported his favorite khaki shorts, the pockets of which were presently stuffed with various tools cadged from Boyd MacAuley's well-equipped tool caddy.

Being an especially perceptive man, Boyd himself was nowhere in sight, having taken Stacy and the girls to the coast for a long, and well-deserved, weekend away.

It was good for Case to have someone to bicker with, Prudy decided as she caught the frustrated glint in his midnight blue eyes. If anyone was Case's equal in strength and forcefulness, it was Morgan Paxton.

It had been Morgan's idea to buy Chloe a jungle gym as a "prebaby" present. Partly to keep Case calm, and partly to please the soon-to-be older sister. He'd been reading about sibling jealousy, he'd explained to Case as they'd ripped open the huge box.

"Nine months ago I never thought of Case as a particularly patient man," Prudy said, watching the muscles ripple in his broad back as he held a heavy pipe aloft while Morgan tightened a bolt at one end. "Now I think he deserves sainthood."

Raine's gaze followed hers. Prudy wondered if her friend realized how much happier she seemed since Morgan had shouldered his way into her life again. Even Case had mentioned the change in their newest neighbor.

"Case is a good man," Raine said softly.

"A better one I think than he knows." Prudy inhaled slowly. The cramp in her belly was getting worse. "Speaking of better men, how are things at your house?"

Raine looked thoughtful. "Surreal," she said finally. "Definitely surreal."

"That good, huh?"

Raine turned to look at her, astonishment bright in her eyes. "Are you always such a Pollyanna?" she groused.

Prudy nodded. "Comes from being wildly in love with my husband. I can't help wanting those I care about to be as happy as I am."

"I suppose you know that Morgan has decided to become a househusband. He has a cleaning schedule, divided into fifteen-minute segments. He's thinking of tackling ironing next."

Prudy laughed. "Sounds heavenly."

Raine let her gaze rest on her husband's broad back. "At the moment, he's still perfecting his cooking skills. He surprised me with a four-course spaghetti dinner last night."

Prudy nodded. "He borrowed some oregano from me. Said your spice cabinet was pathetic."

Raine snorted. "He bought every cookbook in my store. Read them all in a weekend."

Prudy was impressed and let it show. "So how was the meal?"

"The sauce was watery and the pasta was way overcooked." Raine's expression softened. "In other words, it was wonderful."

Prudy laughed, then drew in a breath as a sharp pain stabbed her lower back. "He's spoiling you."

"He's also going to leave me after the babies are born. Maybe before."

"What? How do you know?"

Raine shrugged, ignoring the curl of dread that always wound around her when she thought about the next few weeks. "I recognize the signs."

"What signs?"

"Restlessness. Preoccupation. Phone calls from New

York that he takes in the den. A sour temper when he comes out again.''

"You said he promised to work things out. Maybe that's what he's doing."

Raine glanced down at the cat all but glued to her thighs. Buttercup was the daughter of the MacAuleys' cat, Sunshine, and a true lap kitty. Maybe she should get a pet after Morgan was gone. She touched BC's soft ear and smiled sadly as the cat opened one eye to glare at her before settling again.

"How many phone calls does it take to say 'I quit'?" she asked softly.

"Raine, don't take this wrong, but it seems to me you're asking an awful lot of the man."

Raine felt a flare of anger. "Why, because he's the great 'Morgan Paxton'?"

"No, because he's spent half his life fighting to get where he is. It's only a guess, but I suspect a great deal of his self-worth is tied up in that career of his. Men are like that, you know. I know I can't imagine Case ever leaving the force. Without it..." Prudy broke off to glance at the men bending over the slide portion of the set, then lowered her voice even more. "Surely there must be a way to meet Morgan halfway. Maybe spend part of the year overseas where he could get home more often?"

"Is that what you would do, Prudy? Haul two kids back and forth over the ocean like baggage? Subject them to different food, different germs, no stability?" Raine shook her head. "What kind of a mother would that make me?"

"In other words, you're willing to give up a life with Morgan in order to live up to some idealized vision of the perfect mother?"

Raine frowned and started to answer, only to be interrupted when Case let out a sudden curse.

"Dammit, Pax, I told you to use a shorter bolt on step four."

Both women turned to look at the two large, well-muscled men glaring at one another over the top of the slide.

"I used the screw that was on the schematic," Morgan said in a low, even tone that seemed all the more dangerous for its lack of volume.

"Oh, yeah? How come we need a two-inch bolt to finish the job and all we have left is this piddling one-incher?"

Case didn't bother to keep his voice down. Raine thought he looked impatient and harried and definitely on edge. Morgan looked insulted as he raked his hand through his hair twice before making a fist that ended up jammed against one hip.

"How the hell should I know? Maybe the damn company shorted us on bolts."

Raine looked at Prudy whose mouth was forming a small, shocked O. "I don't believe this," Raine muttered, her mouth twitching. "Two grown men squabbling like little boys over a bolt."

"Too bad Boyd isn't home to referee."

Prudy grinned. "If I didn't know better, I'd figure he'd planned it that way."

Raine looked thoughtful. "Morgan did ask to borrow his tools before they left."

"Hey, you two," Prudy called. "One more word out of either of you and I'll have to send you to your rooms for a time-out."

Morgan looked puzzled. "What the hell is she talking about?" he asked Case in a low voice.

"It's a politically correct form of disciplining one's children. Supposed to be better for 'em than a swat on the butt." Case turned to grin in Prudy's direction. "Right, Mom?"

"Oh, shut up," Prudy called back, grinning. "I'm... Oh my goodness!"

Case froze. "What's wrong? Is it the baby?"

Prudy pressed her hand to her stomach and nodded. "I think so," she said with a nervous little laugh.

"You're sure?" Case demanded, hurrying to kneel at her side. "Maybe it's just a cramp."

Prudy took his hand and placed it where hers had been. "Feel that?"

He shook his head, then snapped his chin up. "Holy hell," he exclaimed, his frown dissolving into pure panic. "We have to go now. Right? To the hospital?"

Prudy nodded. "I think that's a good idea."

"Okay. Okay. Everyone stay calm." Case ran his hand through his hair, then spun around to spear Morgan with a beseeching look. "The car keys are on the dresser in our room. Grab my wallet, too. And Prue's suitcase is in the closet."

"No, by the door," Prudy corrected, beaming at her husband.

"I'll get it," Raine said, lifting the still-sleeping cat into her arms.

"No, you stay here with Prudy and...and hold her hand or something," Morgan ordered, sprinting past her.

"But—"

"He's right," Case interrupted, his gaze fixed on his wife's now-radiant face. Raine felt a pang of envy and fought it down. Morgan had promised to be with her. Perhaps this time he meant it. At least he'll have a good idea of what to expect.

"Someone should call Luke," Prudy reminded them.

Raine all but flung Buttercup onto the chair she'd just vacated. "I'll call him. I have the number memorized."

"Don't forget Chloe," Prudy said, laughing.

"Oh, Lord," Case muttered. "I have to get a grip here."

Raine patted his shoulder before hurrying after Morgan. They nearly collided at the door. "Where are you going?" he demanded, his face pasty.

"To call Luke and wake Chloe," she said calmly before edging past him.

Five minutes later she returned with a sleepy Chloe perched on her hip and found Morgan and Case hovering while Prudy smiled up at them serenely.

"All set," Raine called, hurrying toward them.

Morgan spun around to frown at her. "Here, let me take her. You shouldn't—"

"I'm fine," she protested but Morgan had already swung the little girl into his arms. Startled, Chloe started to cry.

"You scared her," Raine chided, patting the little girl on the back.

"It's okay, tootles," Prudy soothed, trying to get up.

"Don't move," Case ordered, lifting her into his arms. "Damn, I knew I should have arranged for a motorcycle escort."

Prudy started to laugh, only to gasp as another contraction rippled through her. Case turned white. Morgan looked green around the gills.

Raine glanced impatiently from one to the other, then sighed. "Let's go. I'll drive." She picked up Prudy's suitcase and marched down the walk toward the carport.

She heard Prudy's muffled laughter behind her, followed by two ripe male curses.

Raine turned to catch Prudy's eye.

"At last," she said in a disgusted tone. "They've found something to agree about."

Chapter 15

The maternity wing of Portland General Hospital turned out to be a surprisingly cheerful place. Raine had only visited that part of the huge complex once before, early in her pregnancy. It had been a quick trip only, to inspect the facilities where she expected to give birth. At the time all but one of the suites had been empty. Tonight, however, all six were bustling with activity.

According to the motherly, apple-cheeked nurse who'd settled Prudy into the last suite on the left, Luke had two other patients in labor. Prudy, of course, had been amazingly calm in spite of the pains that ripped through her at ever-decreasing intervals.

"I'll be fine," she'd promised as she'd gripped Raine's hand one last time. "Don't let Chloe get too rambunctious while her daddy's busy."

"Not to worry," Raine had assured her.

It had been easier promised than accomplished.

Despite an initial wariness at finding herself in the

strange surroundings of a hospital waiting room, Chloe had adjusted with amazing speed. After that, she'd been a bundle of energy, eager to explore every nook and cranny of this big, new playground. To keep her occupied, Raine had read to her from the children's storybooks stacked on a corner table.

When the sparse selection of books had been exhausted, Morgan had taken her for a stroll to the canteen at the other end of the corridor. He'd returned a half hour later looking frazzled, Chloe's tiny hand firmly clasped in his.

Raine was surprised to see that he was now wearing a faded blue scrub shirt over his bare chest, apparently scrounged from an obliging member of the staff. He hadn't changed his shorts, however, and the tools in the pocket jangled as he walked.

"Chloe have choclit milk," the little dickens chortled with a dimpled grin when she caught sight of Raine still sitting in the same place on the hard blue couch.

"They were out of the regular," Morgan muttered as he sat down next to Raine and lifted Chloe onto his knee.

"A likely story," Raine muttered, returning Chloe's grin.

Chloe's eyes sparkled. "Stowy?"

Raine laughed. "Okay. How about *The Cat in the Hat* one more time?"

Twenty minutes later Chloe was curled against Morgan's shoulder, sound asleep, with her thumb tucked securely in her mouth and her face sweetly relaxed. Only Prudy's wish that Chloe be nearby to see her sister as soon as possible kept Raine from taking the little girl home to her own bed.

The birth of this baby was to be a family affair.

Telling herself not to draw parallels between her situation and Prudy's, she shifted on the uncomfortable seat and tried to ignore the ache in her back. What she wouldn't give to be curled up on Morgan's lap like Chloe, with her head pillowed on that broad shoulder and the heat of his big body soothing her.

Closing her eyes, she tried to snatch a few moments of rest, but random thoughts and stray images from the past kept shooting through her mind. Try as she might to filter those images, she found her thoughts returning again and again to Mike's last hours.

He'd looked so terribly small in the big bed, with all the equipment beeping and pulsing around him. She'd read to him for hours when he was awake. Sometimes she'd sung lullabies and songs from his favorite TV shows. Anything to keep the terror from darkening his eyes.

At least he's not in pain, someone had said to her during one of her rare absences from his side. She couldn't remember who'd actually uttered the words. The remark had been meant to comfort, but she'd exploded in fury.

Of course, he was in pain, she screeched like a madwoman. His damaged heart was slowly failing. He was going to die, and he knew it. She'd seen the knowledge in his eyes whenever he'd looked up at her.

"Raine? Are you okay?"

Morgan's voice was quiet and lashed with concern. Opening her eyes, she forced a smile. "Just a little tired."

He didn't look convinced. "Why don't you ask the nurse if there's someplace where you can stretch out? Or better yet, take a cab back to the house and get some rest. I'll call you when the baby comes."

"No, I'd rather wait here." She forced a smile that felt stiff on her lips. From the concern in his eyes, she had a feeling it looked just as artificial.

Time passed, though slowly, with each wrapped in their own thoughts.

The shift was changing, and the activity beyond the waiting room walls seemed to have become more frantic. Twice someone came in, only to glance around and walk out.

The second time that happened, Morgan scowled at the clock on the waiting room wall before shifting his gaze to Raine.

"Isn't it taking too long?"

She, too, had been watching the clock. It had been over five hours since they arrived at the hospital. A full forty-five minutes since Case had come out of the birthing suite to tell them that the baby was being stubborn. His voice had been calm, but she'd seen the dark overlay of worry clouding his deep blue eyes.

"Babies tend to keep their own schedules," she said quietly.

He furrowed his brow. "According to the experts, second babies tend to come much more quickly."

Because she was feeling more and more uneasy, she felt a need to lash out. "Those 'so-called' experts can be wrong."

He scowled. "Is that right?"

Raine stifled a sigh. "Morgan, you didn't even know Prudy Randolph existed a month ago."

"So?"

"So how come you're behaving like a stereotypical expectant father all of a sudden?"

He narrowed his gaze. "You think I'm...putting on some kind of show?"

She heard the silky note in his voice and knew they were in danger of sliding into a sticky situation. In the past she'd always avoided any kind of confrontation with Morgan. Their time together had been too precious. *Peace at any cost* had been her philosophy, the same philosophy practiced by her mother whenever her father became overbearing.

Things were different now, she reminded herself. Yes, she wanted Morgan back in her life, but on *her* terms this time. And her terms included honesty between them.

"I think you're overreacting, yes," she told him with quiet conviction. "But not deliberately. More like a projection of some other emotion."

He lifted a brow. "Sounds to me like I'm not the only one who reads books written by so-called experts."

Raine felt her backbone stiffen. "I minored in psychology at Bradenton. And my mother was a practicing psychotherapist for years before her death."

"Impeccable credentials, compared to mine, certainly."

For a reason she couldn't fathom, the dry humor in his voice fired her temper. Her precarious emotional state made her careless.

"I know enough to recognize a guilty conscience when I see one," she said in a tight, angry voice that sounded as though it had come from someone else.

He went very still. "Meaning mine, I suppose?"

"You told me once you hated hospitals. That you never wanted to see another bare white wall as long as you lived."

Something flickered in the deep blackness of his pupils. "Go on."

Raine was suddenly exhausted. "Let's forget it," she murmured, her voice devoid of texture. "I'm so tired, I don't know what I'm saying."

He studied her for a moment, then let out a controlled sigh. "Suppose I say it for you, then."

Raine suddenly realized she'd made a mistake. She'd never heard that tone of voice from Morgan before. Gone was the lazy drawl, and the mountain twang had taken on an ominous flat quality.

"No," she said quickly. "This isn't the time or place."

"You're thinking I lied when I told you I didn't hear about Mike's accident until it was too late, aren't you? That I hid behind some half-assed excuse while you had to go through hell alone?"

Surprise at his remarkable insight had her staring at him a split second too long. "No," she said, but it was too late. Morgan had seen the truth in her, just as he'd seen it in so many others during his years of playing hardball in the viciously brutal arena of global politics.

"Hey, don't look so stricken," he said, one side of his mouth kicking up. "You haven't told me anything I hadn't already suspected."

She swallowed, suddenly ashamed. "Morgan, it's not that I don't understand. I mean, you were in that army hospital a long time. From the few things you said, I gather you watched a lot of your buddies die, so it makes perfect sense that you would want to avoid seeing…" She couldn't go on. Instead, she took a deep breath, her hand automatically cupping the swell of her belly where a little foot was lodged.

"Raine, it's okay," he said gently. "I understand. You're not the only one who thinks I'm a self-centered, shallow bastard who'd sell out his own kin for a scoop."

His grin flashed. The cocky, reckless smile that dazzled and reassured at the same time transformed his face—all but his eyes. "Hell, maybe it's true. I've done a lot of other things in my life I'm not all that proud to admit to."

Raine didn't know what to think, what to say. She was appalled at her lack of tact. Her unwitting cruelty. He had every right to be furious with her. Instead, he seemed distantly amused.

She went cold inside. "Morgan, please listen to me. I didn't mean—"

Case's exuberant voice cut across hers. "Hey, you guys, guess what? We have another little girl! Seven pounds, four ounces. Jarrod swears she's a shoe-in for Miss America in about eighteen years."

Both she and Morgan leapt to their feet. In spite of the fatigue lining his face, Case was grinning from ear to ear.

"How's Prudy?" Raine asked, precariously close to bursting into tears of relief.

"Wonderful!" Case exclaimed softly, before a rueful look took over his face. "And telling anyone who'll listen that she's never going to let me near her with 'that big thing' again."

Raine giggled, even as tears trembled on her lashes. "Oh, Case, you know she didn't mean it."

He grinned. "God, I hope not," he said fervently before laying a gentle hand on his daughter's back. "Hey, tootles, wake up. You have a new baby sister just waiting to meet you."

Chloe opened her eyes and looked around, still half-asleep. When her gaze lit her on father, she offered him a drowsy smile.

"Go night-night home, Daddy?"

"Not yet, love," Case said gently as he transferred her warm, sweet body from Morgan's arms to his. "Mommy sent me out to find you because she needs a special hug and kiss from her big girl."

Chloe's eyes lit up. "Go see Mommy?"

"And your new little sister, Lily Angelina." Case kissed her cheek, then tucked her securely against his shoulder and turned his attention to the other two in the room.

"Prudy gave me strict orders that you two are not to haul ass out of here before you get a glimpse of the newest Randolph beauty."

"Bet she used just those words, too," Morgan drawled with a grin.

Case shot him a look. "Damn straight." He took a breath, then taking care to keep from jostling Chloe, stuck out his hand. "Thanks for putting up with a half-crazed expectant father."

"No problem," Morgan answered as he and Case exchanged a hard, fast handshake.

"You, too, neighbor," Case said, leaning forward to kiss Raine's cheek.

"My pleasure," she replied, far too aware that Morgan was watching her with eyes that held absolutely no expression beyond a distant courtesy.

"Sounds like this party's getting pretty rowdy," Luke Jarrod commented from the doorway. He was still wearing scrubs and his face was lined with exhaustion. "You guys celebrating something special or just raising hell in general?"

"Both," Case said, grinning again.

"Have to say you did okay tonight, Randolph," Luke said, winking at Raine. "For a minute or two there, I thought we were gonna lose you under the table."

"Like hell," Case growled, his face turning red. "I was just catching my breath."

"That's what they all say," Luke retorted before shifting his gaze to Morgan. "How about you, Paxton? Think you'll be able to stay the course?"

Raine sensed, rather than saw Morgan stiffen. "Guess we'll just have to wait and see, won't we?"

Luke narrowed his gaze. "Yeah, I guess we will at that."

Raine felt tension swirling around the little room and forced a smile. "Luke, is Prudy well enough to have visitors now, or should I wait until tomorrow?"

Luke's harsh features softened as his gaze rested on her face. "Ten minutes won't do her any harm."

Raine glanced over her shoulder, her gaze locking with Morgan's. "You go ahead," he said with a polite smile. "I'll wait here."

She nodded and quickly left the small room. Her sandals sounded strangely hollow on the linoleum as she made her way to the last room on the left. Decorated in muted pastels, the room was both soothing and homey. A small boom box next to the bed played Mozart, and the lights were turned low. A small padded crib was nearby, along with a bower of flowers.

Reclining against the raised head of the bed, Prudy looked both tired and exultant, with her tiny daughter cradled in her arms. Wrapped in a fuzzy pink and white blanket, the baby looked no bigger than a kitten. Wisps of dark hair were visible beneath the stocking cap pulled over her perfect little ears. Her eyes were squeezed shut, revealing feathery dark lashes.

"Isn't she the most perfect baby you ever saw?" Prudy whispered when Raine approached the bed. "Feel free to gush."

"Absolutely the sweetest little girl I've ever seen," Raine pronounced solemnly as she gazed into the mottled, wrinkled face that only a mother would find beautiful.

"How did Chloe take the news that she's now a big sister?" Prudy asked, her gaze bathing her daughter's small face with love.

"Very calmly, probably because Case had to wake her up to tell her."

Prudy smiled and lifted her gaze. "Just think, Raine. In just a few weeks you'll be holding your own babies."

Raine smiled, but the sudden lump in her throat made it difficult to speak. "Seeing you makes it all more real, somehow."

"Wait until you see me walking," Prudy said with a grimace. "Talk about real."

"Was it bad?" Raine couldn't help asking.

"Now that it's over, no. But when I was going through it, I was sure it would never end." Her expression softened. "Case was truly wonderful. I can't imagine what it would have been like without him."

Unbearably lonely, Raine wanted to tell her. Instead, she lavishly praised both mother and baby once more before taking her leave.

She passed Case and a now-chattering Chloe in the corridor and stopped to offer her effusive compliments, which he accepted without any modesty at all. And then she was alone with Morgan.

"Miss America?" he asked, lifting one eyebrow.

Raine smiled. "A cinch."

His mouth slanted into a tired grin, but his eyes were sad. For an instant she'd sensed a terrible loneliness in this big, self-contained man. It was like a glimpse into his soul. Guilt stabbed at her.

"Why don't you go see for yourself?" she suggested softly. "You're part of the family now."

He shook his head. "I called a cab," he said quietly. "It should be out front by the time we get to the lobby."

They went downstairs together, alone in the starkly sterile elevator.

The cab was waiting, and they rode home in silence. Raine thought she dozed, though she wasn't sure. Her head was fuzzy and her back was one burning ache by the time she went to bed.

Morgan took a quick shower before joining her. She wanted to apologize, but she was too tired to be coherent. Tomorrow, she thought, as he draped one arm over her swollen body and cuddled her close.

She woke up to find Morgan's side of the bed empty and cold.

Feeling uneasy and just a little queasy, she awkwardly maneuvered herself out of bed and went into the bathroom. She was beginning to waddle, she realized with a pang. And her center of gravity had shifted, seemingly overnight.

"Hell's bells," she muttered when she caught sight of her puffy face in the mirror over the sink. Maybe it was just as well she couldn't bear more children, she thought before she resolutely banished the self-pity to some dark hole in her psyche.

A long, hot shower took the edge off of her bad mood, and a cup of herbal tea soothed her stomach. Monday was her usual day off, so she decided to treat herself to another cup before she dressed. Besides, she had nothing better to do.

Morgan had left the house to run errands. Or so said the note she'd found tucked under the coffee mug he'd left for her on the counter. Carrying her mug with her, she unlocked the kitchen door and wandered outside onto the porch, seeking the sun.

It was a perfect day. Warm, but with a delicate haze softening the worst of the sun's rays. The climbing rose she'd transplanted from her mother's garden in Salem was in full bloom, forming a fragrant screen on one side of the porch. A smile touched her lips as she watched an industrious bee flitting from blossom to blossom.

Reaching out a hand, she plucked a perfect bud and carried it to her nose. The petals were whisper soft and scented with nectar. She thought about the sad yellow roses that Morgan had handed her that first day. They'd seemed so puny in his big hand.

It was only the second time she received flowers from her husband. The first was right after Mike's birth. Two dozen red roses with the longest stems she'd ever seen. They'd been faded and forlorn by the time he'd made it home. And she'd never forgiven him for arriving late, she thought suddenly.

Like a squirrel storing away nuts, she'd stored her resentment in a safe place, ready to be hauled out again when she needed it. Over the years she'd added more hurts and resentments to her private store. Missed holidays. Lonely winter nights spent huddled in her bed while the clock ticked away her life. Her son's stifled sobs.

She'd kept them all, nourishing them with the terrible grief she'd felt when Mike had died. Late again, her father had said.

Funny how that man was never around in the rough patches. Almost too convenient.

People commended her on her strength and her courage at handling it all alone. What a strain it must be raising a "difficult" child without a father's steady presence. If she made a mistake, who could blame her? She was doing the best she could, wasn't she?

Even her father had expressed his admiration for her grit.

She'd heard the silent condemnation whenever her friends spoke of Morgan and had said nothing. She'd sat for hours listening to her father speak scathingly of Mike's father without feeling that first pang of conscience.

What a selfish little weakling she'd been.

A fool.

In some deep recess of her mind she'd always known that she carried as much responsibility for the life she'd been leading as he had. But it had been easier to play the martyr. Easier to let Morgan take the risks, and bear the cost. Easier to blame him for her own cowardice.

She felt a kick and bit her lip. She'd felt so smug when she'd laid out her ground rules.

Her house. Her babies.

Her precious grief.

"Oh, Morgan," she whispered, her heart aching. "What have I done?"

Morgan clamped his teeth around the foul-tasting cigar and tossed in his hand. "Too rich for me," he muttered, pushing back his chair. His luck at poker hadn't changed. He was still the big loser.

Tonight, he was playing host in a house that still didn't seem like home, for all his trying. It was a strange feeling.

Raine and Stacy were at Prudy's. Watching racy videos, Stacy had assured him with a demure smile when she'd dropped Boyd off.

Luke Jarrod glanced up, his gray eyes questioning. "You feelin' okay, Paxton?"

"Fine."

Morgan caught the look that passed between the two doctors and scowled. "Anybody want a beer? I'm buying."

"Why not?" Boyd said, studying his cards. "I'm not on call and I'm sure as hell not driving."

"Snag one for me, too," Petrov muttered to Morgan's back as he headed for the kitchen.

"None for me," Case chimed in. "I'm on night patrol."

Petrov rolled his eyes. "Hell, Case, you're just bringing that sweet little darling to her mama, not nursing her yourself."

"Up yours," Case retorted, throwing in his hand to follow Morgan into the kitchen. It had been two weeks since Lily's birth. Since then, Paxton had been wound as tight as he'd ever seen, though the man had been doing a damn good job of hiding it.

Morgan was standing at the window, shoulders braced, his hands tucked into the back pockets of his jeans, staring out at the night sky when Case entered the kitchen. Case had seen enough suffering in his time to know that his neighbor was hurting. Big-time.

"Change your mind?" Morgan asked, turning around.

"Nope. Came to get me some of that motor oil you call coffee."

Morgan snorted as he strode to the fridge. "Help yourself."

Case grabbed a mug from the cupboard and poured. "Guess you're counting the days now, huh?" he said as he replaced the pot on the warmer.

"Something like that."

Case registered the edge in Morgan's voice and considered the warning it conveyed. His cop's instinct told him to back off. He took a sip of coffee and thought about friendship. It wasn't a subject that he knew all that much about. Just enough to sense when a man needed to talk, he decided finally. And listening was one of the things Case did best.

"Prudy said you missed the big event first time around."

Morgan's face tightened as he twisted the top off a tall one. "Story of my life."

"You given any thought to names?"

Morgan popped the top off another beer. "Names for what?"

"The twins."

"Raine has a list. Last I heard, she'd narrowed it down to Matthew and Alexander." He lifted the bottle to his mouth and drained it by half before lowering it again.

"Good solid names, both of 'em," Case commented, his expression properly thoughtful. "Go well with Paxton, too."

Morgan's head shot up, and he lasered Case with a narrowed glance. "You got a problem with that?"

"Nope. Do you?"

"It's not my call." He hesitated, then added grimly, "I signed a waiver. Raine insisted. I thought I could convince her to change her mind after the kids were born."

Case raised a brow. "You going through with the divorce after all?"

"That's not my call, either."

"So you're giving up?"

Anger flared briefly in Morgan's eyes. "I'm a realist, Case."

"What the hell does that mean?"

"It means I was glad when Raine turned up pregnant all those years ago. It made things simpler. More solid. No matter what, we had a connection. Hell, maybe I even had this subconscious desire to give her my baby so that she'd have to take me, too.''

His expression was savage as he finished the beer. Case took satisfaction in knowing his hunch about Morgan Paxton had been dead-on. The man was a volcano inside.

''Prudy was pregnant when I married her the second time. She'd had the flu and it messed up her system, but for a while I thought she'd used me for stud service.'' He glanced down, remembering. ''I was pretty raw for a time. Said a lot of things I wish I hadn't. Never thought she'd forgive me, in fact.'' He glanced up and grinned. ''Guess I'm just lucky I picked a lady with a generous heart.''

Morgan reached for the other beer he'd taken from the fridge, then scowled and dropped his hand. ''What the hell, love is blind, right?''

''So the man said. Or was it a woman?''

''Probably,'' Morgan muttered as he took another beer from the fridge and twisted off the cap. ''Doesn't really matter much, one way or the other since it's nothing more than a fairy tale anyway.''

Case hid a smile. ''What is?''

Morgan looked impatient. ''Love. That 'for better or worse' crap.'' He drew a harsh breath. ''Make one mistake and you're screwed. Hell, you're screwed even if she only thinks you made a mistake.''

Case let out a sigh. ''If ever a man needed to tie one on—''

He was interrupted by the sudden ringing of the wall phone. Case was closer, and reached out to answer it.

''No, this is Paxton's neighbor. Who's this?''

As he listened to the brusque voice on the other end, Case locked his gaze with Morgan's. The man looked years older than he should. ''Hold on a minute, and I'll see if I can track him down.''

Case covered the mouthpiece with his palm before lifting a brow. "Are you at home to some guy named Weinhard?"

Morgan frowned. "Damn."

"Want me to tell him you're not here?"

"No. He'll just call back. Frank's like a bulldog once he gets the scent."

Case nodded, then did a double take. "Frank Weinhard? As in Francis P. Weinhard, the living legend."

Morgan looked embarrassed. "He taught me everything I know."

"Yeah?" Case handed over the phone with a kind of awe.

"Yeah, and I have a feeling I'm about to get a refresher course in loyalty," Morgan muttered before lifting the phone to his ear.

Chapter 16

Raine surfaced slowly. Something was wrong.

She struggled to sit up, only to gasp as her stomach muscles twisted into a hard knot. Holding her breath, she waited for the cramp to ease, her heart pounding.

It wasn't labor. It couldn't be. She had another full month to go. By the calendar and by Luke's own educated guess only two days ago.

Morgan was already up, just as he'd been every morning since Lily's birth. He jogged every morning now, claiming a need to exercise. Rain or shine, he made himself do two miles on the path by the river.

Today it was raining hard enough to rattle the windows. A storm in August. Another indication of the changing weather patterns.

She started to smile, then sucked in as another cramp seized her. It wasn't bad. Nothing to worry about yet. Still, she made herself check the clock and was surprised to see that it was almost nine. She must have been more tired than she'd thought.

When ten minutes passed with no more pain, she began to relax. It had been another false alarm. She'd had several in the past week.

"Good morning."

She turned to see Morgan standing in the doorway, her favorite mug in his hand and a polite smile on his face. He was dressed in jeans and a pale blue shirt with a button-down collar and long sleeves, folded back to bare his corded forearms. Instead of sneakers, he was wearing boots.

She felt a pang of worry before she remembered that he always wore his favorite khaki shirt when he traveled. One of his rituals.

"Good morning." Her voice came out husky. A combination of longing and sleep, she decided. "Finished jogging already?"

Something flickered in his eyes as he came toward her. "Actually I gave it a miss this morning."

"Too wet?" she said brightly, desperate for one of those roguish smiles that used to flash so easily.

"Something like that." He helped her with her pillows, then handed her the mug. She inhaled with greedy pleasure before taking a tiny sip. As usual, it was bitterly strong.

"How're you feeling?" he asked when she smiled her thanks.

"Fine. The boys have been pretty quiet all night."

His smile didn't touch his eyes. "Probably gearing up for a tag-team match this afternoon."

"Probably."

Raine scooted sideways, making more room for him to sit. Instead, he rejected her tacit plea and moved to the window. Turning his back, he gazed out at the dreary day. Raine fought down an urge to go to him and gather that stiff, proud body into her arms. If only she hadn't brought up the subject of Mike's death. She told herself it was the stress of being in a hospital again that had made her careless, but she suspected it was more than that. Perhaps she hadn't healed as much as she'd thought.

"Something's come up," he said. "I need to tell you about it."

"You're leaving," she said, amazed that she was actually very calm.

He turned slowly to face her. His jaw was taut, his hard mouth bracketed by lines that had never seemed quite so pronounced before.

"How did you guess?" he asked with a wry twist to his deep voice.

"Female intuition," she said, desperately trying to match his tone.

He drew a breath. Raine sensed the control he was exercising. It both fascinated and frightened her.

"I had a call from Frank Weinhard last night, while you were next door."

She felt a rush of dismay. "Is he ill?" she asked with genuine concern.

Morgan shook his head. "Actually, he called to ask a favor."

"I see." She wrapped both hands around her mug so that he wouldn't notice their trembling. "Of course, whatever it is, you can't possibly refuse. Not after all he's done for you." She saw his jaw tighten and hurried on. "I mean that, Morgan. In many ways Frank was the father you should have had."

The father he deserved. A kind and compassionate man with a core of inner toughness that matched Morgan's own. A worthy role model for a young man desperate for guidance and understanding.

"If it was just a story at stake, we wouldn't even be having this discussion, but it looks like it might be a lot more than that."

Raine took a careful breath. She felt a slow tug on the

lower part of her belly, followed by a more insistent twisting sensation. To mask her discomfort, she lifted the mug to her mouth and pretended to sip.

"How long will you be gone?" she asked when the contraction eased.

"A week, maybe two. Depends on how things shake out." He shoved his hands into his back pockets, then a second later, pulled them free. "I'll call as soon as I know."

"I'd appreciate that."

"I talked to Jarrod this morning. He's pretty sure you're going to hold off at least that long."

"Yes, that's what he said on Tuesday." Morgan knew that. He'd been with her in Luke's office, enthralled by the images on the ultrasound screen. She'd been touched by his excitement. For all the world, he'd seemed as eager as any expectant father to see the faces in the shadowy images.

"Yeah, well, I figured I'd check with him again, just to make sure." He cleared his throat. "Your dad has agreed to stay with you until I get back."

Raine was so surprised, she nearly let go of her coffee mug. She regained control of her fingers just in time. "You called my father?"

He eyed her warily. "About an hour ago. He'll be here before noon."

She blinked, stunned at the thought of Morgan asking a favor of her father. "Do you need any help packing?"

"No, but thanks for the offer. I packed this morning while you were still sleeping."

Feeling dazed, she glanced around the room, looking for the scuffed, size-twelve sneakers under the chair. The socks on the floor. His worn wallet on her dresser. The room was once again as neat as a pin. Just the way she liked it.

"Looks like you've done a thorough job, but then you've had a lot of practice."

His face tightened, and she felt the prick of tears. "I'm sorry, Morgan. In case you've forgotten, I don't handle surprises very well."

"I haven't forgotten." He stuck his hands in his pockets again, approaching the bed warily.

"You're not wearing your khaki shirt."

He glanced down, his expression rueful. "You said I was too rigid. I'm trying to loosen up."

She smiled. "I see."

He stopped when he reached the bed and looked at her. She felt as though he was searching for words. "I made you a promise and I had every intention of keeping it. Say the word and I'll stay."

Raine felt a wild urge to do just that and had to take a deep breath before it was safely subdued. "And if you stayed, what then?"

He shrugged. "I'd take some flak. Nothing major."

"You'd disappoint Frank."

"He'd get over it."

She almost believed him. Only the tiny flicker of his lashes betrayed him.

"When...when does your plane leave?"

"Eleven-fifteen."

Raine didn't have to look at the clock to know he had to leave within minutes in order to make it on time. "Why didn't you wake me earlier?"

She set her mug on the table and started to throw off the sheet. At least they would have the time it took to drive to the airport to be together.

"I called a cab," he said, stopping her. "He's outside, waiting."

"I see."

He hesitated, then sat down and took one of her hands in his. She felt her body react to his touch, like a flower opening to the warmth of the sun. She knew now that she would always be vulnerable to this man. Married, divorced. It didn't matter. He was a part of her.

"I hate leaving like this, Raine. With things so unsettled between us."

"I love you," she said softly.

His mouth quirked. "Even believing I'm a coward and a liar?"

She felt the blood drain from her face. "Don't say that. It's not true."

He looked at her for a long time, those golden lion's eyes intensely probing. "This is a nice place. Nice people. You belong here."

"And you hate it?"

He shook his head. "I've been doing some thinking. I never realized until I lived here with you these past weeks that every other time I'd been home I was just playing house. I never got involved in your real life. Or Mike's." His jaw tightened, then relaxed. "Not the way Case is involved with his family. Or Boyd. Not where it counts."

"But you could be involved. Deeply involved."

His gaze flickered. "Jarrod may be right to doubt me. Maybe I *can't* go the distance."

Raine took a breath. "I think you can do anything you set your mind to."

His mouth quirked. "Never staying in one place very long, living out of a suitcase or a Range Rover—it started out as a necessity. A way to prove myself. To show the world I'm as good as anyone else. Better." He filled his chest with air and let it out slowly. "If it's just a habit, I can break it. If it's…part of who I am, who I need to be…" He let the sentence remain unfinished. Raine had no trouble filling in the rest.

"In other words, until you know the answer to that question, we'd better keep things open-ended between us."

He narrowed his gaze. She felt the heat of his body and

the hard edge of tension riding him. "It's taken me a while to admit it, but I was a lousy father, and a worse husband. I don't take failure lightly, Raine. It hurts like hell, and I'm not much for pain."

He smiled, and so did she. "None of us are."

"But some have a greater tolerance." He rubbed his thumb over her hand. "You, for instance. Grabbing at life even knowing you might end up bleeding."

"It's not like that."

"Sure it is. And twin boys?" He shook his head. "Now that takes guts."

She laughed softly. "The luck of the draw, so to speak."

He glanced down at the mound of tummy and babies under her nightshirt. "These past weeks, feeling them kick me in the belly night after night, watching them tumbling around under your clothes...I'd all but forgotten they're not mine."

She felt tears welling. "Oh, Morgan—" He stopped her by pressing two fingers to her lips.

"I need a goodbye kiss, honey, to take with me. And make it count."

Her hands weren't quite steady as she reached up to frame his face. She tilted her head, then brought her mouth to his. It was a soft kiss, yet she felt him tremble. She drew back, used one finger to trace his lower lip.

"Your eyes are pure gold. I love your eyes. I love you, lousy coffee, watery spaghetti, quirky rituals and all."

His lashes flickered. "Raine—"

"No, it's okay. I don't expect anything more of you than you've already given me." She let her eyes close as she lifted her face to his again. His lips crashed down hard, and his tongue plunged.

His hands dug into her hair and trapped her, while he explored her mouth with a frantic intensity that took her breath. She was breathing hard when he lifted his head. She let her lashes flutter open, and realized that he was staring at her with an almost palpable longing. "Oh baby, I wish—"

A horn tooted outside, and he muttered a curse.

"Go," she whispered, fighting valiantly to keep her lips from trembling. "Do what you have to do. If you can come back to me willingly, without reservations or resentment, I'll be waiting."

He closed his eyes for a long moment, then with a harsh growl, leaned forward to give her one more hard kiss.

He got up quickly then, and walked to the door. At the threshold, he turned and looked back at her.

"I signed the divorce papers," he said gruffly. "They're in the den. Not because I wanted to, but because it seemed fair."

With that, he was gone.

"More cobbler, Father?" Raine asked with a bright smile.

"No thank you, daughter. I've crammed this old body about as full as I can and still leave room for my lungs to work." Arthur Connelly sat back in her dining room chair and beamed across the centerpiece. "It was another triumph, my dear. I shall be very sorry to go back to my own cooking."

Raine took a sip of milk and glanced toward the twin bassinets placed side by side near the window seat. Both boys had slept through most of their first Labor Day holiday.

September had come in with a whimper this year. All the excitement had happened in August.

She'd been in hard labor by the time her father had arrived a scant forty minutes after Morgan had left. The boys had been in a hurry, arriving just three hours later. Jarrod had performed the necessary surgery immediately, and she'd been pleased to realize she was a fast healer. Luke had pronounced her almost as good as new at her checkup just last week.

"I hope you don't think I'm throwing you out," she told her father with a smile. "I've enjoyed beating you at chess every night."

Arthur frowned. "I beg to remind you that I won both matches last night."

"I stand corrected."

He fiddled with the already perfect knot of his tie. Cleared his throat, sighed, then cleared his throat again. "I'm sorry you haven't heard from him. I thought…well, when I talked to him on the phone before he left, he sounded so concerned about you. I thought maybe things had changed."

Raine felt a whisper of pain in the vicinity of her heart. "At least he left to do something really important."

Her father's seamed face took on a sheepish expression. "I said some harsh things to him when he told me he was leaving."

"I'm sure he knows you didn't mean them."

"Of course, I meant them—at the time," he declared, huffing indignantly. "How was I to know he had a lead on a plot to kidnap the Pope?"

Raine fiddled with her unused coffee spoon. She took her coffee black these days. "He looked terribly tired on TV when he broke the story. I hope he's not still having those headaches."

Arthur coughed into his napkin. Then sniffed. "As you know, I've been periodically checking my answering machine for messages while I've been staying here. There have been several from Morgan, asking me to leave word about you with some man named Bronstein in New York."

Raine looked up, stunned. "Why didn't you tell me?"

"He asked me not to."

"You talked with him?"

"No, he was inaccessible by phone. Bronstein said he was checking in often, though." Arthur offered her a sympathetic look. In the five weeks since the babies had been born, she and her father had grown closer. It was a comfort having him there to rock Matt while Alex nursed or vice versa. But her father was going home tomorrow. The fall semester was starting in a week's time, and he had lesson plans to organize.

"Besides, it's time I got used to being a single parent again."

Her father's soft cluck of sympathy told her she'd spoken her thoughts aloud. "So you're going through with the divorce."

She hesitated. "I think I have to in order to make a fresh start."

"And Morgan?"

She sat up straighter. It seemed to help. "Morgan will always be a part of my life. I don't hate him. I love him, and he'll be welcome to visit as often as he likes."

"So life goes on?"

Raine nodded. "It does indeed. But then—"

The phone rang, startling them both. "I'll get it," Raine said, grabbing a plate in each hand to carry into the kitchen. In the weeks since the babies' arrival, she'd learned to make use of every spare minute.

It was Prudy on the line. "Are you watching?" she demanded without bothering to say hello. "Did you know what he was planning? Why didn't you tell me?"

Raine blinked. "Who? Planning what?"

"Morgan. He's being reassigned. No more foreign assignments. I just saw it on the tube. If you hurry...oh rats! Too late."

Raine realized her knees were shaking. Grabbing a

kitchen chair, she pulled it closer and sank onto the seat. "No more foreign assignments?"

"That's what he said." She heard Prudy's rapid intake of breath. "He was giving an update on that hostage thing about the Pope. About how the Saudis arrested the head of that weirdo group and—"

"Forget those idiots. What about Morgan?"

"I'm coming to that." Prudy sounded offended, and Raine apologized.

"I understand. Anyway, he said it was his last broadcast for the nightly news."

"That's all? Nothing about his plans?"

"Nope. Just that he was looking forward to new challenges."

"What does that mean?"

"Beats me. Maybe he means helping you to raise twin sons, which is definitely a challenge if you ask me." She laughed. "Case agrees. He said the guy's hooked on you big-time and wouldn't be surprised if we looked out the window tomorrow or the next day and saw him pushing those two darlings of yours in the stroller."

Case was sure wrong this time, Raine thought as she guided the big stroller around a puddle on the sidewalk leading from her carport to her back door. It had been two weeks since Morgan's announcement.

Fourteen days of alternating between elated anticipation and deepest misery. She'd expected a call that very night. When it hadn't come, she'd convinced herself she'd hear from him in the morning. When she hadn't, she'd told herself it was the time difference and made sure she was near a phone whenever she was nursing the babies.

Just in case.

But now she no longer jumped when the phone rang. Or ran to the door when the bell chimed.

"Hi, neighbor," Stacy called from her backyard where she was raking sodden leaves. "Want to come in for some coffee? I made a fresh pot."

"Sounds great." Raine steered the stroller off the walk and aimed for the gate in the hedge separating the two properties.

Stacy had put aside her rake and had the gate opened by the time Raine reached it. "Good heavens, I'd swear these two have grown since I saw them two days ago," Stacy exclaimed as she released the safety belt on one of the seats.

"This is Matt, right?"

Raine laughed. "Nope. Alex. His hair is the teeniest bit curlier."

Stacy hugged the sleepy baby and cooed nonsense into his tiny ear. "You adorable darling, you. Makes me want to have a son."

Raine gave Matt a kiss on his chubby cheek before grabbing the diaper bag slung over the stroller's handle. "There are days when I wonder if I wasn't really a tad crazy when I decided I wanted to be a mom again."

"And days when you're so glad you are you want to sing with joy," Stacy teased.

"True, but that's usually when they're sleeping."

It took some doing to get both babies inside, the bulky stroller dried and transported to the kitchen and the babies snuggled into the seats again. Matt fell asleep almost immediately. Alex was more inquisitive, glancing around the bright kitchen with absorbed interest.

Both boys' eyes had started to take on a darker hue. They'd be brown, she thought. Like hers. But so far, their hair was a rich golden color. Like Morgan's.

"Are they always this good?" Stacy asked with something resembling awe on her face as she set a brimming mug of French Roast on the place mat in front of Raine.

"During the daytime, yes. They like to play at night." She sampled the coffee and pronounced it perfect. If a trifle weak, she thought to herself.

Stacy laughed as she sat down, but quickly sobered. "I'm glad I caught you because my conscience has been giving me fits."

"What about?"

"Morgan."

Raine felt a chill. "What do you mean?"

Stacy bit her lip, then sighed. "Boyd told me to use my own discretion about telling you. After all, your divorce will be final in—what? A month?"

"Six weeks." Raine leaned forward, her heart suddenly pounding. "What about Morgan?"

Stacy sighed. "It seems this Saudi doctor called Boyd this morning. As a courtesy, he said, since technically Morgan was Boyd's patient too, and—"

"What's wrong? Is he hurt?" She jumped up and began to pace. "I knew there was something wrong. Those headaches—"

"It's not the headaches. It's some kind of exotic disease. Or parasite. Something like that anyway. Apparently he was sick before."

Raine grabbed the back of the chair and forced her knees to lock. "It was a spore of some kind."

Stacy nodded. "Anyway, I guess he had a relapse. Folded up at the airport on his way home, according to this doctor and he's been in the hospital ever since." She hesitated, then added softly, "In intensive care."

"Oh my God. I have to do something. Call someone." She scowled. "The Saudi doctor. Boyd would have his number."

Stacy leapt to her feet and reached for the phone. "Here, call."

* * *

It was the same flight. Maybe even the same plane. It was definitely the same flight attendant. Apparently she liked the New York to Portland run. Eyes closed, Morgan smelled her perfume as she walked past his aisle, checking seat belts prior to landing.

She hadn't repeated her invitation for dinner, for which he was grateful. He'd barely had the energy to get himself onto the plane at Kennedy and into his seat—a different one, this time. On the aisle, but in the second row. He was determined to change his habits, but it was damn hard work. Almost as hard as shucking that lousy desert bug that had taken a liking to him. As it was, he'd been so whipped from the overseas flight he'd had to lay over a night in New York.

The intercom kicked on, and Cheyenne's dulcet voice recited the landing instructions. Morgan felt his stomach twist and took a deep breath. His hands were icy and his mouth dry. In his mind he saw a slender pixie not quite five feet three inches tall, radiating energy, waiting for him with open arms. He fought down the image, aware that Raine had no idea he was coming.

He was scared and hated to admit it.

She'd told him he could come back. That last morning in her bedroom. He'd replayed her words over and over in his head for nearly two months.

When he'd finally plucked up his courage to call Arthur Connelly the night before last, her father had said she was fine. The babies were fine. The store was fine. When Morgan had probed for more, all he'd gotten out of the old bastard was a weather report. It was lousy.

The wheels touched down, and he glanced out the window. The bastard had lied to him. It was a gorgeous day. Bright and sunny.

Morgan frowned as he undid his belt. Connelly wouldn't

lie about his daughter's well-being. Not even he would go that far. Would he?

The plane was crowded, but one of the perks of first-class was the ability to escape quickly. He felt light-headed and weak as a kitten as he walked up the Jetway. The Saudi doc with the haughty stare had warned him about leaving the hospital too soon, but he hadn't been able to wait any longer.

He had to know, one way or another, whether he was going home. Or simply stopping by for a visit. No big deal, right? Hell, no. Just his entire future. No, his life.

The reception area was full. Damn near everyone was smiling, their eyes bright with anticipation. He'd call Paul John first, then grab his bags from the carousel. With any luck he'd be at her place in an hour.

A flash of purple to the left caught his eye. A small, dark-haired woman was standing there next to a sturdy baby stroller. With two blond baby boys squirming in the padded seats.

He felt a tug in his gut, then another. His steps slowed, then stopped. People surged around him. But all he saw was Raine. She was smiling, and her eyes looked suspiciously damp.

"Hey, look who's here," he said softly. His voice wasn't steady. Neither were his hands.

"Hey yourself," she said, smiling up at him as he made himself move toward her.

"You were supposed to be here yesterday."

She smelled like roses and looked like sunshine. He felt his throat tighten. "How did you know?"

"Frank told me. After I threatened him with a lawsuit for causing me grievous emotional trauma."

Emotions tumbled through him. His dainty little wife with the soft voice and perfect manner had taken on a man feared on three continents for his acerbic tongue and rude manners.

"He, um, didn't mention that to me."

"I told him not to. I wanted to surprise you." She cocked one hip and glared at him. "Next time you change your itinerary, let me know, okay? Do you know how uncooperative those airline people are about giving out information? I had to call the company CEO—"

He couldn't take any more. He dropped his garment bag and reached for her. In his weakened condition he only managed to swing her around three times before his head began to swim.

"You're really here," she mumbled into his shoulder as he hugged her. Her arms were fierce little bands of need holding him. She wanted him, he thought in a daze of disbelieve and elation. She really, really wanted him.

"I've changed jobs," he said as he eased her back far enough to get a clear view of her face. Her cheeks were pink, and her eyes bright.

"I know."

"I'm going to be the host of a new show the network's putting together. A lot like '60 Minutes.'" He risked a grin. "But better."

Her smile was like a rare and precious gift. He hadn't realized until this moment how much he'd counted on seeing it again. "It has to be, if you're part of it."

"It means a lot less travel, and a lot less money."

Her eyes sparkled. "Is that a warning?"

He touched her face and realized it was wet. "Just so you know. You don't like surprises, remember?"

"I remember." She drew a breath, her eyes suddenly clouding. "You look pale."

"You look wonderful." His mouth quirked. "Skinny."

"Not quite, but I'm working on it."

"Stop. You're perfect just as you are."

"Really?"

"Really."

She seemed frozen, her gaze locked with his. He wasn't much better, drinking in the sight of her like a blind man with suddenly restored sight. A cry of outraged impatience broke the spell, and they both glanced down. Two boys stared up at him. Bigger than he'd expected, they were dressed in tiny striped trainman's overalls over bright red shirts, the same color as the basketball sneakers on their fat little feet.

Two little blond boys with big brown eyes.

Morgan felt his heart stop. He felt a rush of pain, a stab of grief. "They look like Mike." His voice was thick.

Raine's hand was gentle on his arm. "At first. Wait until you get to know them and you'll see the differences."

Morgan nodded, already seeing two distinct individuals. Two unique miniature males who happened to look alike. And yet—

"This one's hair is curlier." He started to lean down, then stopped himself.

"That's Alex. Alexander Arthur. His brother is Matt. Matthew Morgan."

He drew a breath. It wasn't enough to dislodge the lump in his throat, forcing him to take another. Someone brushed by and mumbled an apology. A loudspeaker beckoned a traveler to a white phone. Morgan realized they were still standing next to the Jetway. And he still hadn't worked up the nerve to kiss her.

"So, where do we go from here?" he asked, nearly giddy with hope.

She glanced down, then lifted her gaze to his. "Home, to your wife and family."

He grinned, and realized it felt good. "Yeah? Just like that?"

"Just like that." She paused, then pursed her lips in a

little frown that set his blood zinging. "One word of warning, however. If you ever think about leaving me again, I'll have to get extremely severe with you."

Morgan laughed, his exhaustion already lifting. "It's a deal."

He kissed her long and hard, oblivious to the stares of his fellow travelers. And then he reached down and gathered an armful of boys. His sons.

Epilogue

Raine had had a long, arduous day. The spring term at Portland State had just ended, and her store had been filled with students returning books for credit or much-needed cash. She and Ginny had worked overtime. The air-conditioning had quit around two, and her turquoise cotton dress was a wrinkled mess.

She arrived to find chaos. No sign of dinner. No welcoming hugs and kisses from her men.

Her beautiful living room was a mess. Toys littered the rare Chinese rug, and two of the newly re-covered cushions from her sofa were on the floor, one of them sporting a sticky smear of a substance that looked remarkably like chocolate milk.

"Oh my heavens, look at this place." Raine fitted her hands to her hips and tapped an impatient foot.

Flat on his back in the midst of the disaster, Morgan glanced up sheepishly. "Uh-oh, guys. We're busted."

The two towheaded boys busily pounding on their father

paid no attention. Raine hid a smile. Her three men had formed a fierce bond. In every way that counted, Morgan was the twins' father. To make sure there would never be any doubt, he had quietly adopted them.

"I suppose you have an explanation for this...." She waved her hand, at a loss for a precise description.

"It's called free expression," Morgan said, gathering both boys to him for a fierce bear hug before getting all three of them to their feet.

Raine hid a smile with difficulty. "You've been watching the educational channel again, haven't you?"

"Now, honey, don't be mad. We'll clean it all up, won't we fellas?"

Both boys shook their heads. They were growing like weeds. Their pediatrician was sure they'd be tall. Already, at twenty-one months, they were at the top of his charts. Morgan was already talking about teaching them to play basketball—after he learned the game himself, of course. He'd already bought a book—and a video.

"Papa's mess," Alex declared firmly.

Raine speared her husband with an accusing look. "Perhaps Papa has forgotten he's hosting a poker party tonight in less than three hours."

Morgan grinned smugly. His show was in summer hiatus, and he was relishing his time off. "Don't worry, love. I have everything handled."

"I doubt that very much."

Morgan glanced from one bright-eyed son to the other. "Tell Mama the plan, guys."

"Gran'pa's comin'," Matt said with a grin.

"To help," Alex added, his grin fully as smug as his father's.

Raine blinked. "Trust me, guys. Grandpa will take one look at this disaster and faint dead away."

Morgan grinned. "Nah, he's really a pushover. You just have to know what buttons to push."

"What buttons?"

Morgan gave each boy a smacking kiss before setting them on their feet. "Poker. He's hooked."

"You mean you got tired of being the big loser and recruited fresh blood."

Morgan placed a big hand over his heart. Right where he'd gotten paint on his ancient T-shirt this past winter when he was helping her redo the boys' room. "You wound me deeply, wife. I wouldn't do anything so devious, especially to your sainted father."

"Uh-huh."

There was a pounding on the door in the kitchen, followed by the squeaking of hinges as someone shoved it open. "Hey, in there," a male voice sounding very much like Case's bellowed. "You guys ready?"

Alex and Matt were halfway to the door before Raine managed to stop them by blocking their path. "Hey, where do you two think you're going?"

"Pizza," Alex shouted.

"With Chwoe and Wiwy," Matt added, beaming. "And games."

Raine shifted her gaze from the two eager faces of her sons to the smug face of her husband. "Would you care to explain this, Mr. Paxton?"

Her blood heated as he approached, a familiar glint in his golden eyes. "With pleasure, Mrs. Paxton. Case has graciously volunteered to occupy our hellions for an hour or so while we rest."

"Rest?" she asked suspiciously.

He nodded. "In the bedroom. With the door locked. All part of the plan."

Raine felt a rush of anticipation. "I thought you were trying to be more spontaneous."

"Alex. Matt," Case called impatiently. "Get your butts out here, or we're gonna leave you behind."

"Hurry up," Chloe's voice chimed in. "Me and Lily are hungry."

"Me, too, Mama," Morgan said with a grin she could only label lecherous.

"Oh, all right, but you boys behave yourself for Uncle Case, you hear?"

Both golden heads bobbed in unison. "Yes, Mama," said Alex.

"Yes, Mama," echoed Matt before he nudged his brother into a gallop. Seconds later the back door slammed shut and peace descended.

"Poor Case is in for a hell of a long hour," Morgan muttered, as he slipped his arms around her shoulders.

"You're terrible," she muttered, raising her arms to encircle his neck. Her breasts pressed his chest, and his eyes darkened. He trailed one finger along the line of her jaw.

"But lovable, right?"

Raine's heart filled with love. His tone was teasing, but his eyes were wary. He'd been generous and loving and playful during the last year and a half. He'd told her that he loved her in every way he could—except with words.

She would be utterly content, if only he weren't still restless. Still unsettled. She tried not to worry. Tried not to look for the small signs that she knew foreshadowed another leave-taking. But she knew that Bronstein had been calling more frequently. And that Morgan had been terribly preoccupied for the last week or so.

"Very lovable," she said brightly, kissing his chin.

"So you're happy? Everything's good?"

"Very."

When he tensed slightly, her heart sank. He was going to tell her he was leaving. She knew it. "It's okay," she murmured, bracing. "I understand."

The wariness in his eyes took on edges. "You do?"

"Of course. And I want you to know I can handle it, so you don't have to feel guilty."

"Guilty?"

"About leaving. I knew it was only a matter of time, but it's okay. Really. The boys are older now, and I'm very busy, so—"

"Well, hell!" He looked supremely irritated, and more than a little hurt. "You really wouldn't care if I suddenly hauled out my bags and started packing, would you?"

"Of course I care," she said before she remembered her resolve to give him all the space he needed. "It's just that...that—"

"That you're bored with me." He drew back and raked his hands through his hair. She was struck with the realization she'd never seen him look more vulnerable. "I knew that would happen sooner or later."

"What, exactly, would happen?" she asked cautiously.

"It was the glamour you liked, right? The idea of this globetrotting guy who hobnobbed with famous people and had a closet full of awards. It was...sexy to go to bed with a 'name.'"

She saw it then—the insecurity that had driven him. The lack of confidence that had tormented him. Beneath the polish and the amazing intelligence was a ragged little boy who'd known precious little love.

She drew herself up taller and made her expression stern. "Now you listen to me, Morgan Paxton, and listen good. I do not care how many famous people you know, and I do not care how many awards you have shoved in our closet, impressive though they are."

He opened his mouth, but she refused to let him speak. She was on a roll. "I fell in love with a man who made me forget my shyness because he laughed at my pathetic attempts at humor. The same man who made me feel beautiful when I was waddling pregnant. Who cried in his sleep and begged God to take him instead of an eight-year-old boy he adored.''

His eyes flickered, but she refused to stop. It was time they cleared the air. "Yes, you hurt me, but you also healed me. I love you so much that I have to let you do whatever it takes to make you happy. Now, is that perfectly clear, or what?"

When he still looked skeptical, she drew back her fist and punched him squarely in the belly. His breath escaped in a whoosh, and his expression turned fierce.

"It's clear, it's clear," he said, his voice still a little strained. "And for the record, I wasn't planning on leaving—at least not for long."

"You weren't?"

He shook his head. "I can't leave this place. I belong here. With you and our boys and all the rest of the families on Mill Works Ridge."

"You do?"

His mouth slanted. "In fact, I doubt you could blast me out of your life, honey."

She drew a breath. "Then what—"

"I was workin' up to askin' you something," he admitted, his drawl soft. "And I wasn't sure how you'd react."

She drew a breath. "Okay. Ask."

He glanced down, then lifted his hands to her shoulders. "You've heard me mention Josefa Hanan?"

"Your source in Lebanon?"

He nodded. "She, ah, wants to get married to this doctor in Beirut."

"Good for her."

His color deepened. "Right. But there's a problem."

"Which is?"

"It turns out she has this daughter who's almost three."

Raine frowned. Oh no, she thought. Please, no. It can't

be Morgan's. She shifted her gaze to his and felt a sudden overwhelming sense of relief. No, she thought. He wouldn't break his vows, not even for the most important story in the world. "What's the baby's name?"

"Morgana." His gaze was clear and steady. "She's not mine."

"I know that."

He didn't move, but she felt some of the tension leave him. "You believe me?"

"Absolutely."

"Oh, baby." His voice broke, and he cleared his throat. "She won't tell me the name of the father, only that he's American and doesn't want the child. But neither does her husband-to-be. In fact, he won't take Josefa if Morgana is part of the package."

Raine felt excitement race through her. "Yes," she all but shouted. "Yes, yes, yes!"

Morgan blinked at her as though she'd suddenly gone loopy. "You were about to ask me if we'd take her, right?" she said eagerly.

He nodded, looking dazed. "Well, yeah, but how did you know?"

"I know you, my darling. Your stubborn ways and your big heart. And I love you so much, it's scary." She reached for him and he went into her arms. "There's nothing I would change about you."

He drew back to look at her, his eyes soft and full of emotion. "Nothing?"

She pretended to ponder. "Well, maybe one little thing."

He sighed. "I knew it." He straightened his spine and drew in a breath. "Okay, lay it on me. Whatever you want, it's yours."

She felt her eyes sparkling. "Anything?"

"Anything—unless it involves me leaving. Then you'll have a fight."

She felt the last of her doubts and reservations fall away. "No, but about your determination to do the cooking."

He lifted his brows. "Yeah, what about it?"

"Please, please stop. I can't take another lousy meal."

He narrowed his gaze. "You said you liked my cooking."

"I said it was utterly amazing the things you could do in the kitchen. There's a difference."

Morgan drew a careful breath. His darling little pixie wife had just dealt his ego a major blow. And it felt wonderful.

"I'll make you a deal," he said, holding her tight. "I won't cook and you'll let me take the lead in bed one time out of five."

Her laughter was like a soft, sweet caress on his scarred soul. "It's a deal, my love."

He knew then that he was home. At last, and for good.

* * * * *

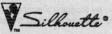

Take 4 bestselling love stories FREE

Plus get a FREE surprise gift!

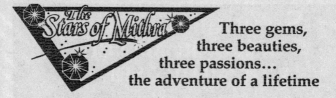

SILHOUETTE WOMEN KNOW ROMANCE WHEN THEY SEE IT.

And they'll see it on **ROMANCE CLASSICS**, the new 24-hour TV channel devoted to romantic movies and original programs like the special **Romantically Speaking-Harlequin® Goes Prime Time.**

Romantically Speaking-Harlequin® Goes Prime Time introduces you to many of your favorite romance authors in a program developed exclusively for Harlequin® and Silhouette® readers.

Watch for **Romantically Speaking-Harlequin® Goes Prime Time** beginning in the summer of 1997.

If you're not receiving ROMANCE CLASSICS, call your local cable operator or satellite provider and ask for it today!

ROMANCE CLASSICS

Escape to the network of your dreams.

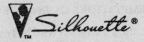